LOVED YOU Once

THE BAKER'S CREEK BILLIONAIRE BROTHERS SERIES

USA TODAY BESTSELLING AUTHOR

CLAUDIA BURGOA

Sign up for my newsletter *to receive updates about upcoming books and exclusive excerpts.*

www.claudiayburgoa.com

Prologue

Blaire

THE ALDRIDGE BROTHERS are like a force of nature. They're like volcanic lightning, fire tornados, bismuth crystals, nacreous clouds, or typhoons echoing through lost caverns. They're passionate and chaotic. They carry the strength and wisdom of redwood forests and the pride and anger of minor gods. Am I giving them too much credit by painting them to be larger than life?

...Perhaps.

It's all about perspective. Some people compare them to a nuclear meltdown.

To say they're interesting is an understatement. The Aldridge brothers are handsome, arrogant, and sinful.

Henry, the hotel mogul, is callous.

Hayes, the doctor, is handsome, nerdy, and detached.

Pierce, the lawyer, is an unrelenting know-it-all.

Mills, the hockey player, is reckless.

Vance, the former Delta Force member, is impulsive.

Beacon, the heartthrob musician, is rebellious.

Make sure to add *as fuck* to each of them. They all have an alpha side that's infuriating,

I haven't heard from them since their brother, Carter, died. Until their father died two weeks ago and they came barging back into my life. Am I ready to face my past?

I don't know. All I care about is what I'll get at the end of this deal. This will be like walking through a rose field under a volcanic eruption. Once I cross the bridge into their world, there's no going back.

ONE

Hayes

———————

"I DIDN'T THINK I'd catch you tonight," Mom says when I answer the phone. "Are you still working at the hospital? Maybe you should quit and just focus on your practice."

Obviously, distance doesn't matter. A mother's nagging is just one phone call away. I squeeze my eyes shut, trying to fight the pounding headache that this conversation creates. We don't speak often so I let it go and just listen. It's nothing a pair of painkillers won't fix once I hang up with Mom, but as she keeps talking, the pounding grows louder. I fight back a groan.

Today has been a long day. I'm tired after the back to back surgeries and almost half asleep. The accident on Highway 5 this morning brought in multiple patients who needed bones reset, consultations, and a couple of amputations. Fuck, I thought being an orthopedic surgeon would be easy, but when things like that happen, it makes me rethink my career.

"I spoke with Hilda Jennings," Mom says on the other side of the phone.

Walking to the kitchen, I grab a tumbler glass and head to my home office where I have my whiskey. I pour two fingers and take a gulp. I remind myself that there's an ocean between us, and she's trying her best to be a part of my life in her own way.

"Sorry, I was working at the hospital, and I had to stay longer than I thought," I apologize, before she lectures me that I canceled my date a couple of days ago.

"Well, her daughter is waiting to hear from you to reschedule," she says. "She's a fashion designer, beautiful and smart, too. You two have a lot in common."

What can I possibly have in common with a fashion designer? I think the comic book author she introduced me to last year was more my speed, and yet, we didn't connect.

"I'm sure she's a nice young lady that comes from a great family," I say in a high-pitched voice that sounds nothing like her, but I try my best.

I hold the laugh when she grunts, "You're not funny, Hayes."

"You love me, Mom."

"Well, I really think she is who you need in your life," she insists.

Obviously, she doesn't understand who and what I need, or she'd be leaving this alone—me alone.

"Mom, just let me be," I request for the millionth time.

"I just don't understand you. There's nothing wrong with the women I set you up with. Is there?"

"I've never complained about them, have I?" I reply with a question of my own, hoping she'll get tired.

"You never called them back either," she says. "What was wrong with Paula Sinclair?"

"Which one was that one?" I swear I don't keep track of them.

They all looked about the same: light hair, slender, beautiful on the outside, but I'm not interested in getting to know them.

"Hayes, I'm doing this because I love you. Every woman I set you up with has a career, a bright future, and is lovely. Why not take a leap and try to find your happiness?"

"Sounds like you screen them well before giving me their contact information. Have you thought about coming out of retirement and starting a matchmaking company?" I try not to sound sarcastic but fail miserably. "You should stop setting me up and profit from it."

"You're thirty-five and still single."

"There's nothing wrong with being single, Mom," I insist, pouring myself another two fingers of whiskey.

If this conversation continues the way it always does, I'm going to be drunk soon and nursing a hangover for the rest of the weekend. I'm glad my next shift at the hospital isn't until Sunday afternoon.

I admit, the social piece of my life is a little pathetic. But dating some socialite from San Francisco won't fix it—it might make everything worse.

"You're alone," she says with a sad voice.

"Oh, Mom."

What else can I say?

I understand she wants me to be happy, but she has to stop emailing me numbers, descriptions, and pictures of all her friends' single daughters, insisting I take them out for dinner and get to know them.

Humoring her isn't hard; I take them out for dinner, but nothing goes beyond a second date. Don't get me wrong, the women she's introduced me to are beautiful, but they're all hoping to be the one who'll get a ring. I'm not in the market to settle down—ever.

Several times I've been close to reminding her that settling down and being part of a couple isn't all that it's cracked up to be. I don't want to bring up memories of our past. Her first marriage—to my father—was a joke. A complete and utter fucking joke. They divorced when I was only seven.

That's when she found out that my father had never been faithful to her and that the philanderer had more children than just my brother, Carter, and me.

"Just think about it. Your life is work and nothing else," she says with a yawn.

"You should go to bed Mom," I suggest, but then I check the clock I have on my bookcase with the time in Sweden, and it's six in the morning. "Actually, why are you awake so early? It's Saturday."

Mom met Lars, her husband, seven years ago at a conference. They dated for two years, and one day, she announced that she was going to retire and move to Sweden with him. Maybe that's what'll happen to me in twenty or thirty years. I'll find a woman to settle in with who already has grown children.

One thing is for sure, I'm not going to be like my father. A man who can't love anyone but himself. I won't bring children into this world who I'll neglect because I'm incapable of love. My father never cared about my mother or the women he screwed. He's never cared about his sons.

Some nights I wonder if he ever cared about us. Why wasn't Mom enough ... or us?

"I set my alarm clock to make sure I caught you before you headed to bed," she answers. "I was hoping you wouldn't be at work at ten o'clock on a Friday. Shouldn't you be out on a date or at least with your friends? You have those, right?"

I can't help but chuckle. "I'm not a hermit, Mom."

Telling her that my friends are spending their weekend with their families will give her another excuse to set me up on another not so blind date.

"We weren't the best example," she continues.

"What's that?" I ask, confused.

"Your dad with his string of mistresses and girlfriends, and I ... well, it wasn't that I was alone. I dated after the divorce, just no one was good enough to introduce to you and Carter," she explains. "Still, I tried to find love, you know—it didn't happen until Lars. He makes me happy. You should try searching for the person you can spend the rest of your life with. It's fun."

"Sounds exhausting," I say.

"Not if you do it right. At least I hope you're having sex, Hayes."

"And we're getting too personal," I complain.

"Sexual activity is important for a man your age," she insists. "You have to get out there and at least have fun with the women you meet."

Is she for real? I'm not sure if this is a European thing, or if she just doesn't care about the lines she's crossing. Mothers shouldn't be meddling in their children dating lives—or their sexual lives either.

"Yeah, I promise to go out more often," I say, instead of telling her that I don't have time to waste on dates that won't lead to anything else than an emotionless fuck.

She said it, I'm thirty-five. Too old to be fucking around.

"In the meantime, why don't you reach out to your brothers?"

My mother asking me about my father's bastards confuses me.

"Look, we might share the same DNA from William's side, but we are strangers," I remind her. "You're the one who tried to force us to become a family."

"Because you guys are brothers."

I don't get why mom keeps pushing this relationship. When your partner cheats and you find out they have other offspring, you don't try to create a family. Do you?

It might've been her upbringing. She was born in Mexico City, the youngest of five. They still get together to celebrate my grandparents' birthdays, their anniversary, and everything in between. They're close, even when they don't all live in the city.

"At one time, the seven of you were close. Until..." her voice lowers.

Until Carter, my baby brother, died. She doesn't finish, and I don't say it out loud either. It's been twelve long years since we lost him. There's a picture of him on my bookcase. His senior portrait. There are a few more of all the Aldridge brothers. Henry, the oldest, Pierce, Mills, Carter, Vance, and Beacon.

I touch the one with Carter and his best friend, Blaire.

My Blaire.

My stardust.

My best everything.

I trace her fine features with my finger. She's not petite, but at five foot four, she's almost a foot shorter than me. In this picture, she looks fragile, but she's so fucking strong. Her big ice blue eyes stare back at me with so much love. Those were the last days we spent together. It was right before I left for Baltimore.

Before we ... before it was over.

Knives carve my insides. The loss of what we had, what we dreamt. A thousand wishes lost forever. I rub my chest, missing my heart. It's been gone for years. Twelve years to be exact.

Every time I have to amputate a limb from one of my patients, I explain about the phantom pains they may have. Their arm might not be there, but for some unknown reason, the twinges, the hurt still happens —and it's normal after the loss of a part of the body.

They might not think I understand them, but I do. I feel those twinges daily, ever since I removed *her* from my life, and she took my heart with her. This picture isn't the only one I have of her, but it's the only one I allow myself to see.

Everything I have of hers is in a box, locked, because I can't seem to be able to forget her. In the past couple of years, I've been tempted to look for her. I went as far as calling her old number, but it's no longer hers. I turn the portrait around, because, today, the reality of not having her hurts too deep to withstand.

Walking to the floor-to-ceiling window, I stare at the dark horizon. The lights illuminate the city, even the bay. There's not one star in the sky, but I know they are there. Just like I know my past still exists, and *she* is somewhere in the country or the world. At least that's what I hope.

Blaire Wilson stole my heart the day we met, and her memory makes it impossible to fall in love with anyone. Perhaps it is the fact that I can't stop loving her.

"Give Dorothy a chance," Mom insists.

It's on the tip of my tongue to tell her the name isn't appealing. It just makes me want to ask where Toto is and whether or not she'll be asking me to join her on the search for the Wizard? I refrain, or she'll lecture me for not taking her seriously.

"Mom, I like my life the way it is," I explain, as calmly as I can. Ignoring the memories that unleash each time I see Blaire's picture.

Maybe that's why I have it there, to punish myself for losing the best thing that ever happened to me. I fell to pieces after what I did to us, but when she chose *him* I ... it still hurts like hell to think about it.

"My work is too demanding to think about having a family," I explain trying not to sound ungrateful. Mom doesn't like to talk about the past, Carter's last days, and bringing up Blaire ... well that's just opening Pandora's box. "But if I change my mind, I'll find the right person on my own."

Maybe when I learn to stop loving Blaire.

She chuckles. "There go my hopes of having grandchildren."

Her statement makes my heart ache because, twelve years ago, I was scared when Blaire said, 'I missed my period.' Today, I yearn to have her back, to have the family we always wanted. The future we planned. What I would give to repeat the last few months we spent together.

Now if she told me "I think I'm pregnant," I'd hug her and twirl her around, telling her how much I love her.

I close my eyes, pain burning me all the way to my bones. When I open them, I look again to the dark sky and touch the window, trying to reach for the stars. Wanting to make a wish, to see her one more time.

"It's Saturday on your side of the world," I say, trying to move the conversation forward. "Shouldn't you be getting ready to enjoy the weekend with your husband. He has grandchildren. I'm sure he can share one or two with you."

"I see that I'm not getting anywhere with this," she says, with a resigned tone. "I just want you to be happy."

"Love you, Mom."

"Love you, too, dear."

After I hang up, a notification pops on my screen, indicating I have a new voicemail. I'm tempted to leave it for tomorrow, but I don't, since it could be an emergency.

"Mr. Aldridge, it's Edmund Smith. I'm calling to remind you that you are scheduled to bring in your Lykan Hypersport tomorrow for service. We'll have a loaner car ready for you when you drop it off."

I sigh because I barely use that car. Maybe I should sell it and donate the money to some cause that might help make the world better, instead of having it in the garage with the rest of my cars. Mom might be onto something; my life is empty, and no amount of surgeries or hours spent in the emergency room teaching residents can help me fill the void inside me.

Since I have nothing better to do, I check the rest of my unheard messages, deleting each one as I listen and scribbling notes if they're important. Then there's one that freezes my blood. I check the time stamp on the screen, indicating that they called yesterday at nine in the morning.

How did I miss it?

I play it again.

"This message is for Hayes Aldridge. This is Jerome Parrish. I'm part of the legal team that handles the estate for William Tower Aldridge. Your father is requesting your presence. He has been diagnosed with pancreatic cancer, and his doctor just recommended at home hospice care. Due to your father's condition, your father is requesting your presence. Please call me at this number at your earliest convenience."

It's been years since the last time I saw William. Hospice care. He's dying. I can't believe it. We weren't close, but ... I'm confused as to what or how to feel. Am I supposed to visit him and make peace with him?

I think about Carter and how I ignored his illness, until it was too late. My relationship with my father is different; still, I don't want to regret not seeing him for the last time.

TWO

Hayes

I ONLY KNEW my father by his absence. He was an entrepreneur. The Aldridge name is synonymous with businessman.

Back in the 1800s, the Aldridge family was part of the Gold Rush. At some point, they settled in Oregon, close to Mt. Hood. They founded a small town called Baker's Creek where they—now he—own most of the town. I'm not familiar with the entire Aldridge history, but the sum of everything is that they're filthy rich.

William Aldridge always wanted to be number one. His dedication to his businesses is impressive. If only he had tried to do the same as a father and a husband. If the man tells me that he owns the world, I wouldn't be surprised. Still, when I arrive at his penthouse, I'm blown away by its extravagance.

I'm not sure what I expected to find, but this luxurious penthouse, in the heart of Manhattan, is impressive. The place sits atop a small, private, and highly coveted, white glove, pre-war building. As the doors of the elevator slide wide open, I step into a room perched high above the city, the floor-to-ceiling window providing a view of Central Park and the Hudson river. There are dramatic high ceilings and an impressive staircase that goes up five floors.

Too busy admiring the magnificence of this place, I don't notice the man standing in front of me. He's a half foot shorter than me, with salt and peppered hair and a slim frame.

"Welcome, Mr. Aldridge," a man greets me. "I'm Jerome Parrish."

"My father's lawyer," I confirm. He nods. "I'm Hayes. How is he doing?"

He lowers and shakes his head. "The nurse called me about it an hour ago, when he died."

I close my eyes as the confusion remains. My stomach feels inside out, and it's not because of the loss of William Aldridge, but the lack of reaction.

Shouldn't I be sad and grieving?

In my private practice, I've never lost anyone. I just set bones and perform ambulant surgeries for the most part. The days I work in the emergency room is when I have to deal with death. I don't do it often, but when a patient dies I have to tell their loved ones that we did everything possible, but we lost them. I can feel their sadness and pain seeping through their pores.

Right now, I'm ... not even numbed.

For fuck's sake, my father died. I should be sad. But, how can I? I barely spent any time with him while growing up, because he was busy running his empire—and having other children. I've held too much resentment to even let him into my life—not that he ever tried to reach out to me.

Anger, that's something I can handle. Sadly, this isn't the first time someone related to me has died and I'm mad. In this case, it must be because my father never cared, and yet, here I am, having to deal with him one more time.

"Did you call his other children?"

"I've been trying to reach all of you," he answers, walking toward a different elevator. "I only heard back from you. If you could please follow me."

Of course, neither of them gave a fuck either.

Why am I here?

I should leave, but before I do, I ask, "Does he have a wife or some other child who we might not know about?" I'm trying to find a way out of this situation.

"He only had one wife—Cassandra Huerta. That's your mother, right?" He answers. "Technically, I could call her."

"No, don't bother her," I bellowed, my voice echoing through the penthouse. "We will take care of him."

As I follow Mr. Parrish, I dial Henry's number—hoping he hasn't changed it. The last time I spoke to him was when Carter died. We've never been close, but since he lives here, I think it'd be best if he steps up and oversees my father's estate and funeral.

"Aldridge here," he answers on the first ring.

"Do you know our father died?"

"Fuck, it's you," he says on a loud exhale.

Well, I'm not happy to hear your voice either, but we have shit to deal with, fucker.

"Where are you?" I ask, trying to keep the conversation civil.

"None of your damn business. What do you want, Hayes?"

"Our father *died*," I repeat.

"I heard he is ... I mean was sick," he says casually.

"Shouldn't you be looking after him?"

"I asked him the same question on my birthday each year while growing up. At least, you had him for a few years," he says bitterly.

"The grass wasn't greener on my side," I tell him.

There's a long silence, and I wonder if he feels like me. Our father doesn't deserve us, but we always tried so hard to get his attention. We should be sad, but this situation brings up the resentment we've carried since we were young.

Finally, he speaks, "Ultimately, I don't give a fuck if he's alive or not."

"Well, he died," I say, in a monotone voice. "We're his only living relatives, and you live in the same city as he does. Would you mind dragging your ass by his penthouse, now?"

The doors of the elevator open on the third floor to a big library. It's an open floor with wall to wall bookcases and large windows facing the park. It might be an office because there's a desk in the middle.

"You're in town?" he asks in a surprised voice.

I walk to the window, staring at the park. Mom, Carter, and I didn't visit Dad often when he used to stay for work, but he lived in a different building. The place was on Park Avenue, and it faced another building.

"Of course, I'm here," I answer his stupid question. I'm exactly where he should be—maybe where all of us should be. "That's what you do when someone calls you to let you know that your father is sick. In his case, terminal. You at least check on him."

"Look, I'm currently busy, and later tonight, I have a date," he states.

"How about tomorrow?" I try to hide the rage.

"I have an early meeting," he says absently. I hear the keyboard on the other side of the line. He's either searching for a time to see me or working.

"We have to meet," I say dryly.

He sighs. "I'll send you my assistant's information. You might be able to squeeze in tomorrow between meetings."

"Could you just meet me for brunch instead of making up shit to avoid what's happening? It's Sunday, for fuck's sake," I say angrily.

"I'm aware of the days," he barks the words. "It's also Monday in Australia. Not that you need to know my schedule. Just know that I am a busy man."

His condescending tone makes my blood boil. He's not the only busy person. I have patients to check on tomorrow and appointments on Monday. A surgery scheduled for Tuesday. I had to find a doctor to cover for me at the hospital.

"People depend on me, and yet, here I am."

"Is it because you're waiting for Daddy's money?" He asks, and the bitterness in his voice doesn't go unnoticed. "Finally, the rightful son is getting everything he deserves."

If he were here, I'd punch him in the face. "How could I forget you're a fucking asshole?"

"Well, this is your reminder. See you in a few years or—never," he says, before the phone goes silent.

Henry: *My assistant is Sophia Aragon. I copied her to this text. Set up a meeting with her.*

Hayes: *I need to be home by tomorrow night. I have a practice to run and patients who depend on me. Our father died. The least you could do is listen to me, so we can make some arrangements.*

Sophia: *I'll take care of the issue, Mr. Aldridge.*

Sophia: *I can squeeze you in tomorrow at one. I'll send you the address and a car if you need it.*

I realize that she sent me that last text outside the group chat, and I think I like his assistant a lot more than I hate him. After I put my phone away, I finally pay attention to the lawyer who is by the desk, waiting for me.

"It seems like it's just going to be me today," I state.

If Henry, who lives here, is not going to come along, I doubt that the rest would join me on such short notice. I don't even know where they live.

"What is it that you need from me?" I ask, because if he called just to hand me my father's estate, I don't want it or give a shit about it.

"Since you're the only one here, you're going to have to take care of your father's remains," he states, matter-of-factly. "There's a final will and testament. But I can't read it until *all* his sons are in the same room —and it has to happen in Baker's Creek."

I cock an eyebrow. "Are you sure about that? Shouldn't it be at your office?"

"That's part of his last wishes. My firm is paid to execute it."

"I can't speak for my brothers, but I don't want anything that belongs to my father," I explain calmly.

He spreads some documents on the desk. A power of attorney is the first one I see. It's under my name.

"Why me?"

"Actually, he signed one for each of his sons, but since you're the first one here..."

I look at the other papers, they're also POAs, but they each have a different name.

"So, I'm fucked," I finish his sentence.

"Look, I don't know anything about your family dynamic," he says. "All I know is that you're officially responsible for his remains. Now, we need to discuss his will. There are a few elements that affect not only his descendants but the town of Baker's Creek."

"Try Henry," I suggest. "He likes money."

He gives me another paper to sign. "Look, this affects the town and whoever lives there. I can't disclose the terms of the will until all the interested parties are in the same room. Do you think you can have them in Baker's Creek in a couple of weeks?"

I rub my temples a couple of times. "Fine. I'll see what I can do."

"Here's the number for your father's assistant." He gives me a card. "She might be able to help you take care of everything."

JEROME PARRISH LEAVES PROMPTLY. I climb up the stairs, heading to the fifth floor where I assume the master suite is, but I stop at the fourth level when I spot a hospital bed. There's a person standing next to the bed, her back to me.

"Was he conscious?" I ask, as I walk toward her.

"No," she answers. "Are you one of his sons?"

I nod in response.

She gives me a sad smile. "Last night he asked if his children had come to visit. It was the first time since I came that he requested water or more morphine. He chatted with me for a few minutes. He was a very pleasant man."

Staring at my father, I realize that he was, for the most part, kind and friendly, but only in small doses. Complete strangers got more of his good side than any of his sons ever have.

"He was ... charming," I agree, finally looking at the bed, staring at the small, fragile man who lays peacefully in front of me.

In all my life, I've never seen him in bed lounging—or even sleeping. He woke up early and went to bed late. He doesn't look like the William Aldridge I knew. I am as tall as my father was, six three. I remember he'd fill an entire room with his presence. Everyone around him respected him. Some even feared him.

Now, he looks so small, so different from the man who exuded power and total control. The doctor in me wants to know what happened. How long has he been sick? He could've contacted us before things got so bad.

Why didn't he?

"Where is his chart?"

She hands me over a binder; there's nothing important other than his vitals, which were taken hourly, and the doses of morphine they administered.

"May I?" I ask her, as she's about to remove the needles attached to his arms.

Carefully, I do it. Just the same way I did it when I was a resident with patients who were about to get discharged.

Why couldn't he call before?

I might not like him, but I would've been here. Fuck, I *am* here.

"Is this what you wanted?" I ask. "To die alone without anyone to give a fuck about you?"

"Are you a doctor?"

"Yes, in San Francisco," I answer. "Did he leave any instructions about...?"

"His assistant already made the arrangements for his cremation," she informs me. "You can call her to see where you can pick up the ashes."

When I'm done disconnecting him from the machines and the IV, I caress his forehead and kiss it. "I'm sorry. I hope you rest in peace."

The employees from the crematorium arrive only a few minutes after I say goodbye. After them, the hospice employees show up to pack and move the medical equipment.

"Are you going to be okay?" The nurse asks while picking up her things.

I pull out my wallet and give her all the cash that I have with me. They don't get paid enough for what they do. At least, this should help her in some way.

"Thank you for staying with him during his last days."

"Money doesn't absolve you from not being here," she says. "No one deserves to die the way he did."

The money isn't a way to ask for absolution, just an extra payment for everything she does. I don't care what she thinks about me. Still, I say, "I tried to make it on time. Not because he deserves better, but because even he should've had someone to hold his hand during those last minutes."

She looks at me, trying to understand how I can seem so callous. But what she doesn't know is that there's always another side to the story. My brothers and I loved our father; he's the one who couldn't love us back.

Once she leaves, I'm left in a big, cold, empty house that looks pristine, and yet, it feels cold and haunted. His bedroom is at the top of the penthouse as I predicted. It has a big four poster bed, and on the nightstand there's a picture of him with the seven of us. Beacon, the baby, is just a toddler. There's also a copy of the one photograph that I have in my office. It's the one Mom took of the two of us when I was a kid.

It's of just the two of us, while we were visiting Baker's Creek. He's teaching me how to fish by the lake. It's one of the few memories I have of him. He looks so much like me. Actually, I look so much like him at that age. The guy might've died alone, but once, he had a wife—a family. I'm as successful as he was, and all my life I've fought to be nothing like him. That's taken me nowhere. I'm really not that different than him, am I?

The pang in my chest has nothing to do with the man in the picture, but the fact that, if I die right now, there'll just be a nurse shutting down the machines and unhooking me before they haul me away. There's no one who would care about me, except my mother, of course, but she has a life in another country.

My mind automatically brings up the memories of Blaire. I can't get her out of my mind. It was long ago, but it feels like everything happened just yesterday. That's a fucking loss I will never recover from.

I crave her, but the best way to quench the thirst is with alcohol. I go back to the library, hoping Dad continued storing his scotch in the bottom drawer of his desk.

Henry and I used to find it there all the time when we were teenagers. Sure enough, I find it. A brand new Macallan. I don't bother to find a glass.

I just open it, lift it, and say, "For you, old man. May you find some peace after destroying so many lives." Then I take a long swallow.

Not sure how much time passes, but when I realize that I've drank half the bottle, I'm also aware that I forgot to eat, and I'm drunk. Inebriated, yet I still don't feel sad about the loss of William. All I can think of is the anger and the resentment that's been eating away at me for all these years.

I'm a fucking wreck.

Is it just me? Maybe my brothers are happily married, or at least have a relationship with someone who, in a way, might fulfill their lives.

Me ... I can't even have a fucking relationship.

"And whose fault is that, asshole? You had it all and threw it away!"

After two perfect years with the most fantastic woman in the world, I just told her it was over.

"Coward," I yell, and my voice continues to echo around the penthouse. "You were a fucking coward."

Yet, the first chance she had she married my fucking brother. She couldn't wait for me.

"Did you ask her to wait?" I continue talking ... more like yelling to myself. "You just left her there, crying, after you told her it was over."

But how could I stay? What if she left me? My father taught me that nothing is permanent, and no one ever stays. Keeping people at arm's length has always been easier. That way, they can't abandon you; they can't fucking hurt you.

Yet, here I am.

Alone.

I remember that book, *Walden* by Thoreau, where he went to the woods because he wanted to live with a fucking purpose. Yet, he realized he isolated himself and never really lived.

That's me, isolating myself from everyone because I am terrified that, at some point, everyone is going to leave me or hurt me.

Years later, my life is inconsequential. It's now when I'm older that I realized it is people who make it worth it. What was the point of avoiding emotional entanglements and evading the messiness that relationships bring? Sure, no one ever disappointed me, but I disappointed myself.

"Look at you, asshole. You're a fucking mess."

I'm fucking envious of my brothers who I'm sure get together at least once a year. It's all my fault. I'm the one who has pushed everyone away.

Now what the fuck am I supposed to do?

"Fix your life. Face your fears."

What if I look for Blaire and I show her...?

Nothing. I'm such a contradiction. I can't just show up at her door and say, *Here I am. Love me.* I bet she's married, with children, and living the life she always planned. I couldn't mess up a good thing. All I want is for her to be happy, and I wouldn't dare to jeopardize her life, just because I am a fucking failure.

How am I supposed to live without her?

After twelve years, I've never even tried to forget her. I still love her with all my heart.

What we had was eternal love, wasn't it? Perhaps we were too young to feel so strongly for each other. Nobody could understand us and what we had.

We existed for each other. I still exist for her.

If only there's such a thing as *second chances.*

THREE

Hayes

MY PARENTS MET IN COLLEGE. Mom was studying pre-med and Dad was working toward his master's degree in business. They dated for a couple of years and married right after she graduated. It was a small ceremony in Baker's Creek, followed by a religious wedding and a huge party in Mexico City with Mom's relatives.

That year, she was accepted at Johns Hopkins, and they moved to Maryland. Well, Mom moved to Maryland, and Dad commuted to New York City. She was busy with med school, and Dad spent weekdays in

New York City where he worked with my grandfather at Aldridge Enterprises.

Needless to say, that's where he met his first mistress—Debra Merkel. The heiress to Merkel Hotels and Spas. That's also when he fathered Henry, who happens to be a year older than me. It's no surprise my big brother resents me.

He's the first born. How is it possible that I got to have a dad, and he didn't?

What he doesn't understand is that I barely saw our father. He was too busy closing deals, traveling, settling into a different city, and fathering more children.

Henry and I have a complicated relationship. When he's not being an asshole, we get along pretty well. Unfortunately, he thrives on being a fucking prick.

I open the door to Henry's office, and his deep forest green eyes, just like mine, stare at me. We both look a lot like my father: tall, chestnut brown hair, straight nose, and well built. It's not like looking at the mirror since I have olive skin, but everyone could guess that we're related.

"You're my one o'clock?" Henry asks, annoyed as I enter his office without even knocking. Just like his assistant instructed me to do.

"I'm surprised your assistant isn't outside waiting for you to bark some orders," I comment, pushing the door closed.

"She'd sue me if I make her work on Sunday."

"Saturday is an option?" I ask sarcastically.

"Sometimes," he confesses, and I'm starting to believe that this guy is worse than me. At least I have the excuse of saving lives, but he ... what is he saving? His fortune?

"You have five minutes," he says. "Use them wisely."

"No, I'm pretty sure your assistant said one to three," I amend and grin when he gives me an annoyed glare.

"Like you, I wasn't a fan of our father. To this day, I still don't know how to feel about him," I say directly without rushing. Though, I'm not sure when he's going to kick me out. "He died. I should mourn, but I'm not. The point isn't how I feel or if I even care to dissect my emotions."

"What's the point of this conversation?"

Last night, while I drank my dad's expensive scotch and reflected on my life, I realized I wasn't much different than him. I don't have one meaningful relationship. Not even with my brothers.

I'm not hoping to spend the next fifty Christmases with them, but maybe, we could stay in touch. Today's goal is to get my brothers together and find out what the old man wanted to do with his beloved town.

"I took care of almost everything. His assistant will be closing the penthouse," I say, taking a seat across from him.

"Are we having a funeral?" he asks.

"Should we?" I refute. "It's not like we were close to him. What are we supposed to say? He was a shitty father and a horny asshole."

He chuckles and shakes his head.

"Well, he had business associates, friends. I'm sure whoever continues the Aldridge legacy has to keep with appearances and make sure he shows that our father mattered."

"Who is going to keep his legacy?" I inquire because I only know medicine, and bones are my specialty. "I'm a doctor. You're the closest to what he used to do. I read that you're a hotel mogul."

He nods. "They left me everything. I had to rise to the occasion."

"They?" I ask, arching an eyebrow.

His face falls slightly. "Mom died a couple of years after Carter. It was a car accident. I began to take over her responsibilities as CFO of the company. Then my grandfather died a couple of years ago, so it's now all mine."

"Sorry to hear about Debra," I say, feeling like an asshole, because she never married, and they weren't that close if I recall.

"Hey, life sucks and you just deal, you know. Mom and I weren't too close. She was always busy, and sometimes, I was just another one of her employees."

My chest tightens when I hear how distant he sounds about the death of his mother. Mom and I might have our differences about my life and my future, but we have a good relationship.

"How's Cassandra?" he asks.

"Mom got married a few years ago. She retired and moved to Sweden with her husband."

"How about you?" he asks. "Are you married with children?"

I chuckle. "Nah, and you?"

He shakes his head. "I don't have time, and I doubt I can be faithful to a woman."

"My feelings exactly." I nod in agreement.

"No, you did have someone. I'm still trying to understand what happened with Blaire—how things ended up all fucked up between the two of you."

Pain cuts through my gut at the mention of her and the memory of our fucked-up ending. How did it really end?

Me leaving, or her betraying me after I left?

If only that's what I remembered about Blaire Wilson: the end when she didn't love me anymore. Not the beginning when I fell madly in love with her, not her cool ice blue eyes that contrasted with her tanned skin and dark hair, but the pain I felt after everything was over.

She broke me. That's what I should remember. Not the times I brushed my lips against her forehead at night while I held her against me as she slept. Those are the kind of memories that sneak up on me at night. The ones where I nuzzled her hair after making love to her. My lips still remember all the times I took her mouth, exploring every corner of it, searching for her flavor as I ignited the fire within her.

It's been over a decade since it all ended, but my body still misses hers. Her soft skin, her heat enveloping me when I was inside of her. Being inside of her used to be my favorite place—the only place I liked to be. My entire being aches, and I don't know what is happening to me.

What I miss the most is talking to her at night before we fell asleep after a long day at school. She would listen to me rant about my teachers or the EMT training I was taking. Sometimes, I'd talk about the latest astronomical discovery or some random scientific article. She not only listened, she also contributed. Deep down, she's just as nerdy as I am.

She'd tell me about her classes, or the kids she visited while she volunteered at the hospital. With her, I was never alone. Blaire was the only person who could make me feel like love existed and that maybe there was more to life than just science. That there were some things you couldn't explain. You just had to believe in them, like faith and love.

I push my mind away from Blaire. She's a bittersweet memory. If I could, I'd shred it. But then, if I do, I will have nothing left of her.

Does it even matter?

The answer is yes. She'll always matter.

"Let's concentrate on our father," I say, focusing on the now and the future of the company.

For the next few minutes, I brief Henry about my conversation with Jerome Parrish.

"You're only coming to me because I'm the business guy, so why not dump the responsibility on him. I have enough on my plate, and I honestly don't care about him or his legacy," he says firmly.

"No, you're misunderstanding. This is a one-time thing. As I said, we meet in Baker's Creek, he reads the testament, and it's over."

"What's going to happen with his fortune?"

I shrug. "Who cares about it? We'll sell, donate, and walk away from everything."

He cocks an eyebrow. "You don't want his money?" he asks, suspiciously. "You're his *legitimate* child. I guess you deserve the name and all the shit that entitles."

This should be the part of the conversation where I tell him that his perception of my position in the family is outdated.

Who the fuck cares about being the legitimate child? I don't think that's even important in modern life. We were all the same to William Aldridge—nothing. Just products of his irresponsible sex life.

"Why should I care about his money?" I ask. "I make half million a year. I haven't touched the trust he gave me."

I don't know why Dad gave us three trust funds. Out of guilt, a way to say I'm done pretending we're a family, or just because he had too much money. Either way, each one of us received three different amounts. The first one when we turned eighteen for two billion dollars. The second for the same amount when we turned twenty-one. The final payout to happen at twenty-five for six billion dollars. We each have ten billion dollars—except Carter, who only received the first because he died at twenty.

"Good point," he agrees and runs a hand through his hair. "Send a text with the town's information and the date to Sophia. I'll meet you in Baker's Creek."

"What about the funeral you suggested?"

He sighs. "I guess people are expecting that from me."

I arch an eyebrow. "Which people?"

"Father and I haven't spoken in years, but we ran in the same circles. Everyone knows I'm William's child." He rises from his seat and walks around. When he stops, he says, "I don't want anyone I know there. Let's do it in Baker's Creek. We can make an excuse about the wake. Maybe something like, he only wanted us—his sons—present."

"Sounds like a plan." I agree and check my watch.

I'm all tapped out for today and my flight doesn't leave until tonight. Maybe I'll go to the airport, and while I wait for my flight, I can call the other four.

"Have the others agreed to see you?" he questions before I leave.

I shake my head. "None of them have answered my calls."

"Who is next on your list?"

"Honestly, I don't have an order, but we should contact Pierce," I answer.

He scratches his chin. "Give me a second. I think Mills is in town."

He pulls his phone closer, pushes a few buttons, and the speaker comes to life. The dial tone is the first noise heard, followed by some beeps.

"It's Sunday," an annoyed female voice answers the phone. "What do you need?"

"Where are the Orcas playing this weekend?"

"They're at Madison Square Garden," she answers screaming, "GO DEEP!"

"How do you know?"

"Because I'm here and you're interrupting the game. You owe me a pair of tickets for the next home game, since you're ruining it."

"I'll get you season tickets, Ms. Aragon," he says, rolling his eyes, "If I ask you to call Stewart to ask him for a favor?"

"What do you need?" she grunts.

"I need a word with Mills."

"Aldridge?" she asks curiously. "You told me you weren't related."

I arch an eyebrow, and he shrugs answering, "It's complicated."

"Well, your non-relative has been out for the season ... no, no, fucker, the net is the other way."

I can't help but laugh. This woman is passionate about her hockey.

"So, he's not here," my brother confirms.

"He's here, but not playing. If you're related to him, get me an autograph, and I might forgive you for breaking the rules."

"Well, I might have to live without your forgiveness, won't I?" He says and hangs up the phone.

"Do you have his number?" he asks me.

I try it, and the call goes to voicemail.

Fucker 2: *Mills, I'm in New York. Can we meet?*

Mills: *No, I don't give a fuck if the old man is dying.*

Fucker 2: *HE DIED YESTERDAY. Henry and I need to speak to you.*

Mills: *Where do you want to meet?*

"Where can we meet?" I ask Henry.

"I have work to do," he responds.

"I'll ask him to come here. In the meantime, order some food," I request.

Fucker 2: *Here are the details. How soon can you arrive?*

Mills: *I'm on my way. Apparently, the fact that my old man died gives me a pass to leave the arena early. Lucky me.*

FOUR

Hayes

DAD WAS A MOVING BODY. His home base was Baltimore, where he shared a place with his wife and newborn, me. He traveled every other week to New York, but while he was doing business with the Merkel Hotels and Spas, he was also sharing his life with Debra Merkel—and Henry.

Needless to say, the Merkels trusted him. Mom's theory is that they were hoping to fuse both families—through marriage. He was working his way to become the CEO of Aldridge Enterprises while managing some of the Merkels' acquisitions. During those deals, they wanted to buy a resort in Aspen, and they sent Dad to close the deal.

He closed the deal and also hooked up with their Colorado lawyer, Sara Bryant. During the process, he acquired a brewery too. His excuse to return to Colorado. Hence, he had to buy a house in Denver and establish yet another residence. It had nothing to do with business and a lot to do with his new mistress and his son, Pierce.

And then, we were three.

So, while we wait for Mills, Henry suggests contacting Pierce. Even though they don't get along, he knows how to reach out to him. According to Henry, he is one of the partners at Bryant LLP, which is the Pierce family's firm. I can't believe they still handle the Merkel's hotels in Colorado. Instead of calling him, Henry sets a video conference.

His hair is jet black, his nose has a small hook on the bridge, but he has the same green eyes we all share. He has a fucked-up temper like Henry. I guess we all do. And just like me, he doesn't want to do shit with our father or his inheritance. He claims to be too busy to deal with any family affairs.

He doesn't specify if it's Aldridge family affairs or any family in general. Do any of us stop working to be around our families?

I love Mom, and yet, I haven't taken any time off to visit her in Sweden.

"You're not the only one who has to work," Henry says, squeezing a stress ball. "I get it, Pierce. You don't give a fuck about him—me neither. However, we have to at least see this through and close that chapter."

"So what if you miss a weekend at the slopes," I say, as I look at the snow mountains behind him. "Where are you? Aspen?"

"My life isn't any of your business," he says. "Baker's Creek is a place I would rather avoid. I don't want to attend his funeral. Who cares about his last wishes? He never cared about any of my wishes. Nothing he leaves me is worth the trouble."

The door to the office opens; it's Mills. He's a couple of inches taller than me, and he's the blonde of the family.

"Great, fucker one and two are here," he says. "We're having a fucking family reunion. Where are the rest?"

"Who is that?" Pierce asks.

Henry moves the monitor, so he can see Mills. "Oh, the jock. I heard your career is over. You should be the one taking on Aldridge Enterprise and Dad's assets. Aw, you can be just like Daddy."

"It's not fucking over, fucker number three." His voice makes the entire room vibrate. "I'll be back next season."

"Original, you know. We do all have actual names. Fucker has nothing to do with them. But what can I expect from you, a stupid jock?"

Mills is smart, but he grew up in Vancouver, Canada, where hockey is a religion and not just a sport. The guy knew how to skate almost at the same time he learned how to walk. It's understandable that growing up in such a culture he'd end up playing hockey.

"Can you two stop the nonsense? You're grown men," Henry orders.

It's always been like this between them. I guess it's because they're only a few months apart. Daddy didn't stay in Colorado long enough. I'd like to blame the Merkels for trusting him to work in their best interest. Dad acted in his own interest. The deal in Vancouver fell through, but Marie Tremblay became part of his life, giving him son number four.

Honestly, I wonder if our father ever used a condom because how in the fucking hell did he keep knocking up these women?

"What do you want from me?" Mills asks.

I go ahead and explain everything that transpired in the past couple of days.

"It's just a quick trip to Baker's Creek," I conclude, clasping my hands behind my back as I look outside the window.

I can see the Statue of Liberty from here. It's pretty cool to at least look at something beautiful while you're working. I, on the other hand, don't have the time or the view.

"Do you know how many times I begged him to come to see me play while growing up?"

"You're not the only one, Mills," I say, exasperated. "I get it. He was an asshole who didn't care about any of us. Dad missed games, practices, recitals, science fairs, and so much more. It wasn't only you. He did it to all of us."

"So, I have to act like a loving son and follow his wishes?" Pierce asks with sarcasm. "Or what's the plan?"

"We go in, pretend to give a shit during the funeral, sit down while the lawyer reads Dad's will and decide how to get rid of his money—unless one of you needs it."

"The jock might need it since he's too stupid to do anything other than punch assholes for a living," Pierce says.

"Stop!" I order.

"We're not teenagers anymore. Even then, it was shitty the way you treated each other," I say, trying to put some order. They're thirty-three and yet, they behave like they're five. "Can you get through this without fighting or punching each other?"

"I can if the bloodsucking lawyer keeps his trap shut," Mills agrees. "My issue is Arden."

"Arden?" I ask, confused.

"My son, he's with the hockey wives right now. They help me watch him during the games, but I don't have anyone who can help me if I go to Baker's Creek."

"You have a son?" we all ask at once.

"Yeah, well, shit happens. Condoms break, and I have a fourteen-month-old kid who shouldn't be at a funeral."

"Where is his mom?" I ask.

"She's not in the picture—long story," he says dismissively.

I don't say more, but I have so many questions as well as respect for him.

When Blaire scared the shit out of me saying, *I think I'm pregnant,* I wanted to bolt. Don't get me wrong, I adored her, but the kid part scared me. In fact, even though she wasn't pregnant, I bailed on her and left for Baltimore. Johns Hopkins was waiting for me, and I couldn't risk *my* future by having a baby.

Blaire was too young, and I was ... an idiot, because what I wouldn't give to have her and a baby with her.

"We'll find someone to watch him for a couple of hours," Henry says with a smirk. "Actually, I have just the person for the job."

"I'm not leaving my son with a stranger."

"Sophia isn't a stranger. She's my assistant. I've known her for a couple of years. She has nieces and nephews. I'm sure she's capable."

"How about you?" Henry asks Pierce. "Any children or family we should know about?"

"A wife," he says and clears his throat. "Ex, if she wasn't stubborn and would sign the fucking divorce papers."

"Sorry, Man," Mills says. "That's tough. Mom went through a few divorces, and it was never easy."

"How is your mom?" I ask curiously.

"Happy with husband number five. They live in Calgary. I see her often," he says. "Do you have any kids, Pierce?"

"Are Beacon and Vance going to be at this party?" Pierce asks, changing the subject. "Because I don't see them here."

"It seems like everyone ignored Dad's lawyer," I state the obvious.

"Except the nerd," Henry says, staring at me. "The good son."

"Fuck off," I warn him and pull out my phone, calling Vance.

"Hey, it's Hayes." I start speaking right away since voicemail picked up on the first ring. "I'm with Henry and Mills. Dad died yesterday, and we want to speak to you."

"What about me?" Pierce protests. "I'm here, too."

"Right," I say, rolling my eyes. "Pierce is on Facetime. We have to talk. The funeral is in a couple of weeks—in Baker's Creek. We need you there—it's not optional."

I hang up, wondering if Vance will even show up. He's the quiet one of the seven. He's baby boy number six. Carter was five. When Carter was alive, those two were very close. If things had been different, I'm sure Carter would know how to reach out to Vance.

Scrubbing my face with both hands, I try to find my footing. I don't like emotions, and they have been fucking with me since Friday. I miss Carter so much. Wondering how things would've been if he hadn't died is useless, and yet, I can't stop playing the different scenarios.

I was three when Carter was born. My memories about that time aren't many. It's understandable, since, according to my mom, I was a busy toddler. All I can remember is a baby crying, and my parents fussing over him. I liked him, and I was a proud big brother.

A few months later, Dad started making a few deals down in

Atlanta, and that's where he met Addison Belle Holmes. The daughter of a decorated general. That's when Vance was conceived. Dad was lucky that the general didn't shoot him once they figured out that my father was a womanizer and an asshole.

"I just texted Vance, too," Mills says.

"You're in touch with him?"

He shrugs his shoulders. "Yeah, I saw him once at the airport while he was traveling to Germany. Back when Atlanta had a hockey team. We chat sometimes."

"What does he do?" Henry asks.

"He's part of the military. Not sure if it's the Army, Navy, or ... he doesn't talk about it," he concludes. "We just text a few times a year."

"Why him and not me?" Pierce protests, making Henry and I snicker.

"You two fight like cats and dogs," I respond. "You're fucking unbelievable. I could ask the same. Hey, why didn't you invite me to your wedding?"

"Yeah well, I guess we're not that kind of family, are we?" Pierce answers.

I shake my head.

"Vance is out of the country," Mills informs us. "He wants you to text him the information, and he'll see what he can do."

"Tell him it's not optional," I press.

"Okay, one more call," Henry says, somehow encouraging me to continue.

"Aww, we're calling the baby," Pierce mocks me. "He might be sleeping. Isn't that what rock stars do during the day?"

Beacon plays for one of the most famous bands in the world, Too Far from Grace. At almost thirty, I think he's the most successful one of all of us. I admire the kid because he's at the top under his own merit. Even though he's Hollywood royalty, being the grandson of the famous actor Kirk Fitzpatrick and the son of the famous singer, Janelle, he made it on his own.

The guy never used the Fitzpatrick name, his mother's connections, or the last name Aldridge. He doesn't talk about his roots. If anyone figured out who he is, it'd be all over the news, and I think it would affect everyone—including us. How he has kept the secret under wraps is a mystery.

His mother was a huge pop star back in the late eighties and nineties. I don't know how Dad ended up knocking her up. We never learned the story, but because he got tangled up with her, we learned that he had more than one family. At some point during their relationship, his picture ended up in the tabloids, along with the news that he's the father of Janelle's baby. A kid no one ever found out about until that day.

That's when everyone realized Dad was a scumbag.

"Beacon's phone, how can I help you?" A cheery female voice answers.

"Is he available?" I ask.

"It depends," she retorts. "Why are you calling, asshole number two?"

I chuckle. "Is that how my name comes up on the caller ID? He catalogues us as assholes, just like Mills calls us Fuckers."

"No, it reads Hayes. However, when your name flashed, he just said, 'Fuck. First a lawyer calls about my father and now it's asshole number two,'" she explains, trying to imitate a male voice but failing. "I answered because I guess things are not going well with his dad, and he can only ignore him for so long."

"I can ignore him forever," Beacon says on the other side of the line. "Leave it alone, G."

"He's sick, and you have to at least say goodbye. It'll be good for your soul."

"I'm soulless, so it doesn't matter," he argues while she grunts in response.

"And you are?" I ask intrigued.

"Beacon's Jiminy Cricket," she answers.

"Just less green, sassier, and cuter," he says mockingly. "Hang up, G."

"What is it that you need to tell him? I'll convey the message."

"Can you at least put me on speaker?"

"Fine," she sighs. "Speak."

"Beacon, our father died yesterday morning."

"Tell him I don't give a fuck," Beacon says.

"When is the funeral?" His friend or girlfriend asks.

"In two weeks, in Baker's Creek," I inform her. "We need him to be there—it's not optional."

"Hmm, I know where that is," she says. "You hear, Beac, we're going to Baker's."

"There's no fucking way I'm going to that damn town," he says.

"Umm, we were there just a couple of weeks ago," she says and then screeches after he says, "That's it, you asked for it, G."

"Stop!" She bursts into laughter. "Put me down, Beac!"

"You know what to do," I hear him say.

"Uncle!"

There's a long pause and the laughter coming from the phone fills the entire office.

"Look, asshole," Beacon speaks. "I don't give a shit about the old man."

"We agree, Beacon," Mills says. "Yet, we're here trying to deal with his shit one last time."

"Mills?"

"Yeah, and Henry is here, too," he responds. "Just do this once, okay?"

"Fine. Send me the info. I'll be there," he promises, and I wonder how close Beacon, Vance and Mills are. "Now, if you'll excuse me, I have family shit to do."

"Your wife?" I ask, wanting to know more about the woman he's with.

He laughs. "Nah, I don't do that shit. My best friend invited me to have brunch with her family. See you later, assholes."

"You know what's sad?" Mills asks after Beacon hangs up.

"That we're getting together just because our father died?" Henry responds with an unamused voice.

"Other than that," he amends his statement. "That we're all alone."

"I'm married," Pierce protests.

"Are you in all honesty happy with your life?" Mills asks, and there's no animosity in the question.

"I will be when she signs the fucking divorce papers," Pierce responds.

"We're pathetic," I conclude.

"We have 'daddy issues,'" Mills chuckles. "Really. That's what my therapist says. Well, he doesn't use those words, but it's all the same, you know."

"You're going to therapy?" I ask, impressed, because at least one of us is trying to do something about our screwed-up lives.

"Hey, I'm trying to be a good father. I had a shitty one, so I have to figure out how to do it right, you know," he says. "So, I go to a guy who tells me I'm an idiot and an asshole in a constructive way, so I can change."

We all laugh. I'm sure that's not the case, but he's getting help and that's a step or two above any of us.

"I hate to kick you out of my office, but that's all the time I have for you," Henry says when his phone buzzes. "I have a videoconference with the manager at the Bora Bora resorts."

It's on the tip of my tongue to tell him that we have food coming in, but I choose to let it go.

"See you in a couple of weeks," I say, taking my jacket and leaving the office.

"Hey, wait." Mills walks behind me. "I don't need to go to the airport until later. Let's get Arden, and we can have a late lunch or something?"

"That would be good," I say.

FIVE

Blaire

"MS. WILSON, this is Jerome Parrish. I'm part of the legal team for William Tower Aldridge. I called to inform you that Mr. Aldridge died two weeks ago tomorrow. We're sorry for your loss. The funeral is this upcoming Wednesday. Your presence is required. Please call me at your earliest convenience so we can discuss all the details."

SIX

Blaire

––––––––––––

WHAT DOESN'T KILL you makes you stronger. That is my motto. Not many things can bring me down. Really, I'm a survivor. It's not a joke. I could even write a book on how to survive in the Amazon Rainforest. It's not easy. Let's start with the animals you have to be on the lookout for. Like piranhas, boa constrictors, jaguars, and poisonous arrow frogs. There's an anaconda or two hanging from the trees. My biggest enemies are mosquitos. Those suckers carry a lot of nasty diseases.

After all my travels, I'm used to wearing long pants and long-sleeve shirts, even under the heat and humidity of the jungle.

"I can survive everything," I say out loud, as I drive the rental down the road, taking me to Baker's Creek. "I'll make it through this day unharmed."

I've been to the quaint little town with a few thousand citizens—at best—a couple of times. If I recall, they organize the most outrageous festivals to keep the flow of tourists visiting, even when it's not ski season. This place is a two-hour drive from Portland, near Mt. Hood.

The landscape is spectacular, but at the moment, it's hard to enjoy it. It's been a long time since I've driven a car, and these steep curves and narrow roads are reminding me why I prefer to walk. The first thing I'll do when I arrive in town is kiss the ground and maybe search for a home to stay forever, because there's no way I'm driving back again.

What if I rent a bike and ride all the way back to Portland? Walking would take me more than a day and I'm not sure if this area is bear free. Are bears awake in May?

This trip better be worth the hassle. All the things I could do with— What is it that they're going to give me? Who cares? I'll put it to good use.

Right when I'm thinking of what I could do with the money I might inherit, my phone rings. It's a good thing I listened to the guy at the rental car agency and connected the Bluetooth.

"Blaire speaking," I say, as I push the answer button on the steering wheel.

"Hey, Boss," Victoria, my right-hand and best friend, greets me. "Are you in Baker's Creek yet?"

"No. According to my phone, I should arrive there soon. But *soon* is relative, since I'm driving at turtle speed."

She laughs. "You should've hired a car service or let me do it for you. You're a shitty driver."

No kidding. I learned to drive at seventeen. I didn't have much practice during college because I didn't own a car. Back then, my boyfriend let me drive his truck, but not too often—he was afraid I'd smash it against a light pole. After graduation, I moved back to San Francisco, choosing to walk or use public transportation. It's good for the environment and the other drivers.

When I travel, there's always a designated driver who knows the area better than me.

"Someone has to stay behind in case I don't make it out of here alive," I say jokingly, kind of.

"It can't be that bad."

"Oh, but it is," I argue, sounding dramatic, because she doesn't know who I'm about to meet and the story between the Aldridge family and me. Or how long has it been since the last time I had any contact with William ... or Hayes.

Twelve years.

"Why are you even going then?"

"According to the lawyer who contacted me, this guy left me some money. We could use it, Tori."

I sigh. If anyone who doesn't know me heard me say that, they'd think I'm a gold digger who's just been waiting for the old guy to die. I'm not. In all honesty, I haven't thought about William in a long time. Ultimately, the money is going to whatever project needs it the most.

"That's true. Your to-do list is getting longer, and our benefactors' list has decreased. I told you we should try a charity event."

She's always full of great ideas, but they require an initial investment I can't afford. Let's just hope this inheritance is real. This is exactly why I'm eating my pride and setting up my mind into survival mode. Entering the Aldridges' world is like willingly diving into the Amazon river. There's no way to avoid the piranhas, black caimans, or anacondas. There's little hope to make it out alive.

Should I tell Victoria to send a rescue team if I'm not home by tomorrow?

Hopefully, that's not the case. Vance, one of the youngest brothers, is going to be there. He and I are on good terms. If someone can take down his siblings, it'd be him. He's a former army captain—at least that's what he tells me. Everything he does is classified.

Not that I need him to fight my battles. I can take care of myself. Am I anxious because Hayes might be there?

How could I not be?

He was my first everything until, one day, he decided he didn't love me. That man did a number on me. I fell for him so hard and so fast. He became my universe, and then one day, poof. He decided to push me away. Metaphorically speaking, he threw me into a black hole and forgot all about me. The last time we saw each other he was cruel, distant, and hateful. I'm not in love with him, but my heart never quite recovered from what happened between us. The pangs of pain happen often—if not daily. I don't think they'll ever go away; they'll stay right next to the love I'll always have for him.

There are things in life that are impossible to forget, like your first love and your soulmate, no matter how painful it is to remember.

As the exit to Baker's Creek comes in to view, so does a sign that says, *Welcome to Baker's Creek. Home of the best... Find Out.*

I push the break and read the sign again. Thankfully, there's no one driving behind me, or this reckless move would've caused an accident. I read it again. It's new, or at least twelve years old. Who put that in there? It really reads *Find out.*

I'm not sure how to feel about that sign. Is it a warning or ... why would they have that?

The best serial killers, the best blackberry pie, the best ... I'll figure it out and suggest they change it. I'm good at playing chess, puzzles, and solving mysteries.

Following the instructions of the navigation system, I continue down the road and then turn left toward the bridge. The lake is beautiful, and the view of Mt. Hood makes it magical. It's as if you leave the world behind, and you enter into a new dimension. The evergreens surround the area. I spot maple trees too and a variety of flowers. Like red currant, red columbines, and a trail of lavender that extends toward the east. I wonder how far the resort is since the snowed mountain looks farther than I remember.

"Blaire, are you still there?"

"Yes, sorry I was—"

"Daydreaming, I know," she answers. "I'll leave you to it. Call me when you are settled in and know more about your new net worth."

"It wouldn't be mine," I clarify. "I'm poor as a country mouse. The last time I checked, I had about thirty dollars on my savings account. Not enough to pay rent, in case you're going to ask me for it."

I'm thankful that the legal firm that represents William paid for my ticket, or I couldn't have afforded the trip—or this car. I even flew in first class. Do they need me here that badly? The lawyer said, *"There are a lot of futures at stake, and the Aldridge brothers can't do it without you."*

"Good thing I'm leasing your room to a doctor who works at San Fran Medical," she laughs. "That's code for: you are staying on the couch until your next trip."

"That sounds like a plan," I answer absently.

"Yep, you're not even paying attention. Drive safe, Blaire."

The place makes me want to extend my stay to explore the area.

As I drive along the narrowed road, I'm in awe by the look of the historical buildings. It's a mix of the old west and the Victorian era. Nothing has changed much, but I feel like now that I'm older, I appreciate the architecture and the vegetation a lot more than I did when I first came to visit.

I remember Hayes telling me the Aldridges founded this back in the late eighteen hundreds. They owned most of the town. I wonder if that's still the case. Wouldn't it be wild if they say, *you've inherited the town since the sons don't give a fuck about it?*

I can see the six brothers fighting over the money, the assets, and the companies outside this magical place.

The question is why am I being called? Obviously, it has to do with Carter—my late husband. But why here and why is my presence mandatory?

How can the brothers need me? Most of them hate me.

That's what the lawyer said. I'd be helping people. The Aldridge brothers need me. To say that I'm not curious would be a lie. It shouldn't matter to me. I just need the money, and we can be done with these people forever. The word *help,* though ... that pulls me like a magnet. I thrive on helping others. My parents say I'm a philanthropist by nature. Not that they like it—in fact, they hate that I dedicate my life to serving others.

The sight of the bakery makes me almost push on the break. They have the best cookies in the world and their croissants are to die for. I drive slow enough so I can look at both sides of the street. There are a few stores I don't recognize, but others I am familiar with, like the bookstore and the diner.

I hope the small diner still has its original furniture. It was a trip to the past when we dined in that place. The wait staff and the cooks dressed in clothing from the 50s. If I could, I would stay a couple of extra days, but two days is all the time I have. Unless, I get kicked out before I even settle into my room.

Tori booked a room at The Lodge. That's the family ski resort and where the lawyer is expecting me at noon.

"Ugh," I groan.

I only have twenty minutes to arrive, check-in, change, and head to the conference room. I pray that it's just the two of us. I don't want to see any of the brothers. The last time I saw them, everyone was in a bad place. Words were said, hearts were broken, and friendships forgotten. No, that's not true. My heart had been broken way before that day. I guess that day those fragmented pieces were pulverized.

As I arrived at The Lodge, I turn off the engine and take a deep cleansing breath. I leave my sleeping bag and my hiking backpack in the trunk and pull out the duffle bag. I'll come for the rest later. It's a good thing I'm close to the mountains where everyone is backpacking and planning on camping. I won't look like an odd tourist.

Is it camping season?

Maybe not. The only time I camped here was during the 4th of July. There was some celebration over the weekend that we skipped while Hayes and I remained in the woods. My cheeks heat just thinking about him and that weekend. We didn't explore the area, but we explored each other pretty well. I fan myself because I shouldn't look flustered thinking about sex or Hayes while walking into the conference room.

Am I ready to see him?

No. If the memories of him affect me so much when he's away, how am I going to react when I see him? My heart stutters at the thought of seeing him again. Back in Brazil, it was an idea that I swept under the rug. When I boarded the plane, it worried me. During the drive, I was brave and ready to attack. But as I step into the lobby, I fully accept that I'm not ready for Hayes.

I grab onto the sting of humiliation during our last encounter. His rejection, his hate. It's not emotionally healthy to hold onto such nasty feelings, but I don't have any other options. If I don't raise some walls, the alternative might be throwing myself into his arms and telling him that it's been hard to forget him. I learned that in life it is best to forget the bad and stick to the beautiful parts of your life.

He was one of those parts. Not that he'd care, which is why I have to pretend again. Like I did when Carter died. I have to fake that I don't love him. That he doesn't affect me. That he's inconsequential.

"Good afternoon," the guy behind the desk greets me. "The hostel is on the other side of town."

"You have a hostel in this town?"

He gives me a shrug. "It's a shelter, but it sounds better calling it a hostel?"

I glance at myself and sigh. I look and smell like I've been in the jungle for two weeks. That doesn't give him the right to send me to a shelter because he doesn't like the way I look. I'm a guest.

"Blaire Wilson," I announce, taking my ID and credit card out of my wallet.

He scrunches his nose and says, "We reserve the right to deny accommodations."

I slam my hand on the counter. "Listen, I don't have time to deal with you. I have about ten minutes to take a shower, change, and go into a meeting."

"If you don't leave the premises, I'll call the sheriff," he threatens me, placing a hand on the telephone next to the computer monitor.

"What do we have here?" My breath stills at the familiar baritone voice.

Please, don't be Hayes, I beg.

The concierge gives me an arrogant glare and then looks at the new arrival. "I'm explaining to this ... lady that we reserve the right to deny accommodations."

I turn still hoping that it's anyone but him. My heart stops. Lungs collapse and the entire room spins. I grab onto the counter since my legs can barely sustain me.

Hayes.

Tall, dark, and breathtakingly handsome Hayes Aldridge. His green-eyed gaze focuses on me as my heart thunders inside my ribcage.

Hayes gives me a tight smile, his dimple showing, taking my breath away. He's still annoyingly handsome. No, he's even more handsome than when I met him. I want to run a hand through his soft chestnut colored hair and kiss the stubble of his chiseled jaw. Of course, the want has to do with my lack of sleep and lack of human touch. Nothing to do with the man.

Do I want to ask how he's doing?

Maybe because it's been twelve years and his father just died. I have no idea how things ended between them, but while we dated their relationship was rocky. Hayes denied how much his father's absence hurt. I want to just hug him and say, I know it hurts but it gets better.

I don't speak for several seconds, or maybe minutes. I can't even move. We just stare at each other. It's truly painful to be here in front of him as a stampede of memories rush through my head. Stepping back a bit, I remind myself that he's my past, and he shouldn't affect me in the present. I loved him, but now, he's just another guy.

"Oh, it's you," I say, trying to mask the plethora of feelings fluttering inside me.

His bright green eyes meander along my body before he speaks, "Charming as usual. Why are you here?"

I can't help but scrunch my nose. Charming is a word he uses a lot when he doesn't like someone, but that person is pleasant. Suddenly it's all too much, his scent, his presence, and the memories.

Reluctantly, I respond, "I'm guessing for the same reason as you."

He studies me, and I hate that I can't read him well. "You look like you've been in the woods for a week."

"The Amazon Rainforest," I correct him, my eyes meet his as I find some balance. Clearly, I wasn't ready to see him, but I can handle the jungle, I should be able to handle him. "And it was two weeks."

He frowns and blinks a couple of times.

"Long story," I answer his silent question, wanting to tell him more. Everything.

It's been twelve years, and he's still the first person I want to talk with after something exciting happens to me. When I started to travel, I created a blog, and every time I write for it, I imagine I'm talking to him. He was the best listener and the best problem solver, too. The thing about Hayes and I is that we just function perfectly together. We fit perfectly until he decided I wasn't the piece that completed his puzzle.

But we're strangers now, and there's nothing that we can do or say that would fix the past. Is there?

I turn around to the snobbish guy and ask, "Now, can I have a room, or should I go to the lake to clean myself?"

"Nick, give her the key to one of the suites," Hayes orders the guy then grabs my ID and credit card inspecting them. "You live in San Francisco?"

"Sometimes," I respond and turn to the guy. "A normal room works. I can't afford the suite."

The law firm is reimbursing the room and my meals, but I doubt they'll pay for a suite.

"It's on the house," Hayes says, giving me back my stuff. "Give her a suite—and make sure that any room service is charged to the house account, not to her."

Grudgingly, Nick gives me a keycard and instructions on how to get to the elevator bank. I give him a sweet smile and make my way to the elevator.

"Aren't you going to thank me for getting you the room?" I hear his voice following behind me, its huskiness stealing the oxygen around us. I walk faster because I don't think I can have a conversation with him—not yet, or ever.

Who knew he'd be provoking such emotional havoc in me by just being in his presence for only a minute? I should've known, though. My physical reaction to his memories haven't changed over the years. It's logical that my response to him would be, at least, as strong.

"Thank you for coming to my rescue, oh noble Hayes Aldridge," I say mockingly, pressing the elevator button several times.

"Blaire."

I turn to look at him, trying to keep the little annoyance I can fake because really all I want is ... *him*. We have so much history and such a disastrous ending that I should stay away. I play the cool, yet annoyed woman—a role I hate. Faking and lying are two things I despise.

Faking that he's not affecting me is harder than I thought. I take a good look at him. In another reality, if we drifted apart and we found each other again, we'd be thrilled to see each other. This should be the part where we hug, we kiss, and we say how much we missed each other. But we don't.

My heart wants to reunite with its soulmate. My body wants to be held by Hayes, but my mind knows it's impossible. Heat rushes through my bloodstream at the memory of what we shared so long ago. And that curious gaze he gives me reminds me of the first day we met.

THIS IS my first-time flying solo. College seems like the right step, but it's also a huge step for someone who's been homeschooled and away from her peers since middle school. It's fine, though. College has to be a way better experience than the last four years of my life.

At least, that's what I keep telling myself.

Deep breaths, one foot in front of the other. Nothing is impossible.

You can carry thirty boxes to your room—even if it takes you an entire day.

I'm so worried about how I'm going to open the door, since both of my hands are occupied, that I don't notice the boxes in my path.

In seconds, I'm tumbling, falling forward, and the boxes I hold fly forward too. An arm that feels like a bar of steel secures me by the waist, breaking my fall.

"You okay?" A deep, rough, almost gravelly voice asks.

Heart pounding and mortified about dragging the attention of anyone around, I try to straighten myself and recover from the fright.

"Umm, yes." I try to play it cool.

Nothing happened, Blaire.

Hopefully, no one will remember this incident by the end of the day. So maybe I have to repack my boxes in front of everyone and I'll finish moving in by midnight. It's all good.

I tilt my head and try to look unphased and say, "Thank you."

I'm taken aback as I spot a heart-stopping smile. My breath falters.

He's not exactly your average college boy. At least, I didn't see a guy like him during freshman orientation.

He's gorgeous. Sculpted cheeks with dimples. A strong, hard, chiseled jaw. He also has the most striking green eyes I've ever seen.

BEING SO SHELTERED, it only took a matter of seconds for him to capture my attention, and, soon after, he stole my heart. I lived in a cloud of firsts: love, passion, and dreams. Until I fell from it, slamming back down to earth, with so much more than a broken heart.

The chiming sound announcing the elevator has arrived brings me back to the present. He hasn't said a word, but his gaze keeps holding mine. I pivot and take a step into the elevator.

"It's good to see you," he says, surprising me, because the last time we spoke, his hatred annihilated me.

As the doors close and he remains outside, waiting for me to respond, I'm speechless. What am I supposed to say?

Is it good to see him?

I don't know, because it took me years to forget him. Yet, it appears that I did a terrible job.

SEVEN

Hayes

MY STOMACH CLENCHES. My heart thumps fast and hard against my ribcage. I lean on the wall for a moment, closing my eyes as I calm down from the emotional hurricane I just endured.

It's been twelve years. Twelve fucking years since the last time I saw her. She's more beautiful now than the first time we met. Her body has changed. Her hips are wider, her legs are stronger. Her dark hair is long, and instead of a hat, she's wearing a big headband, but it's all the same. She's covering her head.

There are things that never change. Her voice is still sweet, raspy. Soothing. In some ways, it feels as if nothing has changed, and yet, she's changed a lot. My feelings for her, though, they are just as strong as they were when I chose to move to Baltimore. When I chose my future over her.

Fuck, she's here.

Blaire Noelle Wilson is here.

My Blaire. But she's no longer mine.

Her striking blue eyes look a shade darker than I remember. I can't tell what she's feeling for me. She was acting strange.

Why is she here?

Because since my father died, I've been doing what I've never done before. Praying for a miracle. For her.

It's probably something less magical and more practical. Like my father saying "Fuck you, Hayes" in his own way. Well, the joke is on him because seeing her doesn't make me angry. It makes me everything but.

If only I knew why she came. But that shouldn't matter now. She's here, and this is my chance to be back in her life. And the only way to do that is to earn her trust, and show her I am different from that coward she dated in high school.

But can we become something more?

What if she's happy?

I can't ruin her new life just because I did that with mine.

Running a hand through my hair, I decide to go to the conference room. First, I need to know why Blaire is here, and Mr. Parrish can answer my questions. But when I enter the conference room, Henry is speaking and already making some decisions.

"I vote that we sell the ski resort. It needs too much work."

"We don't know who gets the resort," I remind him.

"What if he split his fortune in equal parts?" He asks. "I'm not running a fucking resort for you, assholes."

Isn't it obvious that he should be the one running it?

"You own Merkel Hotels and Spas," I remind him. "You could potentially buy our shares and do something with it since you have experience."

"Fuck no!" He growls. "It's a money pit."

He's always growling like a wounded wild animal, pushing away everyone, in case they're around to hurt him. I glare at him as a way to remind him I'm not part of his staff or in the mood to tolerate his fucking attitude. I wish his assistant, Sophia, was here. She seems to know how to control him. Instead, she's in town with Arden, Mills' son, and we get to babysit her asshole boss.

"Have you heard from Vance?" I ask Mills.

"No. I have a friend searching for his unit," Henry interrupts. "He's a fucking Delta Force or some special forces officer. Did you know that?"

I look at him. "Our little brother is a badass?"

"According to my sources, he is, and he's not easy to track down," he answers.

"As I said, we need everyone to be here in order to read this testament," the lawyer says in a monotone voice and checks his phone. "Just a reminder, you're running out of time."

"We don't even want the fucking money," Beacon says. "Keep it, man."

His green eyes, which look just like everyone else's, spit fire, even when his posture seems relaxed.

He sits next to Pierce. Both wear suits, but even though they look alike, it's easy to see the differences between them. Pierce seems like he's in his element while Beacon is about to rip off his clothes because he hates wearing suits.

It's surprising how six guys, who came from the same father, can be so different. I'm thankful that fifty percent of our DNA comes from a different source.

Science, gotta love it.

Blaire used to say I was the nerdy one of the seven, and she wasn't wrong. Mom is a doctor. My grandparents were scientists. Science is all I know.

I could even explain to her why I loved her through science. Once upon a time, Blaire loved me because of that.

Blaire said it wasn't just DNA, but the sociological and geographical elements around us that made the seven of us so different. We didn't grow up together. We only saw each other twice a year up until Carter died.

"We get it. You're important and have shit to do for your fans. I am a busy man, too," Henry yells. "You're not all that, you know."

I look at Henry and say, "You could be less…"

I don't finish. Why even bother. This might be the last time I see him, and there's no point in telling him that he's a fucking asshole.

"Excuse me if I'm not trying to be pleasant. Us faking being a family was over a couple of hours ago, once we buried William," Henry grunts. "Just because we came from the same asshole, it doesn't mean we're brothers."

"Well, this might be our last day faking it, so can you try for once in your fucking life to be human?"

He storms out of the conference room, and I wonder what's really upsetting him. He's an asshole, but he's not as soulless as he likes to pretend. Clearly, he's having trouble adjusting to something. Maybe Dad's death affected him more than he wants to admit.

His mom died. We're really all he has, and yet, he acts as if he doesn't need us for shit. Maybe he'll end up like our father, or he'll be the one seeking us during the holidays.

Who the fuck knows what's going to happen after today?

I learned early in life to be ready for the unexpected. Hope isn't a word I use often. Not even when I explain to my patients what to expect after surgery. Too many times, the outcome isn't what they expected. The damage is irreversible. I studied medicine to save lives, but truthfully, I don't feel like I've done any of what I set myself to do when I embarked on this journey.

I don't even remember what I expected when I chose medicine. Maybe it had to do with saving lives, but I haven't saved anyone, not even my loved ones. I wonder if my father learned anything in his lonely, selfish life or while he was dying. If I could tell him something, it would be the fact that money can't buy you everything. Not the love of his sons or his health.

Is that how I'm going to end?

Alone with not even one of these fuckers giving a shit that I died.

Without *her*.

"Oh, fuck," Beacon says, his eyes open wide. "This is going to be fun. How are you, Gorgeous?"

"Hey, kid," I hear Blaire's melodic voice greeting my little brother.

I turn around to see her. The first thing I notice about her is her long dark hair, covered by a black beanie hat. Even when it's braided, I can spot a few pink strands mixed in. She wears a long skirt that accentuates her curves, and my entire body is aware of her.

"What the fuck are you doing here?" Henry asks, as he enters the room.

"Do you think I'm happy to be here?" Her voice is smoky, soft, gentle yet firm.

She tosses her hands up in the air. "Why don't we just get this over with?"

"If my father left you anything," Pierce threatens her. "I'll make sure you never touch it."

"She's right. Let's get through this last family reunion." I swiftly put an end to the nonsense because if any of these assholes insults her, I'm going to punch him.

"Hayes," she whispers my name, and all the emotions I'd buried deep inside my head when I entered this room unleash at the sound of my name.

I want to hug her, to kiss her, to tell her that nothing has been going well since I left her. That I...

"Why is she here?" Pierce asks no one in particular.

"Your father stated clearly that this can't be read unless his seven sons were in the same room," the lawyer explains, handing over a package to each one of us.

"That document is outdated," Pierce states. "Our brother Carter died twelve years ago."

"Let's get this over with, so I can go to bed," Blaire says. "Tomorrow, I have to drive back to the airport."

"It's only noon," Henry says exasperated.

She huffs and ignores him.

"We have to catch up, Skittles," Beacon says, calling her by her old nickname. "If you want, I can give you a ride. Where are you going?"

"You were always my favorite," Blaire states. "San Francisco. I'm sure it's out of your way but thank you for the offer."

"Nothing is out of the way. I'll do it," he assures her with a serious expression.

Beacon was almost fifteen when Blaire came into our lives. We might not have the same mother, but our mothers and his grandparents tried to push us to have a relationship. Not that it worked that well.

In any case, these guys met Blaire almost at the same time I did, and they adored her. She has a way with people, but especially with children. She's sweet, charming, even enchanting. I've seen her in action. She volunteered at the hospital while in college and would visit the kids in the oncology ward, playing with them for hours while bringing them treats, mostly Skittles. She always carried a few bags with her.

"Mr. Parrish, would you mind reading the will," she says, ignoring everyone.

"And please explain her presence," Pierce reiterates.

Please do, because even when my heart has been waiting for this moment, my mind wasn't ready to see her again. The wheels turn in my head; my father did something very, very stupid. And, whatever he tried to do, it's going to come back and fuck us all the way through Sunday. The disconcerting excitement of seeing Blaire dims by the thoughts of what's to come.

"As I explained earlier, Mr. Aldridge wanted all his children present when his testament was read. In the absence of his son Carter, he requested the presence of his widow. Blaire Noelle Wilson."

The old pain comes back. Carter's widow. That's so fucked up, and it's my fault because she was mine and I pushed her away. Can I get past their marriage and everything that transpired while he was sick?

"You're fucking kidding me. She gets part of the cut?" Henry, who is the businessman of the group and so much like my father, protests. "She's not getting more money from us. I'll contest the will. Pierce, get ready to fight her."

"Can we skip the drama and act like grownups?" Blaire sighs and crosses her arms.

"Where is Vance?" the lawyer asks.

"He was striding into the hotel when I was sauntering toward this room," Blaire informs, looking at the closed door.

In that moment, the door opens again, and it's Vance, looking even worse than Blaire did when she arrived. He's even bloody. What is it with these two?

Did he just come from the war or some battlefield?

"Sorry for the delay, the guy at the entrance didn't want to let me in. According to him—"

"He did the same to me. Tried to send me to a shelter," Blaire complains and looks at all of us saying, "I suggest you train him or fire him."

"Hey, Skittles," he greets Blaire and even hugs her. "You look better than the last time I saw you."

"Took a shower, avoided a kidnapping, and I even texted my mother on my way into the conference room," she says jokingly, and I wonder what that means.

She touches his arm, which has a bloody rag tied around it, and asks, "You okay?"

"All good. I'm glad you're here because I'm too busy to go and search for you," he says, casually dismissing her question. "What have I missed, other than the funeral?"

"Nothing," I answer.

"Shall we start?" Henry asks.

The lawyer lists my father's assets. The Lodge in Baker's Creek, and the properties he owns around the town. He pretty much owns the entire town and the one next to it, Happy Springs. He also has a multitude of houses: a mansion in Seattle, another in San Francisco, a penthouse in Manhattan, another in Vancouver, ranches in Colorado and Austin, the manor house in North Carolina, The Hacienda in Los Angeles, a plantation in Atlanta and a house in London.

Is it ironic that he has a house in every place he had a child?

I wonder if he has any sons or daughters who we're not aware of because it's obvious that he owns more than six homes. He has properties around the world, including the factory that operates in Happy Springs. Not to mention several bank accounts with billions of dollars.

"To receive this inheritance, you have to spend the next eighteen months sharing the Aldridge mansion located in this town. You also have to share the responsibilities of The Lodge, the factory, and Aldridge Enterprises."

"She doesn't deserve a penny of my father's hard-earned money," Henry protests.

The great thing about having a money-grabber asshole as a brother is that he can look like a fool while saying what everyone else is thinking.

Blaire rolls her eyes and shakes her head. "Do you have any idea what I can do with that money?" she asks rhetorically. "Maybe end world hunger, and as much as I'd love to do it, I'm out. If Carter was here, he wouldn't want any part of it either."

"Then, you didn't know him at all," I tell her defyingly.

"I did, and he'd get a kick out of seeing Henry fight for the company and maybe The Lodge. Watch you tear each other apart for money you don't even need. That's Carter, the one who threw the match and enjoyed watching you fight."

She gives us a sad smile and shrugs. "This was interesting. Let's never do it again."

Her eyes find mine and we stare at each other in silence for a couple of breaths. She gives me a slight nod and turns around heading for the door. I have this impulse to stop her because we should talk. She can't just walk into my life for a few seconds and disappear forever. I wanted a moment with her. This is my chance to at least find out if she's happy.

"Ms. Wilson, I haven't finished reading the will, and as I told you over the phone, a lot of people count on you," Mr. Parrish says, stopping her right as she's about to close the door of the conference room and leave us behind. The lawyer looks at the entire table and repeats. "*All of you*. Let me finish reading."

She sighs and turns back around, looking at him intently. I pull the chair out next to me and tilt my head. She takes a seat and crosses her arms.

"For the next eighteen months you're to live in the Baker's Creek property. Pierce, who is the only one married of the six, should live with his wife, Leyla Faye Aldridge."

"Wait, he knew I'm married?" Pierce asks confused. "How? I haven't spoken to him in years."

Mr. Parish ignores him and continues. "Mills should bring his son, Arden, along."

Pierce asks, "Did he know about your boy?"

Mills shakes his head, but Blaire is the one who speaks, "If you follow hockey, you know he has a son. This guy is considered the hottest single dad in hockey history."

"So, you're a hockey fan?" I ask curiously.

"No, I'm a Mills' fan. He's like my baby brother."

Mills gives her a smile.

"May I resume?" The lawyer asks.

We all nod.

"You will share the responsibilities of the companies. You should manage the properties and do what's best for the towns of Baker's Creek and Happy Springs. After eighteen months, everything will be divided into equal parts. If one of you walks away before the term is over, all the assets will be liquidated and donated to various charities."

"I vote that we take the charity route. Let's sell everything right now," I propose.

There's no fucking way in hell that I'll be away from my practice and my life for eighteen months, especially when it consists of living with my brothers, who I can barely stand ... but I could make the sacrifice if Blaire is here. This could be my chance to win her heart.

Would she give me the chance?

I glance at her. She's biting her lip, staring at the table, either daydreaming or wondering how she's going to escape this room.

I want to reach for her, grab her hand and hold it like the way I used to when she was this close to me.

Fuck!

It's so hard not to touch her. I'm hungry for her kisses—for her. I want us to talk, for her to tell me everything that's happened in the past twelve years.

How can I be harboring this craving when we've been over for so long?

There's always one obvious answer. Because I've always been hers. Since the beginning of time.

Because I never stopped loving her.

"I don't think you understand what's at play," the lawyer says.

"Well, then tell us the stipulations, so we can figure out how to end William's game," Pierce encourages him.

His eyes stare at the document Mr. Parrish reads, and he's about to snatch it away from him and read it himself.

"In the event that one or all of you decide not to commit to this town, the employees, and the properties, everything will be sold to the pre-approved buyers assigned by William Aldridge. That means The Lodge will be demolished and the land will be donated to the state of Oregon with the condition that nothing is built in its place.

"The properties he owns in Baker's Creek and Happy Springs are going to be sold to a developer. All the small businesses in these towns who lease from your father will close, since the developer plans on changing the..."

I tune him out because what he's saying is that he'll ruin the town if we walk away. However, it's not Dad who'd ruin it, but us, for not following his fucking instructions. He was a soulless bastard when he was alive, and he's fucking insane if he thinks we're going to do his bidding when he's dead.

"In short, he's holding us hostages," Blaire concludes and closes her eyes, because if there's something Blaire Wilson can't do, it's turn her back on those in need.

It's pretty simple, she's going to stay.

"So, we put our lives on hold because the asshole who spread his seed around the world feels entitled to play with our lives?" Henry asks. "You're out of your fucking mind if you think I'm going to live in this godforsaken place."

"Put aside the grudges you hold, try to find what little humanity you have left in that dark heart of yours, and think about someone other than yourself," Beacon speaks. "I'm not saying let's move in together and make this work, but we can find a loophole to save the town."

"Can we take turns?" I ask the lawyer.

"No, it has to be all of you or nothing."

"Can you contest the will?" Blaire asks Pierce. "Modify the terms, so you can donate everything to the town, and they can run their own lives."

He looks at her and then at the table but doesn't answer.

"Someone has to take charge of the factory and the resort," Henry says, his voice booming inside the room.

Blaire looks at me as if asking me to shut him up. She hates when people yell just for kicks.

"Henry, calm the fuck down," I warn him in a low voice. "Pierce, can you find the loophole?"

He shrugs.

The lawyer says, "Other than contesting and seeing if you can win, there's nothing else that you can do. You have thirty days from tomorrow to get your affairs in order and move into the property."

"Can they buy out William's assets?" Blaire asks.

"No. Only the approved buyers can do it. In fact, the prices he set are below market value. The charities, who are getting the profits, won't get much once everything is said and done."

He's not giving us any options, is he? He's still fucking with my life, even from the grave.

EIGHT

Blaire

IF ANYTHING HAS BECOME clear to me, it's that nothing can be planned. We live trying to understand why in the world we're here.

While growing up, I always changed what I wanted to become: an astronaut, a teacher, a singer, a zoologist. I was thirteen when I was diagnosed with leukemia, when my future became uncertain. In the blink of an eye, my life changed drastically. It went from swim meets at five in the morning, followed by six hours of school and ending the day with lacrosse practice to not being allowed to leave my house and my mom becoming, not only my teacher, but my only companion.

Not even my brothers were allowed near me in case they carried any germs or viruses that could get me sick. Some days were better than others. I became tired of needles, treatments, and isolation. My parents tried everything to fight for and with me after the first doctor said that there's only a forty percent chance I would beat it.

I was fifteen and in the middle of chemotherapy treatment when I decided to go into the healthcare sector—if I survived cancer. It was the doctors and the nurses who, unlike my parents, stayed with me during those treatments and made me realize that they do not just cure you, but they give you emotional support too. They matter in so many different ways.

During those days, I learned from books but also from the people who surrounded me. I found faith and started to trust in fate. I knew that miracles existed and that magic was all around us. It became clear that we should believe in science, but it wouldn't do us much good if we didn't have hope. I confess that, during those days, I lost my optimism one too many times, but I held onto my favorite moments. Those reminded me that it was worth it to keep fighting. That if I endure the treatments, maybe I'd get to collect more happy memories and live a long life.

The nurses' station had frames with several profound and uplifting quotes, and two resonated with me: "There wouldn't be stars without darkness," and "There's a sunrise after every sunset." I held onto those words, and they kept me fighting. I even graduated high school early and convinced my parents that I was ready to go to college.

My freshman year of college, I was still undecided about my future, but I had a goal: to become the best health provider I could be. After talking with several doctors and nurses, I decided to go into nursing. Those four years would help me decide if I would become a nurse or study for another eight to ten in order to become a doctor.

Hayes and I began dating only a few weeks after I started my freshman year. He always wanted to be a doctor, and his enthusiasm convinced me to follow his path. Together, we made plans. They included specializing in pediatrics, setting up our own practice, and getting married. Everything started to crumble, though, when he got accepted to Johns Hopkins—I didn't know it at the time, but when he left for medical school, he said goodbye, forever.

During our senior year of college, Carter was diagnosed with stage four melanoma—most of his organs were already affected when they found it. His death was yet another turning point in my life. I had come to terms with my mortality during high school. When he died, I came to terms with the rest of my life, however long that might be. I had no idea if the leukemia would ever come back, or if I'd live to be a hundred years.

After I said goodbye to him, I finished nursing school and became a physician's assistant while taking some business classes online. Once I was ready, I started a non-profit, similar to Doctors Without Borders. Now, I cross off my life bucket list while traveling around the world to small towns, orphanages, and refuge shelters where I give basic medical attention to people in need. I love what I do. I wouldn't trade my life for anything.

Honestly, I never thought I'd stop doing what I do. Until now.

When Carter was diagnosed, his mother and father dragged him from one doctor to another trying to find a cure. Every doctor they visited gave them the same prognosis. Against Carter's wishes, they started him on chemotherapy and radiation. It didn't matter that the treatment wouldn't give him more than a few months. Carter didn't want to live his last days destroyed by the chemicals. William though, he was fighting against his wishes and wouldn't listen to reason.

William struck me as a narcissistic man who liked to have everyone under his thumb. Everyone should do what he said, on his terms. His sons fought back and won most of the time. Apparently, this time there was nothing they can do.

If this was a chess game, he could be saying from hell, checkmate.

He won.

Whatever we do will transform our lives. We'll be the ones who either destroy an entire town or who sacrifice their lives for others.

"When you say we have to live here, does that mean we can't travel for business or pleasure?" I ask the lawyer, pulling out my small notepad and my pen.

He frowns. "What do you mean?"

"Well, I'll be happy to move into Baker's Creek if that's what he wishes," I expand, trying to find my own loophole. "But I have work to do, and I want to make sure that I can continue."

I turn toward Pierce, who was in law school when I met him. "Could you contest the will, or do you know anyone who could at least help us modify it?"

He nods in response, giving me a thoughtful look.

Yes, buddy, I'm not the enemy.

"Are there any stipulations about traveling outside the town or the state of Oregon?" I continue poking around, trying to make this work at least for me.

"You have to change your residence," the lawyer answers. "Your ID should state that you live not only in Baker's Creek, Oregon—but the Aldridge property."

I pull my driver's license and set it on the table. "This says I live in San Francisco, California. I spend three weeks of the year at this address. The rest, I spend it working around the world. Can I do the same?"

"What do you do?" Hayes asks, his eyes studying me.

"It's not important," I answer, dismissing him. "I need to know if I can keep working or if I have to find people to do what I do? I assume it is the same for you guys."

"I'm not fucking staying in this forsaken place," Henry protests. "I own resorts all around the world. I have to check on them periodically."

"There's no fucking way I'm uprooting my son's life because the fucker who donated his sperm went insane before he died," Mills adds. "Can we overturn this and claim insanity?"

"Where is he?" I ask Mills.

"Who?" he responds confused.

"Your son," I answer excitedly. "I want to meet him."

"Strolling around town with Henry's hot assistant," he says, pulling out his phone and showing me a picture of a toddler with the same Aldridge green eyes and a smile that reminds me so much of Mills when he was young. "You can meet him later today."

"It's spelled clearly here," Pierce says tapping at the papers. "We're expected to live on his property and become residents of the state of Oregon and the town of Baker's Creek. We're free to work on our businesses *remotely*. However, the factory, the resort, and managing the properties is our first priority."

"How about Aldridge Enterprises?" Henry asks.

Pierce laughs. "Fucking William. That too. We have thirty days to gather our things—my wife will be happy about this."

"You know," he pauses, tapping his chin and staring at the ceiling. "This might work. Leyla will give me the divorce immediately. She hates small towns. I might be in."

Pierce burst into a maniac laughter.

"What will happen to everything when we're done?" Hayes asks, ignoring his brother's sudden outburst.

"Focus on the present," Henry orders.

"I'm a surgeon," Hayes protests. "What the fuck am I supposed to do, perform surgery on the spreadsheets?"

I chuckle and then suggest, "You could ask the local doctor to hire you." Then I close my mouth, regretting what I said, because *I* should be the one applying for the job.

"If either one of you two decides to practice medicine in town, it's allowed, as it's considered a service to the town," the lawyer says, looking at Hayes and then at me. "You can't travel to San Francisco to perform surgeries or check on your patients."

"What about my job?" I ask the lawyer, who is aware of what I do for a living. "Too many people depend on me."

"Sorry, you'll have to find other ways to help."

"If I organize a gala?" I ask him, wondering if I can try to arrange it myself, raising funds to hire doctors to help me with what I can't do for the next year and a half.

"Sorry, Blaire, but you can only use the next thirty days to make an appearance. He restricted you *a lot*." Pierce is the one who answers that question. "You're not allowed to travel—not even short trips. Oregon is as far as you can go and only for the day. You don't get thirty days after the first six months are over like the rest of us."

He frowns as he reads, then takes his phone out, taps it and browses it. After a minute or so, he looks at me with a little more respect than he had a few seconds ago. "If you need money for the operation, tell me how much and I'll just write a check."

His sudden change surprises me, but I smirk, wondering if I can get a million dollars out of this act of generosity. "I might accept your money."

"What about those thirty days?" Henry asks. "Do we have more than that to pack?"

"No. We all have to be here in thirty days," Pierce explains. "After we spend six months living together, he's allowing us to travel outside for thirty days. We can split them among the twelve months left at the time. Or take off all at once."

"I can work with that," I say, because, even if I can't travel outside the country, I can go to San Francisco and help Tori.

Pierce looks at me and shakes his head. "You don't get that time, Skittles. I'm sorry."

My eyes trail down to Hayes' hands, wanting to reach for them, asking him to hold me and promise me that we can find a solution. Maybe he can help me fund my foundation because, if I can't go, I have to pay someone to do my job. Letting out a long breath, I simply continue listening to what everyone else says.

"How about Portland?" Hayes asks. "If I ask my clients to meet me there for surgeries?"

"I guess that's something we have to handle on a case by case basis," the lawyer responds.

"I'm a musician," Beacon says. "We have tour dates set starting this September. I can't cancel. That will destroy my career."

"You're Beacon," I say reassuringly. "People will wait for you. Also, you can stream from here. Bring your band."

"You can commute," Pierce says. "It's right here in the will. As long as you only do it twice a week and you're back the same day, you can do live appearances. Fucking William Aldridge. He has to be laughing his ass off at us from hell. Mills, it says that your son could benefit in this environment, and it'd be good to be around his uncles and aunts."

"Which aunts?" Mills asks confused.

We all stare at Pierce who responds with a frown, "Leyla and

Blaire." He exhales and closes his eyes briefly. "Let's hope that Leyla doesn't come."

"What's the plan?" Henry asks, running a hand through his hair.

"Let me see what I can do," Pierce answers, taking a copy of the will. "I'll take it home and have my team look into it."

"Listen, he made this foolproof," the lawyer explains. "You can hire the best attorney in the country, but at the end of the day, there's nothing you can do to stop me from executing this next month—if you're not here everything will be sold. You can either mobilize or waste your time. The decision is yours."

I put my notebook and pen away in my purse and look at everyone before I speak. "Look, eighteen months isn't a long time to be away from home."

"Easy for you to say when you're never home," Hayes says, looking at me.

Easy?

There's nothing easy about putting my life on hold to do this nonsense. My home is ... the world. My kids need me. All of them. Years ago, before I started my new career, I would've never guessed that the world would become my home, or I'd have a family as big as the one I have now. Project after project, I arrive at a place where I can help, where I can give, not only medical aid, but love, too.

"It's eighteen months," I answer. "Not sure what kind of medicine you practice, but I'm sure you can refer your patients to one of your colleagues for that period. Maybe you can use your father's money to set up a hospital here and do surgeries."

Then, I turn to the rest. "Yes, it's hard to leave the comfy life you have, but you're a bunch of privileged guys who can afford employees to cover for you. Think about the town. They're depending on you."

"Where are you going?" asks Hayes.

"To make some calls. I don't have your resources, and my kids depend on me."

"You have kids?" He asks confused and maybe even a bit sadly.

I could explain to him that the kids aren't mine exactly, but there's no point in expanding. This, having to share the same space with him for the next eighteen months, is going to be hell when I know he hates me and I ... I still feel more than I should. It amazes me how my heart and body respond to him even after all this time.

"Keep me updated," I say, to no one in particular and leave the room.

When I'm outside the conference room, I look at the ceiling and say, "No good deed goes unpunished, does it, Carter? I'm still paying for saying 'yes' to marrying you—asshole. 'What could happen?' you said. 'It's for a good cause,' you continued. 'It'll be fine.'"

I walk outside The Lodge and yell up at the blue sky, "It's not fucking fine!"

NINE

Hayes

"IF YOU'LL EXCUSE ME," the lawyer says, gathering his things, "I have a plane to catch this evening."

"That's it?" Mills asks. "Here are your father's last wishes, deal with them, and you wash your hands of it and of us?"

"It's not his fault," Pierce defends Parrish. "When did they diagnose our father?"

The lawyer looks at him confused or maybe disgusted. He's judging us, but clearly, he doesn't have the complete story. "Maybe his assistant has that information. I'm not family or a friend of his."

His tone sounds accusatory, and I don't blame him for assuming that we're a bunch of assholes who don't give a shit about their father. Jerome Parrish doesn't know our side of the story. Personally, I choose to keep it to myself.

My father can die being the martyr; I don't fucking care. He barely cared for us, and we just stopped trying to get his attention and his love at some point in our lives. Mine was around high school. I don't know about the rest of them though.

"Why does that matter?" I ask Pierce.

"He had cancer, right? Remember Carter's hallucinations?"

"We already tried to use that excuse to stop Blaire from getting Carter's trust fund. It didn't work that well," Henry says bitterly.

"He was in his right mind when he requested us to draft his will a few years back," the lawyer says. "He made a couple of adjustments three months ago, adding the potential buyers and the criteria they should follow to be eligible. Everything else has been in place for years. As I said, you can exhaust all your resources, but my firm has everything in place to sell in thirty days if you choose to ignore his last wish. We get paid the same rate either way."

"Do you even care about what happens to the people in this town, Jerome?" Beacon asks.

"It's not my job to care, but, because I do, I gave you two weeks to get together for this meeting," he admits. "Off the record, your thirty days should've started when he died. That means that, as of today, you would have only around thirteen days to move into your new house. There are too many people depending on you, so I gave you extra time."

"So, you waited for us?"

"On record, I stated that we had to wait for Blaire Wilson. She's busy doing more for the world than the six of you combined."

"Hey, I pull my weight to save the world, too," Vance speaks up for the first time. He stands and looks around the room. "I'm not sure if I'll stay. Let's hope Pierce finds a loophole because being around you isn't my idea of having a good time. In any case, Blaire gets to keep the money. You try to pull some shit on her, and we'll have a problem. Understand?"

"Great. Another sucker who fell for her," Henry sighs.

"Keep your trap shut." Vance pins him down to his chair. "I can make you disappear, and believe me, brother, no one will miss you."

He walks out of the conference room, and I follow him.

"Vance," I call out, and he comes to a halt, turning around and glaring at me.

"Be careful of what you say or ask. I'm not in a good mood."

I raise my hands in surrender. "Have you thought about anger management therapy?"

His nostrils flare. "The guy at the front desk needs to go," he says.

"So, you're staying?"

He chuckles. "If you guys can't find a way to avoid the eighteen-month incarceration, I might stay. That doesn't mean I have to put up with stupid people. I just finished a job and flew directly to this forsaken place, and the guy tried sending me to a shelter because I don't look the part. How are you supposed to look when you come into this hotel?"

"Less bloody," I offer. "You look like you should be at a hospital. Do you need medical attention?"

He looks at his arm that's wrapped with a piece of cloth that is bloody.

"I was going to look for Skittles and see if she can patch me up," he says.

"What does she do for a living?"

It guts me that he knows more about her than I do. From what I gathered during the meeting, she travels, and she might practice medicine. I'm not sure about her specialty, though. Maybe pediatrics ... but she travels. I want to know more—actually, everything—about her.

He grins. "I can't tell you."

"Why did she come from the jungle?"

"Fuck if I know, but even if I knew, it's none of your business," he answers.

"How about the kidnapping shit she said?"

"Dude, you're going to have to talk to her," he insists.

"You were involved. It's your story, too," I retort.

"Classified," he answers and smirks. "Listen, Skittles is under my protection. You already hurt her a lot so stay away from her. Do you understand me?"

"Is that a warning?"

He nods and walks away. I follow right behind him.

"What do you want, Hayes?" He asks, heading toward the exit.

"You need medical attention," I insist.

"Mr. Aldridge," Nick, the guy at the front desk, calls.

We both stop and turn around. "Yeah?"

"Are we expecting more … people like them?" He looks at Vance in disgust.

"Do something, or I'll do it, and it won't be pretty," Vance says with a warning look.

"Take the day off. We'll talk tomorrow about your attitude, Nick," I say, hoping I'm doing this correctly.

There's no way we can function without Nick. He's the manager—and, apparently, the only person William trusted in this town. That should be a red flag. If he's anything like my father, he might be just another asshole. Still, I don't know how to run a hotel. Henry does, but he might be packing his bag right now and flying out of here without even batting an eyelash.

"But I'm the manager," he protests.

"You tried to kick two of the owners out of the place because of their looks," I respond. "Either you change the way you treat our guests, or you're out."

Before I can say anything, Blaire walks into the hotel carrying a hiking backpack. I had no idea she was outside—or that she hikes.

"Your blood or someone else's?" she asks and then I realize that she's unwrapping Vance's arm. "This doesn't look good at all."

"A bullet grazed me," he answers, flinching, as Blaire touches him lightly.

"Let's go to my room. I'm going to have to do more than clean the wound," she says. "I went to the car for my medical kit."

As we walk by the front desk, she looks at Nick and says, "Find me rubbing alcohol. Do you guys have a clinic in town?"

Nick shakes his head. "The doctor's office is on Main Street, but he only works Tuesdays and Thursdays. He's retiring. There's one in Happy Springs."

"It's not that bad," I tell Blaire. "I'm sure we can fix him."

Actually, I should say: I *hope* we can fix him, if not we can rush him to Portland. Honestly, it's hard to tell since I don't know how much blood he lost. I don't think we have the equipment to do a blood transfusion. Fuck, I don't even know if any of us share the same blood type.

"Well, send over lots of clean towels and chicken soup. Two chicken soups, please. I'm hungry, too," she requests.

Nick looks at me and I say, "You heard the lady. Also send a gallon of orange juice, vanilla ice cream, whip cream, chocolate sprinkles, and strawberries, too."

"That's not part of the menu," he tells me.

"Find everything and send it upstairs now, if you want to keep your job."

Then, I catch up with Blaire and Vance who are about to board the elevator. I have so many questions for her, and we need to fix my brother.

TEN

Hayes

"WHAT WERE YOU DOING? It's time to retire and do something else. We worry about you," Blaire talks to the guy who happens to be a foot taller than her as if he is a little kid.

Who exactly is this 'we' she speaks about? Are they friends?

"Someone has to do it. It might as well be me," he answers, as we walk out of the elevator and toward her suite.

She's right across from the one Henry, Pierce, and I are occupying for the time being. Yesterday when we arrived, we went to the old house because there was no point in using a room at The Lodge. Except, the place is a dump. We have to hire someone to renovate it if we plan to occupy it soon. Thirty days might not be enough time to make it comfortable enough for all of us.

I don't even know how many people are going to stay there. We have eight rooms. Henry said that if he had to move, his assistant would have to come along. Arden needs his own room, too. Pierce is going to have to share with his estranged wife. I don't care if they kill each other during their stay.

That takes care of one of us, right?

"Help him take a shower," Blaire orders.

"The wound?"

"I don't think it is deep enough that he lost too much blood, but just cleaning around the area won't be enough. I want him to shower before we stitch him. Where were you, Vance?"

"Classified," he answers her question.

She rolls her eyes and grunts. "Ugh, did you at least call your mom?"

"I will once I have a decent meal and some sleep. I don't want to lie to her because I don't want to listen to her lecturing me about my job. You've done plenty for her."

Helping him into the shower is easy. "Do you have any clothes?" I ask, looking at the pile of rags he dropped.

"Nope," he answers, as I put his bloody clothes in a laundry bag.

"Blaire, can you ask Mills if he has a spare change of clothing for Vance, please?" I request.

"I don't have his number," she yells from the bedroom.

"Use my phone," I say, walking to where she sits and handing it over.

"What's your passcode?" She looks at me sternly.

I sigh. "One-zero-zero-nine," I answer, hoping she doesn't think much of it.

No such luck, because once she unlocks it, she looks up at me, and I can see the sadness in her eyes. Her birthday.

"Hey, can you text Henry about Nick, too," I ask her while she's typing.

"What about Nick—the jerk manager?"

I explain the deal with him, while walking back to the bathroom.

"Just tell him we need someone to cover for him today—and to train him tomorrow. I'm going to keep an eye on my brother."

"You can leave," Vance orders when I enter the bathroom. "I've been in worse shape."

"Is that your only injury?" I ask, looking closer. He's still bleeding, but as Blaire said, it's not a deep wound, and I doubt he lost too much blood. "Your shirt was bloody too."

"Yeah, that was someone else's," he states.

"Let me guess. Classified."

He chuckles. "You're getting the hang of it. So, what are you up to other than being a fancy doctor?"

"There's not much to say," I answer.

"The lawyer said you're not married, but what about an ex-wife, children, or at least a dog?"

"No. And you?"

"Mom wishes," he answers.

"If she's anything like mine, she's already been trying to find you a wife."

"Not yet. She's told me that it's okay if I'm gay," he says with a chuckle. "She loves me no matter what."

"Are you?" I ask casually.

"I'm bi, but I keep that to myself because of the general. He's a traditional man," he answers, and I can't imagine what it'd be like to have a general as a grandfather. "He still believes in the 'don't ask don't tell rule.' And no, I don't have a significant other."

It doesn't take long for him to finish his shower. When I go into the living area, Blaire gives me a pair of jeans and a t-shirt. She already has a pile of towels, a plastic container and rubbing alcohol on top of the coffee table.

"Do you have needles and—"

"I'm always prepared," she interrupts me, opening a plastic container. "Room service should be here soon. Henry will take care of your reckless decisions."

"Is that what he said?"

"Something like that. He needs a chill pill and to get laid," she says.

"Make sure that Vance only puts pants on. After I treat him and cover the wound, he can put on his t-shirt."

Vance dresses; he looks paler than he was earlier. Blaire gives him a hand towel to bite on and starts cleaning the wound. I wash my hands, sterilize them with alcohol and open the kit that has everything I could need for surgery, well, except anesthesia.

"You're prepared," I admit, grabbing the needle and thread.

"Almost. I didn't go home to replenish it. Hence, I don't have local anesthesia," she states when Vance groans. "Sorry, Van."

"What is it that you do again?"

"I work for a non-profit that is similar to Doctors Without Borders. We distribute food, clean water, medicines, and whatever they need. We help the communities we visit as much as we can."

"Communities in the heart of the jungle," I guess.

"Some of them are there," she confirms, watching me close the wound. "Wow, that's a good technique. You have to teach me."

"Any time," I offer. "So where are you going after this is over?"

"It depends how long I have to stick around," she answers. "I might have to cancel the next mission because it's hard to get doctors to donate their time on such short notice. I can't afford their salary."

"If you need money, I'll wire you some," Vance speaks.

She laughs. "Don't tempt me. We could use some money. That's really why I came. My wish list and projects are immense, and we don't have enough equity to fund them. I only receive so much from Carter's trust fund every year."

"Can you withdraw all the funds at once? I can," Vance asks, giving her a curious glare. "I mean, you have two billion dollars at your disposal."

Blaire glares at me. "No. Some people made sure I didn't have access to it because, God forbid, I would enjoy the money."

"It was William's idea," I defend myself, poorly, because I supported him and Henry who were upset about Carter's marriage to Blaire, and that she became the beneficiary of the trust fund after he died.

"You supported them," she says, her voice carrying some anger.

"You married my brother," I match her tone.

"You fucking married my brother," I repeat resentfully. "You were mine."

"First of all, I was single when I accepted Carter's proposal. You dumped me because you wanted to be free to date while living in Baltimore," she reminds me.

And I flinch because there's some truth behind it. It wasn't so I could date, but rather so she could date and be sure that I was the one. To ensure she wouldn't be tied down to me and then regret our relationship. Also, what if I couldn't be faithful to her—like my father. That's the only example I have of a long-distance relationship, and I saw how much it hurt my mother.

Are you done making excuses? I ask myself. You did it because you were a coward. *Still, she married my fucking brother.*

"So, you married my brother to get back at me," I conclude.

"You're so arrogant," she complains. "The world doesn't revolve around you—and when I said yes, I didn't even think about you."

"Fucker," Vance mumbles through the towel.

"Sorry, I didn't mean to squeeze hard," I apologize.

"It was never about you. I did it because your parents were torturing him," she answers, and her voice resonates through the room. "He was done. It was over. Do you have any idea what it's like to go through chemotherapy and radiation? It's painful, and when there's no hope, what's the point to live through such a horrible experience."

"They were trying to save him."

"Do not defend them because you weren't there. You don't know Carter's side of the story. He was terminal. There was no way to save him," she fires back with an anger that's very 'un-Blaire' of her. She's usually calm and sweet, even when things are rough. "They wanted to extend his life for a few more months—a year, if possible. He wanted quality over quantity. He had just a few months, and he wanted to enjoy them the best he could, but your father said he was mentally incapable of taking care of himself and was filing to become his guardian. I'm pretty sure it was your mother's idea. Never seen two people who can barely stand each other work so well together to destroy someone's soul."

"That's why you married Carter?" Vance asked.

She nods. "Yeah, he tried to call his big brother, but he was too busy in London. His semester abroad was more important than Carter."

Her words remind me of how much I fucked up and failed my brother—and, apparently, her, too.

"I didn't know how bad it was. Mom said he'd be okay. That I should—"

"Look, I don't care about what happened then. I did what I could for my best friend. Once I married him, I became his next of kin. The one who could make decisions for him. Your parents had no say anymore. He was free to live his last days the best way he could—and he did.

"While he was sick, I was reliving my own illness. All those years going in and out of the hospital, not knowing if the treatment would work. If I would make it to my next birthday. I made it, but I wasn't living my best life. It wasn't about the money, but when we realized that the trust would go to me, we made plans.

"Med school wasn't important anymore. I could spend a few more years in school to become a pediatrician or find a way to treat children by changing my career path. The latter sounded better, because my cancer can always come back—or I can choke while eating. You never know when it's going to be over.

"When I told Carter about my idea, he encouraged me to use his money. He was happy to know that something good would come out of his trust. He called it his legacy. That's why it's called Carter's Kids Foundation. It could help if I could just take whatever I need whenever I need it, but ... I make it work."

Working for that non-profit sounded badass. Founding it is admirable. I have a high regard for her even more now. Thinking about what she's doing and how I could help her feels like fresh air. An infusion of vitamins—even a new life. I've spent years working on setting bones and becoming one of the best orthopedic surgeons in the world. My waiting list is long, but really, I don't help as many people as I could —not the way she does.

The guilt that she can't access Carter's money angers me, and it's in part my fault. I have to do something to fix it.

"So, you've been managing for the past twelve years with what little you can access?" I ask, as I finish the last stitch and feel like a complete asshole.

"More like nine, I had to finish college and... Yeah, that's what I do," she says, covering Vance's wound with gauze and medical tape. "You can't get this wet for a week. Let's try to meet, so I can take out the stitches."

"Yes, doctor," he says mockingly.

Looking inside her raggedy hiking backpack, she produces an orange bottle. Takes out two pills and gives him a bottle of water. "Swallow them."

"I don't need pain meds," Vance protests.

"Good thing I'm giving you antibiotics because I never carry pain medication," she tells him. "We want to prevent an infection. As we were just told, they don't have a clinic in town to treat you if you go into septic shock."

I take the bottle and see what she is giving him. Keflex, it's a stronger antibiotic than amoxicillin, but she only has six pills, and he needs a lot more than that.

"You don't have enough for ten days," I inform her.

"There has to be a pharmacy in this town," she says. "If not, I'll call my assistant, so she can send them over."

"You're upset because the family practice is closed and they don't have a clinic, aren't you?"

"Well, yeah. The only doctor works twice a week. You're in a small town, but this hotel is designed to receive at least two hundred families at a time. What if they have an accident or...?"

"There's a clinic in Happy Springs."

"That's beside the point," she says. "Hypothetically, what'll happen if you send a head trauma to that clinic because there aren't any services here? You already lost at least thirty minutes or more while you transport them there. If you need to move them to Portland, that's another two hours. What do you think will happen to the patient?"

"I get it. I didn't design the town," I say almost apologetically. "Do you want me to build you a clinic?"

She huffs, and before I can say anything more, there's a knock on the door.

"Room service," the person on the other side of the door says.

When I open the door, it's Nick with the food we requested.

"Thank you," I say.

"Mr. Aldridge and his assistant are taking over the front desk," he says. "I'll report tomorrow at nine, if that's okay with you?"

"I'll pay good money to see Henry in charge," Vance says, yawning.

"Eat your soup and drink your juice," Blaire says, pushing the cart closer to him. "Then take a nap. You don't look well. When was the last time you slept?"

He shrugs. "I don't keep track while I'm working."

"You can stay in the second room. Unless you have a room assigned," she says.

"Thank you. We can be roomies," he says and begins to eat.

"Have you eaten?" I ask Blaire, as I start putting together her sundae.

"Here," I offer. "Do you want me to order you some fries?"

"Thank you," she says and smiles. "Hold the fries, though. I'm just eating the soup after this and taking a nap."

"When was the last time *you* slept?"

"If you don't count the nap during my flight from Dallas to Portland ... last Monday," she answers, while eating the ice cream.

I gather all the biohazard material into a bag and email my assistant, requesting the medication for Vance and asking her to research the Carter's Kids Foundation.

"Call me if you need anything," I tell them, heading to the door. "I'll check on you in a few hours."

ELEVEN

Hayes

MAYBE OUR FATHER did this to screw with us one last time, but I now see it as an opportunity for me to fix my future after I screwed up my life so badly. I lost the girl—more like I pushed her away from my life. I lost touch with my family—these five assholes are, after all, my brothers.

I won't take all the blame for not keeping in touch with them, but it is partly my fault. I should've tried harder. I lost the passion to save lives —now I just fix bones.

Blaire is here, and my feelings for her haven't disappeared. This is my chance to get to know the woman she's become. The opportunity to make her fall in love with me again. To remind her that we're soulmates. We were forged from the same star. We've loved each other since the beginning of everything.

There's so much I have to do to convince her to give me a chance. I might not deserve it, but if anyone has a heart big enough for forgiveness, that's Blaire. I have to start somewhere, and the house is the first step. We have thirty days to make sure it's livable so we can all move in.

I go to my room, email my boss at the hospital, handing him my two-week notice. Then, I send a second message to my partners, offering to sell them my share of the practice.

This is crazy, I say out loud when I shut down my computer.

I just quit my life in San Francisco, and it took less than five minutes. But it's what I need to do because now I have time to create a new life where Blaire is the sun and I'm just a planet orbiting around her. After shedding the suit, I take a shower and dress in a pair of jeans and a t-shirt. I leave the room and head to the staircase.

"What the fuck?" Henry asks, when I walk by the front desk. "You disappeared after almost firing the manager and sent a ridiculous text to fix your shit. Where have you been?"

I check my phone to read the text. Earlier, Blaire set it on the coffee table, and when I found it, I just put it back in my pocket without even checking my messages.

Hey, fucker. I let Nick take the day off without pay. Since you're the hotel guru, can you take care of the place? I'm busy playing doctor with Vance.

I almost laugh at Blaire's ridiculous message. She loves to upset Henry.

"Well, it's self-explanatory. We were patching up Vance," I inform him. "If you didn't notice, he had a bullet wound."

His eyes bulge, and his color drains. "Is he okay? Do you need me to fly him to Portland?"

"Nah, it's okay. You can keep your toy on the ground until we leave," I tell him.

He rented a helicopter to fly from Portland to Baker's Creek. I had no idea he had a pilot license—for small jets and another one for helicopters.

"Still, you could've helped me here," he says upset.

"Well, you have everything under control," I say, dismissing his fury.

"I have a plane to catch," he says, grinding his teeth. "We're leaving in a couple of hours, if you want a ride."

"Not anymore," his assistant reminds him, while typing on her laptop. "We're flying out Friday night, because you need to train the employees and update the computer equipment of this hotel. We have to do an inventory of the place and create a list of things we have to replace immediately. All your meetings have been rescheduled."

Not sure what computer equipment and which employees she's talking about, but I'm glad they're doing something for this place. It looks like a blast from last century and not in a well-preserved way.

"I told you we should try to switch them to videoconferences, Sophia."

"I don't appreciate your tone," she protests. "There's a cute book-store that can keep me busy until Friday and a Bed and Breakfast in Happy Springs where I can stay away from you. Don't tempt me to leave you here to manage everything on your own."

"I should fire you."

"I should quit, and yet, here we are," she tells him with such calm-ness that my brother's face turns red.

"I like you," I tell her.

"Take your paws off my assistant, Hayes," he warns me. "She's not allowed to date my brothers."

"To think I could choose between a hockey player, a hot musician, and a famous doctor," she jokes.

"You forgot the broody and dangerous Delta Force officer," I say, teasing Henry, not even knowing if there's such a thing as a delta officer. The only thing that matters is Henry's angry face.

She sighs in resignation, and the flint in her eyes makes me laugh.

"I'll have to keep my hopes up that I'll find something better on Tinder," she says.

"Swipe your phone during off hours," he warns her. "I don't have time to deal with your personal life."

She rolls her eyes but doesn't answer back.

"You're a saint for putting up with him," I tell her, ignoring Henry.

"No, I happen to have good taste in expensive shoes, a huge debt, and I hate change. You know what they say, better the devil you know..."

I laugh, and my brother doesn't look amused.

"If we stay eighteen months in this forsaken place, I'm going to have to absorb this shithole, add it to the Merkel Resorts line and bring it into the twenty-first century."

"Do you have to stay?" Sophia asks, a deep frown in her forehead.

"I hope not," he answers and changes his attention to me. "What are you going to do for the rest of the day, Hayes? I can use some help."

"Where is everyone else?" I ask, ignoring his question.

"Pierce left for Colorado. He thinks he can find the loophole," Henry answers.

"We need to fix the house in case he fails," I inform him. "The other two?"

"Beacon knows the town and promised Arden to take him to the petting farm," he answers, banging the bulky computer. "Sophia, what happened with the IT department?"

She rolls her eyes and moves his hands away from the old monitor on top of the check-in desk.

"They can't send anyone until tomorrow," she says, with a condescending voice. "I sent them all the information they requested, so they can bring the necessary equipment. You have to be patient. We already agreed that banging objects is a big no. You might break them, not fix them."

"So, you got this," I conclude before I leave.

"I'm not staying, Hayes," he calls after me. "We can't just do what William wants and pretend it is okay."

I halt and turn around, staring at him. Does he understand what's at stake or is he so out of touch with reality that he thinks these people don't matter?

"Unless you find an alternative, we'll be living here for almost two years," I assure him, more like warn him.

"Are they worth it?" he asks, glaring at me. "I don't fucking know these people. Why would I sacrifice my business for them?"

"Because if we leave, they'll have nothing left—they'll lose everything. Because as Beacon said, deep down buried somewhere inside your dark soul, there has to be a human."

"You can't leave your practice. You're Hayes fucking Aldridge, one of the best orthopedic surgeons in the country."

I don't correct him and say, the world, because the title means nothing. I don't tell him I already quit my job at the hospital and offered to sell my part of the practice.

Our father was William Tower Aldridge, one of the top ten richest people in the fucking world. He died and not one person gave a shit about him—not even us, his children. He built an empire, accumulated billions, and owns multiple properties all around the world. Yet, in the end, he died alone.

"And you're Henry Aldridge, the owner of Merkel Hotels and Spas, resorts and spas. Is it really going to matter when you die, alone?"

Henry's jaw sets. He turns red.

"This round goes to the doctor, ladies and gentlemen," Sophia says like a sports announcer. "Such a shame that I won't get to witness who stays alive at the end of the eighteen months."

"If I have to stay," Henry grunts. "You're staying with me."

I laugh because, if she stays, he's going to be the first one buried in our backyard, after she kills him.

TWELVE

Hayes

STEPPING OUT OF THE LODGE, I breathe in the fresh air. It's been a long time since I took some time off and just enjoyed my day. I look toward the parking lot, wondering if I should use one of the resort golf carts to drive to the house, but then I decide to walk. Baker's Creek is small enough that driving isn't necessary. The distribution of the town is pretty simple.

The Lodge is on the east side of town, the closest to the lift, so the skiers can easily access the slopes. To the west is the entrance of the town. On the north side is the Aldridge property and the residential area is on the south side of town.

Bakers Creek isn't big; everything is within a five to ten-minute walk distance. At least, that's how it used to be back when I was forced to visit my father. It was an annual event my brothers and I had to do because our mothers organized it. They sent us with him to bond as a family. What they didn't know is that dear old dad was almost never here. We ended up spending time with my grandmother or the maid. Grandma was fine, but she was detached, just like my father.

Jesus, no wonder we're all emotionally impaired. I've only loved one woman, Blaire, and maybe it's because she's the sweetest person I've ever met. Everyone who meets her loves her instantaneously. After her, I haven't been able to care about anyone.

My brothers don't seem to do well in the relationship department either.

Is it a curse?

Carter used to say that, and I always thought it was some fucked up conspiracy theory. He was full of them. But now, I'm starting to think he might have been right.

"Good afternoon, mister," a kid riding a bicycle greets me, and the one following him does the same.

I don't remember the last time someone greeted me while walking in the streets of San Francisco. It feels weird to be called mister. Back in the day when we visited, we weren't allowed outside the house. Dad had rules, and one of them was to keep away from the town. As of today, I don't understand why he imposed them.

When I was in college, I visited a few times with Blaire. It was easy to drive up here to get away for the weekend during summer. It upset my father a lot since we would be walking around town and either camping or staying at The Lodge. Carter joined us some of those times, too.

Dad even flew in once to kick me out when he found out I was here, but then he realized I was an adult and he couldn't force me to do anything.

Is that what he's doing now?

He's showing us that he can force us to do his bidding and that he's better than us. He was certainly delusional.

Now that we're here, it'll be interesting to see how people will treat us when they learn we'll be managing the properties and the businesses.

We own most of the land around here. After listening to the lawyer, I understand we also own the shops. Maybe once we fulfill the stipulations, we can sell those properties to the current occupants.

A lot of people look my way as I walk by, and I'm not sure if they recognize me as one of Aldridge's sons or if I'm just being paranoid. I stop when I find a sign that reads, "Baby Blue Eyes Flower Festival is coming up soon. Have you registered your business?"

What kind of festival is that?

I pass the medical building. The door is closed, and I chuckle when I read the office hours.

Tuesday and Thursday from 9-12. In case of an emergency, call the clinic in Happy Springs.

I wonder if there's more than Dr. Garrison's practice in that building or if he occupies the entire first story. Blaire and I could buy him out, and since we own the building, we can add a second floor. We'd create not only a medical practice, but a clinic too.

Would she be on board? She was pretty upset about the healthcare provided in town—or lack of it.

First, we have to sit down and clear the air between us. The yelling match we had earlier, where I found out more about her marriage to Carter, wasn't enough. I couldn't even tell her that I was sorry for leaving her alone to handle my brother's last days and for not being there for her after he died. They were close. Carter adored her. She was like a sister to him. He was fucking mad at me after I broke things off with her.

"How could you let the best thing that had happened to you go?" Carter called me furious when he found out.

"You can't possibly understand," I said.

"You're a fucking idiot, and when you realize your mistake, she'll be long gone."

He was right, but she's here, and this is my chance to fix what I fucked up. Eighteen months seem like plenty of time to work things out with her, but we have to at least become friends before we start living together—and I swoon the shit out of her.

I have to ask for her forgiveness. Redeem myself, not only for what happened after Carter died, but for breaking up with her when I went to Johns Hopkins. With new determination, I hurry to the house. When I finally arrive, I spot Beacon and Mills by the gate. Beacon is unlocking it. Mills carries his sleepy son in his arms.

"Why are you here?" I ask them.

"Pierce said it's a piece of shit. We have to make a plan just in case," Beacon answers. "Also, I have to find a place to set up my studio because there's no fucking—."

"Language," Mills reprimands him. "Arden is young and impressionable."

The baby is asleep, does it really matter? But since I'm not a father, I keep my mouth shut.

"Why are you here?" Beacon asks while he studies me. "More like, where did you disappear to after the meeting?"

"We treated Vance's wound," I explain to him. "Now I'm here to assess the house."

"Yeah, I tried not to overreact, but that arm looked nasty. I'm sure it's just another Wednesday for him, but what was he doing before he came to town?" Beacon asks, giving me a what the fuck is Vance really up to look.

I shrug because, from what I gathered, everything about Vance is classified. "Do you want to walk through with me?" I question, tilting my head to the main house.

"Dude, we have to find another solution," Mills says. "How do I explain to you that my kid can't be moving around?"

"He goes with you to every game—including international games," Beacon argues. "He could use an eighteen-month break from the hectic life of a hockey player, and so could your knee. We can find you a nanny or we can help you take care of him. You can build an indoor rink on the property and train—once you recover."

"What happened to your knee?" I ask, regretting not asking about his injury back in New York.

I accept it. I'm a shitty brother, and there's no excuse for the way I've behaved with my brothers. Something has to change. Things between us used to be different.

"I blew it," Mills answers.

Since he's wearing shorts, I squat to look at it closer. It's slightly swollen. He should be wearing a brace and not carrying his son. I don't find any scars, still, I ask, "Did they do surgery on it?"

"The doctor said it wouldn't help much."

I straighten up, taking Arden into my arms. He moves just a bit but doesn't wake up at all.

"I could take you to my office, examine it," I offer. "You could have come to me when it happened."

He looks at me with resentment but doesn't say a word.

What did I do wrong now? I choose not to ask, and we all go inside the house. Beacon takes notes for me as we make our way to the kitchen. The place doesn't have any furniture. Some of the walls need to be repaired. The kitchen is empty, the cabinets are broken, and the appliances are gone. The bathrooms need to be replaced.

"This house was so different back when we used to visit," I mutter, wondering when this happened. "He pretty much abandoned it. His penthouse in New York looks like a palace compared to this place."

"I could live in New York for a year," Beacon says. "Can we at least switch the location? Dude, this town is one of those places you visit because of their crazy festivals and ski season, not because you want to live here."

"When was the last time one of us was here?" Mills asks, ignoring Beacon's rant.

Beacon shrugs. "I was seventeen, the only idiot left from the bunch. He wasn't here. The maid wasn't here either. It was just me. It still had some furniture if I recall."

"Did you stay?"

He shakes his head. "Nope. I called a friend, and then I flew to Europe."

"To party?" Mills asks. "Poor rich kid."

"No, she was studying abroad—she's a musician, too. Her mom pulled some strings, so I could join the program."

"Music nerd," Mills says.

"Yeah, well, I'm more famous than you."

"You wish," Mills answers.

"I can prove it," Beacon contends, challenging him. "We post our pics on Instagram at the same time and let's see who gets more likes?"

I look at both of them. They're taller than they were when they were younger, and yet, they're still trying to prove who is better with dumbass challenges. At least they're not trying to eat their weight in hotdogs, blackberry pie, or ice cream, like when they were twelve and ten.

"Stop this nonsense and help me finish the list," I scold quietly, hoping that Arden doesn't wake up with their nonsense. "We have thirty days to fix the house, or we'll be living in a dumpster. I don't even know if they have a contractor in town."

While we assess what's more important, I juggle the kid and my phone, so I can google contractors around the area. I find a local one, thankfully. He doesn't have many reviews, but the few he has are raving about him. Also, I realize the cellphone connection is crappy in some areas of the property. However, I'm able to email him a request.

"There's no way we can get this done within the next thirty days," Beacon decides, taking some photos of the house. "Can we at least stay at The Lodge?"

I scrub my face with my free hand, trying not to wake up Arden. Beac is right. Unless we can find someone who is efficient and has not only the manpower, but the resources... How can we accomplish so much in so little time?

That's when I remember one detail. We have enough money to make things happen quickly.

"We all have the financial freedom to hire the right people and ensure the project is completed within a month. It might help the town's economy, too," I remind them. "I hate meetings, but we should get together tonight to decide our next steps, in case Pierce can't fight the will. How long are you guys staying?"

"Sophia convinced us to stay until Friday," Mills responds. "She needs us to stay at the hotel tomorrow while Henry goes to Happy Springs to visit the factory."

"Well, we have a couple of days to find a good contractor."

I hand the baby to Beacon and shoot a text to Sophia.

Hayes Aldridge (yummy doctor): Can you set up a dinner meeting with my brothers tonight at seven, please?

Sophia Aragon: Any food preference?

Hayes Aldridge (yummy doctor): You can choose. Though if you can order Reuben sandwiches or tacos, I'd appreciate it. Also, have some kind of dessert ready.

Sophia Aragon: I'll do a taco bar. What kind of dessert?

Hayes Aldridge (yummy doctor): Whatever you find that goes with Mexican food. Churros or flan could work—get whipped cream too.

Sophia Aragon: Anything else?

Hayes Aldridge (yummy doctor): Guacamole. I think that should cover everything she likes.

Sophia Aragon: By she, I'm assuming Blaire.

Hayes Aldridge (yummy doctor): Thank you for your help.

Sophia Aragon: Should I contact your brothers, or will you be able to do it?

Hayes Aldridge (yummy doctor): Just make sure Henry is there, I'll take care of the rest.

Sophia Aragon: Text me if you need anything else.

Henry: Leave my assistant alone. She's mine.

Hayes: We're just setting up a meeting to make sure everyone is on the same page. Did you lick her already to claim her?

Henry: You're an asshole.

Hayes: Takes one to know one. See you at seven.

"We're meeting tonight at seven," I inform them.

"What about my studio?" Beacon asks. "Can we see if there's anything I can use while I live here?"

As we walk around the property, I realize the land is bigger than I remember. I wonder if I could build a house close to the lake that's on our property. First, I have to figure out the clinic, though.

"Are we going to use the barn?" Beacon interrupts my thoughts.

"That's up to the others. As far as I know, none of us has animals," I confirm.

"Okay then, I'll use that as my studio."

On our way back to The Lodge, I get in touch with Dr. Garrison's assistant, who sets up an appointment with the good doc tomorrow at seven thirty. Then, I receive a notification that Easton Rodin, the contractor, has replied to my email. He could see me as early as tomorrow morning. I reply explaining what we're looking for, including the current condition of the house.

Beacon texts me some of the pictures he took, and I forward them as well. Easton suggests he drops by the house early in the morning to look at it. I tell him that I have an early appointment with someone else, but we can meet once I'm done. He asks if he can start looking at the property while he waits for me, so he can have a timeline and price estimate ready.

The moment I step into The Lodge, I feel confident that, if Pierce doesn't find a loophole, I have a chance to start something new—to create a future for Blaire and for me. Not what we planned when we were young, but something that fits who we are now. I know she's not the same person, but I also know that I still love her.

None of us asked for this mess, but perhaps there's a reward at the end of this ordeal. It'll be more valuable than William's money. This is my chance to find my own path and not continue the legacy that William left or follow into his shoes.

THIRTEEN

Blaire

I'D BE LYING if I said that Hayes getting me ice cream didn't make my heart beat faster. He still remembers that dessert always comes first. But I sober up quickly when *I remember* who he really is. He's not that much different from his father.

Nothing is permanent for guys like him. I love you forever doesn't mean much to them. Forever is two years, if you're lucky. I'm not sure how many hearts he's broken after mine, but he definitely destroyed me.

Vance doesn't say much after finishing his soup and drinking the whole pitcher of orange juice. He goes into the bedroom I assigned him in the suite and shuts the door.

I march to my own room, change into a pair of pajamas, and plop myself onto the bed. It's not my soft as a cloud bed, but it's better than the seat of an airplane.

Closing my eyes, I hope I fall asleep, instead of tossing and turning for hours while I think about William, the will, and well ... Hayes. Thankfully, I'm too tired to even care about them or what my life might be like in thirty days.

When I wake up, it is already dark outside. I stretch before leaving the bed and go into the suite's living room. There's a note on the coffee table from Hayes.

B,

We're meeting at seven in the conference room to have dinner and discuss the move. I want to be ready—in case Pierce can't find a way to get us out of this mess.

See you there,

H.

THIS GUY IS EITHER clueless of what he's doing to me or just trying to open the wounds of the past. Probably the former, because he didn't call me *love* or *stardust*. Maybe I'm reading too much into his behavior, and this is just the way he operates with everyone.

I shake off the funk and change into a pair of leggings and a long sweatshirt. Brushing my hair, I choose to leave it down and put on my blue beanie. I slip into a pair of flats and walk down the stairs, instead of using the elevator. Once I reach the main floor, I make a quick note on my phone about asking the maintenance team to change the lightbulbs that are broken.

When I enter the conference room, there's a buffet set up in the corner, several laptops on top of the table, and everyone is talking over each other. More like the brothers are yelling at each other. There's a woman next to Henry eating nachos, while watching the guys with amusement.

When she spots me, she rises from her seat and walks toward me. She's a few inches taller than me. At least, that's what I think, until I spot her killer high heels. She's beautiful. The definition of classy and elegant. Big brown eyes and long lashes with long curly hair that is darker than mine.

"You must be Blaire," she says enthusiastically. "I'm Sophia Aragon, Henry's assistant."

"Blaire Wilson, it's nice to meet you," I answer, wondering why Henry had to bring her and if she hates me because the asshole can only say ugly things about other people.

"Please, make sure to get yourself some food. I ordered a taco buffet, but if you—"

"Tacos are one of my favorites. Thank you for taking care of the food," I interrupt her, rubbing my hungry stomach. Then I turn my attention toward the center of the room where the five brothers are in a heated conversation with the big monitor on top of the table where Pierce's face appears. Neither one of them looks happy.

"How long have they've been fighting?"

"Since Pierce..." she wiggles her nose and taps her chin. "I think he's the lawyer."

She pulls out her phone and shows me her list. "Is this right?"

Hayes yummy doctor

Pierce hot lawyer

Mills I want to eat him hockey player

Vance broody smoldering (who is he?)

Beacon heartthrob musician

I burst into laughter. "That sums them up," I confirm and hand over the phone.

"What would it say about Henry?" I ask curiously.

"Satan's spawn," she answers with a smirk. "I thought he was the devil in the flesh, but it sounds like his father was worse."

I shrug because I have nothing good to say about William. The first time I met him, he tried to run Hayes and I out of the town. He was a huge asshole with us. The next few times were while Carter was sick—and when he fought me for the trust.

"What did Pierce say that has them bickering like cockatoos?"

"That doesn't sound very manly," she observes.

"The best way to tease them is by comparing them with animals," I say. "It drives them crazy."

"That's good to know," she says, giving me a mischievous look. "Pierce said, 'I'm trying, but I think we're fucked.'"

My stomach drops because what's amusing to her is a life sentence to me. Eighteen months with these men.

"They're entertaining," she adds, and I realize she's having a blast observing these morons.

"They have their moments," I agree.

"How long have you known them?" She asks.

"Since I was seventeen," I answer. "I met them during my freshman year of college. Carter was moving into the same co-ed dorm that I was. My parents didn't have time to help, so it was me and thirty-some boxes. Hayes took pity on me and made them help me."

"Sounds like the beginning of a nice friendship."

"Or a nightmare. They are hot as sin, but vicious when provoked," I say and walk toward the buffet, picking up a little of everything and a lot of guacamole to go with my chips.

When I turn to find a place to sit, there's only one chair available, and it's right next to Hayes. There's also a plate set with a flan and a few small churros. I lick my lips, wondering where I can find some of that because there was none on the buffet table. Maybe Sophia can tell me later. Even though I hate to eat my dinner before dessert, I take a seat.

Hayes pushes the plate with sweets in front of me along with a bowl filled with whipped cream.

"What are you doing?" I mumble, so only he can hear me.

He turns to look at me with a confused expression. I tap the dessert, and he smirks. I flash him an angry glare.

"Finally, Princess Blaire decided to grace us with her presence," Henry says.

"Cool it," Hayes orders. "We just started, and she was resting."

"That's what nights are for," Henry states bitterly.

Sophia rolls her eyes and says, "And yet, you use them for work. Stop judging others for not following your habits."

"It's been two weeks since I slept in a bed. You're lucky I woke up at all," I explain. "Do you mind doing a recount? Oh, Henry the great."

Sophia chuckles, and I realize that I really like her.

"Don't encourage her." Henry glares at me, and I'm not sure if he's talking to me or Sophia, but, either way, I think she's his kryptonite, and he hates that more than me.

"As I mentioned," Hayes speaks, redirecting the conversation. "We just started this meeting."

In no time, they bring me up to speed. Pierce can't find a way to contest the will or modify the stipulations. If we try to contest the will, we might not be able to stop the lawyers from selling the properties on time. All the contracts are signed, and the deals are almost closed. William thought about everything. Asshole.

The house where we're supposed to stay needs a lot of work. They pass along some pictures that Beacon took earlier today. The place is totally rundown and doesn't have any furniture or appliances.

Did William know the condition of the place?

If he planned on shoving us all in there, the least he could do is give us enough time to make it a home.

"We need a crew to come and perform a miracle," Hayes explains, giving them an entire list of what the place requires to be livable. "If we hire the right people, it can happen."

"I'm not investing a cent in that property," Pierce protests.

"We're all going to live there," Hayes says in a calm, cool voice. "I'll pay upfront, and once we move in, we can discuss how much you owe me."

"Who is going to see this through?" Henry asks. "I don't think you understand my situation. You're asking me to move to this town and manage my father's businesses, while I manage my own. If I agree to stay here, I only have thirty days to prepare my people for my absence."

"I'll take care of the factory," Mills says. "I have a business degree. You could give me a hand until I get the hang of it because I don't have any experience. What else do you need?"

"Before you continue playing the martyr in this situation," Hayes speaks. "Let me remind you that we can hire anyone from a CEO to whatever else is required to work for us. You need to delegate, or you won't last long enough to see this through."

"You mean, stop being a control freak?" Sophia asks. "Good luck with that one."

Henry clears his throat and glares at her. She gives him an innocent glance.

"The resort needs a lot of work. Am I supposed to pay for it, or are we all going to pitch in?" Henry asks.

"Before everyone gets all worked up about who is paying what," Pierce interrupts, "we can access the assets and cash of the companies if we need it. Jerome Parish, who is the executor of the will, has to approve all the transactions, though."

"I'd rather pay for the house from my own money," Hayes says. "I don't want the lawyer to be fucking with it because he thinks he has some authority over it."

"I agree," Henry declares. "Anyone in favor of that decision, raise your hand?"

"As much as I want to raise my hand, I can't afford fixing the house," I inform them.

"You can pay us when you get your cut of the inheritance," Hayes offers.

"So, we're doing it," Pierce says over the phone.

"Is there any other option?" asks Vance. "I'd give my fortune to skip this ordeal."

"We have to do it," I repeat. "Unless we want to see the people of this town... Actually, I'm not sure what's going to happen to them. They'll have to move to Happy Springs, Portland, or... Do they even have money to relocate and start over?"

Hayes runs a hand through his thick brown hair and exhales loudly. "We can't let that happen. It's no longer about William. It's about the town."

"As I said earlier, we don't even know them," Pierce says.

"That's not the point," I speak. "You don't have to know someone to be kind to them."

"In conclusion, we stop living our lives, so the town can survive?" Mills asks. "I mean that's practically what we'll be doing."

"Did you stop living when you hurt your knee?" Hayes asks him, and Mills shakes his head in response. "It's the same thing. We'll restructure the way we do business, create music, deal with legal cases, and/or care for our patients. We'll rebuild the house, so we can live comfortably. The contractor in town doesn't have the infrastructure to renovate the house in thirty days, but he knows enough people to lead the project. I'll be speaking with him tomorrow."

The entire room goes silent, and we all look at Hayes. It seems like he's been busy working on plan b. If I were Pierce, I'd be pissed because he doubted him. However, I'm me, and it's hard not to want to kiss him for trying to make this work and thinking about the town. Still, I focus on finishing my delicious churros. I can't deal with this swoony feeling right now. In fact, I have to push it away.

"Can he convert the barn into a studio?" Beacon requests.

"I need the barn," Pierce interrupts. "Leyla won't move without the kids. Find another place for your music. That's mine."

"What do you mean by kids?" I ask, slightly confused and horrified. There was no mention of them having children earlier today, and why would they put them in the barn.

"She has two horses, an alpaca, chickens, and two dogs. They are like her children, and she won't move to Baker's Creek without them," he says. "You can have the barn if she signs the divorce papers before I move in—but I doubt she'll let me leave, so I can start anew."

I wonder about his relationship. He sounds so eager to get a divorce, but the way he came forcefully fighting for the barn for her animals sounded off. As if he was saying, my woman comes first.

"We can build you a studio, Beacon," Hayes offers. "You're allowed to commute. Maybe you can try that until it's ready."

"He can only commute during concerts," Pierce corrects him.

"Can I have the garage?" Beacon asks hopeful.

"Sorry kid, as I told you earlier, we all need a place where we can park our cars. We might even have to expand it," Hayes says and taps his yellow pad. "Any special requests other than the studio."

In a way, I feel like I don't fit into this conversation. Really, give me a room with a bed and I'm happy. Instead of listening to everything they need, I continue eating.

As soon as I finish dessert, I drink some water and tackle the guacamole, which is amazing. There's just the right amount of lime and salt with a balance of tomato, onion, and cilantro. Whoever made it deserves a thumbs up. Pretty soon, I run out of tortilla chips, and Hayes goes to fetch a few more. Ugh, I want to hate him, but he's being so nice to me.

To fight the butterflies fluttering inside my stomach, I try to pay attention to the conversation. I just can't. They all have requests. Space for their home office, their own garage. I tune them out and send a message to Tori.

Blaire: *Hey, can you find me doctors for our next project? We need to figure out how much they're going to charge and start creating a budget for everything we need for it. I might be able to get enough funding this time.*

Tori: *I'm sure we can cover it. We received a generous donation.*

Blaire: *How much is it?*

Tori: *Check your email.*

When I do, I gasp and start coughing. Ten million dollars. Someone just donated, not one, but ten million dollars.

"You okay?" Hayes asks, patting me on the back and handing me a glass of water.

"I'm fine. The tortilla chip went down the wrong pipe." I touch the base of my throat, trying to recover my breathing. "Thank you."

"You'll tell me if you're not okay, right?" His eyes are filled with concern.

I nod. He's always worried about my health. When we met, I had been cancer free for only a year, and I had just received the news of my second six-month checkup. My doctor had sent some balloons, wishing me a happy healthy year.

He has always been cautious and vigilant about my health—even a slight cough worries him. To distract myself from the past, I return to Tori and the mysterious ten million dollars.

Blaire: *Is this a joke?*

Tori: *No. The money is already in the account. With this money and* *whatever the old man left you, we can cross a lot of items off your list. Wait, why do you need doctors? Are you staying home? Because I wasn't joking about your room.*

I read the email again and confirm that it is ten million dollars. That's ... a lot. Hayes asks me something, but I'm too busy thinking about what we can do with the money that I only nod and say a couple of uh-huh's. It's not like I can bring much to the table. Can I?

Blaire: *About that ... I need to stay in Baker's Creek. I'll explain everything tomorrow, when I'm back home. Send me the resumes of the doctors who apply in the meantime. We need to be thorough.*

Tori: *You got it.*

"So, we agree," Henry concludes. "We all have our assignments, and we'll meet here in a month."

I look up, feeling like I missed something important, and yet, the conclusion is just what I expected. There's nothing left to do but to move in within thirty days. Henry and Sophia are having their own discussion. Vance, Mills, and Beacon are talking about buying some tequila and bourbon at the liquor store. I guess this meeting is adjourned.

"Do you want to take a walk?" Hayes asks, as I finish my last taco.

"Not with you," I answer, sounding defensive—maybe I should be less confrontational. "Listen, we have to interact with each other for the next eighteen months, but let's not pretend that we are friends, okay?"

"Maybe we should clear the air," he suggests.

"What's there to clear?" I ask, standing from the chair and starting to clear my dishes.

"Leave those there," Sophia suggests. "The crew is coming over to clean in a few minutes."

"Thank you again for everything," I say.

"Can we continue?" Henry asks with a groan. Sophia rolls her eyes, and her attention goes back to him.

I leave the conference room. Hayes is right behind me, and he says, "There's a lot to clear, Blaire."

"There's nothing, really," I insist. "We'll just coexist until it's over. Have a good night."

Instead of heading upstairs, I leave The Lodge. I do need to take a walk. It's a habit of mine, or more like something I have to do, or else, my day isn't complete. After dinner, I always take a walk.

This old habit began back when I was sick, and I refused to eat. It became an incentive for me to finish at least a meal. My parents tried to keep me indoors and away from germs since my immune system was compromised. I was allowed to go out for a small walk after dinner, as long as I ate something.

Mom or Dad would take me if we were home. At the hospital, the nurses would either push me in a wheelchair, or if I was strong enough, I'd be walking on my own with one of them supervising. In college, I walked with Hayes most nights.

"There's nothing left between us," I say and walk faster.

"How much do you hate me?" He asks, and I notice he's still right behind me.

I halt and look at him in surprise. "I thought you were the one who swore to never forgive me or stop hating me for what I had done," I reminded him, using some of the hurtful words he threw at me like arrows after Carter's funeral.

Since I'm not interested in whatever he's selling, I continue walking.

"Look," he says, without acknowledging what I just blurted. "They're beautiful."

I stop and turn around to see what he's looking at. You never know when a snake or some dangerous animal might appear that he might think is cool. The guy is a nerd and, believe it or not, a nature junkie.

Hayes is actually looking up at the sky. When I follow his gaze, I see all the constellations shining. It's beautiful—magical.

"It's been years since I've seen them this close," he says.

"Hmm," I say in response. "How? You like stargazing."

He looks down at me and gives me a sad smile, and then I remember. When we met, it became our thing. Then, the memories of the first time we went out to Monte Bello Preserve, which is one of the best places to stargaze in the Palo Alto area, come back to me. It wasn't a date, but it might as well have been because, from that moment on, we became inseparable.

FOURTEEN

Blaire

IT'S FRIDAY, I just finished the third week of my freshman year. So far, I've adapted to the rhythm and the atmosphere of college life. Tonight, I'm on my way to the ice cream shop when I bump into Hayes Aldridge. I didn't think I'd see him any time soon, even though his brother lives right across the hall from me.

"Pink?" He asks, pulling down the beanie hat I'm wearing. "Do you have one in every color or one for each day of the week?"

I frown, confused, because how does he know I have so many different *beanies. We haven't seen each other since he helped me move, and that day, I was wearing a baseball cap.*

"Hi," I say, instead of quizzing him.

"Hey, Blaire," he says with that raspy syrupy voice of his that makes me a sticky mush. "Where are you going?"

"Getting something for dinner," I answer.

"That's an ice cream shop," he states the obvious.

"Life is too short. I always start with dessert and then make my way toward the rest."

He gives me a strange look and then says, "I was heading to the sandwich shop. Why don't we buy food and get out of this town? We can find a spot to eat."

His invitation tempts my dormant wild side. Being in college is different from living at home with my parents—homeschooled and isolated from everything and everyone. I wasn't a rebel during middle school, but I tried to keep up with my brothers who loved to raise havoc. Once I got sick, my parents never let me go anywhere without them.

It's the first time I'm on my own in seventeen, almost eighteen years. The past is behind me. I don't have to be afraid of getting pneumonia because someone walking by me sneezed. The weight of my parents' marriage was stripped from my back once I moved out of the house and into campus housing. The burden of getting on with the program, even when I wanted to give up, because I was tired of the medication, the needles, and my parents' fights, is over.

Done.

I'm free.

I can allow myself to feel any way I want without worrying about my mother nagging me about always smiling because I'm still alive. Keeping a positive attitude while struggling is hard—sometimes impossible. Hey, I'm grateful for all my blessings, but I'm also human. We can't be all smiles and positive thoughts twenty-four seven.

This new future is different. I'm supposed to be cautious. Mindful of my studies and my health. Still, my doctors and nurses recommended me to have fun, to truly live. Tonight, I want to just be Blaire, not the sick, cautious girl. I choose to be semi-reckless, and I agree to go with Hayes.

"Where should we go?" he asks, once we have our food and are inside of his truck.

"Monte Bello Preserve," I answer, without even thinking.

He doesn't ask where that's at, he just drives to our destination. In the meantime, we listen to his music, which isn't that bad. Coldplay, Linkin Park, Bush, and the Killers are some of his favorite bands, but he also likes classical music and old classic rock. I'm not ready to tell him that I love boy bands. My brothers used to say I was lame for loving them. Surely this guy is going to think the same—or worse.

When we arrive at the park, we eat, we talk about my classes, and once we're done, we enjoy the view.

Being here, laying on a blanket, watching the stars is a new experience for me. At least everything looks different. Brighter. The last time I visited this place was with my parents and my brothers. It was ... before.

"What are you thinking?" Hayes asks.

Too many things, but I don't answer. He doesn't know that I never thought I'd see the stars again like this. Or that maybe they look even more beautiful because I had an almost near-death experience—or because he's here with me.

It's the place, not him. The sky looks so different from my bedroom—or the hospital room. A part of me has been waiting for what feels like my entire life to witness this wonder of nature: a sea of stars.

Galaxies billions of years away from us. An experience I thought I would never get to live again. But here I am looking at this miracle.

The stars.

A million wishes waiting to be professed to the darkness. My one wish is to be able to experience life. For the cancer to never come back.

Today is enough, though.

I've been waiting my entire life to experience the freedom that was snatched from when I turned thirteen. I'm free to dream, to hope, and to do as I wish.

At least for now.

"Are you always this quiet?"

"Only when I'm in front of greatness, or I don't have anything good to say," I answer.

"Which one is it?" His voice is low, and the words slide through my ears slowly like warm syrup.

"The former," I answer with a chuckle and turn my attention to him.

His mouth turns up at the corners. "It's like a dream, right? I don't think there's anything more relaxing than watching the sky at night."

"Some nights, when my parents took me camping, my family and I would spend hours looking up at the sky and trying to search for our constellations. I wanted to be my own."

"You wanted to be a star?"

"I guess, if you put it that way, it sounds ridiculous."

"No, it's just strange. Do you know that stars always shine brighter seconds before they fall apart?"

"Well, aren't we a glass half empty kind of guy."

"No, sweetheart. I'm a who the fuck needs a glass kind of person."

"Still, I'm telling you I wanted to be a constellation, and you're telling me that I'd explode if I shine too much."

"You are, in fact, part of a star," he says. "So no, that's not what I meant."

"Now I'm confused."

"Well, it depends on how you want to see it. According to an article in National Geographic, we're made out of stardust. Most of the material we're made of comes out of dying stars. I'd guess you originated from one of the biggest, brightest ones."

"It feels like you're giving me a compliment," I say. "A very nerdy one."

He laughs playfully. "I know, I'm a nerd."

"A sweet nerd," I reply, staring at his profile, as he continues looking up at the sky. His chin dusted with facial hair, his lips slightly open. It makes me want to kiss him.

How would that be? I've never been kissed. A kiss from him might be the beginning of a long fantasy or the start of a heartbreaking tragedy. Because what if I fall for him, but then, like the stars, I die?

Should I push him away?

According to the young adult novels, fiction books, and romance novels I've read for the past five years, by now I should've fallen in love at least once. I should've had my heart broken twice. Suffered from unrequited love several times. Have a million crushes, if not, at least five of them.

After my parents' marriage broke, I stopped believing in love the way I used to. I don't believe in love at first sight. Lust might exist, but I've never experienced it. Swooning ... I've only read about it. I didn't believe in those crackle sounds that some hear when there's a hot guy around them making them fall in love—until I met this guy.

Hayes is making me question myself. I feel an energy surrounding us that pulls me to him. It might be pure imagination. He's older, I have to remind myself. Much more experienced, and he knows how to entice women older than me. I'm just a small fish.

"I like your smile and you," he says. "But your eyes ... I can get lost in them forever."

"You don't even know me."

"But I do," he answers. "We originated from the same star."

"Does that line work?" I ask skeptically.

"You tell me, beautiful."

I laugh hard. Not sure if it's because I'm nervous, happy, or because he's actually funny.

"I think this is it," I say, as I'm calming down from the hysterical laughter.

"What is it?"

"Favorite moment of the day," I tell him.

"Favorite moment?"

"I collect them, in my journal. I started doing it when I was about fourteen. Back when the days were dark, and I felt like I could barely hold onto this life, I'd read them. They helped me get through the day. I still collect them. It's a way to remind myself that there's always something good, even on the darkest days. That it's okay that not every day is bright, but there's always brightness within it."

"Seeing you," he says. "Every time I see you around campus is my favorite moment of the day."

STARGAZING with Hayes was always special, but that night is still one of the top ten favorite moments of my entire life. Is it possible that everything that's been happening is just pure coincidence, or...?

I look at him, and I'm positive that he's trying to reenact our story.

"What are you doing?" I ask him suspiciously.

His face is solemn, but his eyes hold a little mischief. Bingo!

I finally caught him. He's trying to recreate us: our past, how we met. Even our favorite moments. But why?

"Desserts, the walk, the stars..." I list the small things he's been doing.

"I don't know, Stardust," he says with a low voice that makes my entire body tremble.

I can't succumb to his charm. He can't be doing this to me. Not now —or ever. How dare he call me that when he's the one who relinquished the right to be mine and broke my heart.

"All I know is that for the first time in years, I..." He shuts his mouth and looks at me anxiously. "Listen, I fucked up royally. I understand that it is twelve years too late to ask you to forgive me, to let me love you again. But if anyone believes in second chances, it's you. I promise to do the impossible and prove to you that I'm worthy of you. I just hope I can convince you that I am truly sorry."

That huge donation we received today, I'm positive that he sent it.

"It was you who left me. Now you're sorry, and you're sending me money to show me your remorse?" I can't contain the anger. "Ten million dollars doesn't mend a broken heart. It doesn't erase the ugly memories, nor wipe the tears. Are you becoming your father? Here are a few millions, please forgive me for skipping your graduation. In my case, sorry for breaking your heart and breaking my promise."

"That's a low blow, Blaire. Never compare me with that asshole," he says offended.

"The truth hurts. You broke up with me so you could be free to fuck around. You said I was your soulmate, and then you left me."

"It was for your benefit. I was your first," he says, raising his voice. "First boyfriend, first kiss, first love ... first everything. You hadn't lived at all. There was a moment when I wanted to marry you, but I didn't want to repeat our parents' mistakes. My parents married after Mom graduated. Your parents had to marry because..."

Dad knocked up Mom. There's my answer. The pregnancy scare.

"It was the baby," I match his tone. "I wasn't pregnant, and even if I had been, I told you that I could take care of myself and our child. You said it was okay, it wouldn't matter. That even though kids weren't in your plans, we could handle it. But those were all lies. You were afraid that I'd trap you. So that's why you broke my heart?"

"I confess, being a father back then scared me. William was an asshole—he never changed, Blaire. What would happen if I followed in his footsteps? I was twenty-two and stupid. Things were happening too fast—and I wanted it all with you. At some point, med school didn't matter, it was just you. My star. My heart. My love. But what if one day you realized I wasn't worth it? If you met someone new and left me?"

"No matter how you spin the story, Hayes, you left me. You weren't any different from my parents or my brothers who decided I was too much work to stick around."

He shakes his head. "No, I swear that wasn't it. It was everything but that, Love."

"Do not call me that!"

"I'd give up everything I have to have one more day with you. I'd give up my career, my fortune. All. In exchange of a lifetime filled with favorites with you. Our forever."

"Stop!"

"Seeing you again," he says.

"What?"

"My favorite moment of the day is seeing you again."

"Don't do this to me. It took me years to learn how to live without you. You have to stop this nonsense," I beg him, walking away.

I need to put some distance between us, because my heart is just like every muscle, it remembers Hayes, and if I'm not careful, it'll remember how to love him.

FIFTEEN

Hayes

BLAIRE DOESN'T JUST WALK AWAY; she practically runs away from me. Next time, I should approach her with caution and try to keep things friendly between us. At least until she realizes I'm still in love with her.

She's right. I intentionally recreated some of her favorite moments of us to refresh her memory. I wanted her to remember the good times. To remind her that, even when she wants to give up, it's worth it to continue. And maybe that's where I failed. We need new moments—a different approach to our second chance.

Heading to my room, I decide to call Mom. I promised to do it no matter the time. Knowing her, she's awake, waiting by the phone to see what my father's last testament was about.

"Hayes," she answers on the first ring.

"Hello, Mom," I greet her. "Did you sleep at all?"

"I did my best. How is everyone doing?" she asks. "The boys—are they okay after... I still can't believe that your father died. He swore he'd live to be a hundred."

She sounds sad, and I wonder if she still loves him. Maybe I'm wrong and there's one person who grieves his death—Mom.

"Well, there are things money can't buy, like health or love," I say. "He died alone and with no one to mourn him. Unless, you still love him."

"Not him," she says with a whisper. "I mourn the guy I met in college. I'll always miss him. He was different. William made every day we were together special. I fell in love with a sensitive man who knew all the right moves and all the right words. Later, I figured out that he just didn't understand love. His family was focused on the bottom line—and he strived to please them because he'd be the next Aldridge to own it all."

There's a long pause, and I don't speak. I wait.

"He cared in his own way," she continues. "When Carter was diagnosed ... he came back to me. The same guy who would do anything for his family. For me. After your brother died, I realized it was all an illusion."

"I'm sorry," I say, not sure if I'm saying, *I'm sorry for her loss or that she fell in love with a guy incapable of love.*

There's no point trying to explain to her that him knowing what to say and how to behave doesn't mean he really loved her. Then again, maybe he did love each woman he dated—or married—in his own twisted way.

"So, how are your brothers?" she asks, her voice back to normal. "Are they in denial like you or—"

"Everyone is fine, Mom. I'm not in denial," I protest. "We weren't close to Dad, so there were no tears, if that's what you're asking me."

She sighs, but instead of pressing on the subject, she asks, "When are you going back to San Francisco?"

"About that ... he fucked us all up," I inform her, and I proceed to recount the events of the day, and while I'm doing so, I notice my anger is gone. Though Mom stops me when I mention Blaire.

"She shouldn't be there," she snaps, her voice high pitched. "Not after what she did."

Mom hated Blaire for what happened when Carter died. She's the one who told me everything that had transpired between Blaire and Carter, and now I realize she gave me her version of the events.

"And what exactly did she do, Mom?" I ask, because her side of the story is so different to Blaire's and I want to believe my mother, but Blaire doesn't lie. She always said that life is too short to tangle yourself between fake words and lies.

Mom told me that they married without her permission, and that Blaire didn't let her see my brother. According to her, Blaire only wanted Carter's money. It sounds cold and calculated, and Blaire is anything but those things.

"You already know what happened," she answers. "She kept Carter away from us and didn't let him get his treatment. It's because of her that he died so soon."

"Mom, would you like to stick with that story or give me a more accurate description of the events?" I question, and it feels like I just dropped the weight of the world on her shoulders because she gasps.

"Who are you going to believe?" she asks with a challenge in her voice.

"Whoever is being honest about what really happened during Carter's last days, Mom. He's dead, but I'm sure Carter would be disappointed if we were holding onto lies, instead of the good times we shared with him. It's been twelve years. He's gone, and I miss him. Can we be honest with each other, please?"

"Why are you doing this?"

"Because I need the truth, Mom. Did you really try to force him to get treatment against his will?"

"I... There was hope, but Carter didn't want to listen. He insisted that the only person who understood him was Blaire, and when I called your father, he said we could just claim he was mentally incapable to make any decisions on his own so..."

"He got married," I finish her sentence.

"Yes, but she kept him away from me, and she—"

"Carter," I amend. "Carter is the one who didn't want to see you, and he shielded himself behind her. Do you know why Blaire understood him?"

"Because they were having sex," she answers, and I'm not loving her tone.

"Blaire had leukemia when she was a teenager," I tell her. Although it is something Blaire hates to share, I feel it's important to tell my mother, so she can understand why Carter did what he did.

"She lived what Carter was living. The only reason she didn't give up during her treatments was because there was hope, but she knows how painful that process is and how it takes away what little energy you have, as well as the will to continue."

"I wanted to save him." She starts crying. "She didn't let me."

"It's easier to blame someone else. It was painful to lose him. He had an energy that not many have. People loved him the moment they met him." I speak with a calm voice. I'm not upset with her, just worried that she hasn't been able to let go of what happened—just like me.

"Remember the time when one of my patients sued me because he lost his leg?"

"It wasn't your fault," she says, still angry, because he went after my medical license.

I almost lost everything I had built because of the resentment he harbored. It wasn't malpractice; it was a decision the medical team made and his family approved of. Yet, he tried to hurt me because he hurt.

"He did it because he couldn't stand the loss. He couldn't admit that it had been his reckless behavior that caused the accident. Amputating his leg saved his life, but for him, it ruined it. He had to blame me because he needed someone to take the blame for everything that had changed and that part of him he will never get back. I think that's what happened to us."

"What are you saying?"

"We blamed Blaire," I explain, but, actually, she's the one who blamed Blaire, and I just took Mom's side. "She just did what was best for Carter. She gave him what he needed: the best last months of his life."

"Are you going to forgive her?" she asks.

"No, I'm going to work hard to deserve her forgiveness," I answer.

"This is the grief talking. The pain of losing your father," she says. "You're not thinking straight."

"You're wrong, Mom. Losing William isn't the reason why I'm working hard to fix my life. My reasoning might not make sense to you, but it does to me. This is the first time in years that I'm actually thinking outside work and my career," I correct her, because what is thinking straight? Love never makes sense, does it? "Just a couple of weeks ago, you wanted me to be happy, and guess what, *happy is Blaire*."

"Hayes..."

"Yeah, Mom?"

"What if I can't?"

"I believe in you, Mom. I'm going to send an email with some links. You should take a look at them, and I hope that you find peace, because we can't live the rest of our lives like this. It's time to let go of what happened during Carter's illness and realize that Blaire was just doing what was best for him. I'm actually thankful that someone was there for him. He could've just left everyone behind, Mom."

"He was always too independent."

"And you tried to clip his wings. You know that never worked with Carter," I remind her.

"He was stubborn," she continues.

"Love you, Mom," I say, before I hang up the phone.

For the next few hours, I research Baker's Creek, how to set up a practice, and go through all the links I sent Mom about the Carter's Kids Foundation. Blaire has a blog and social media. I've been reading all her entries, looking at her pictures, learning about her travels, and looking at all the places and the children she's been caring for since she started the foundation.

As I read every entry, I can hear her voice telling the story, feeling her excitement, celebrating her triumphs, worrying about the struggles she faced. After reading so many entries, I know her a little better, and yet, I've just touched the surface of what she's been doing during all these years. And I want more.

Everything.

Why hadn't I look her up before?

Because I was in denial and angry. Carter's death pained me to the point that I wanted to hate the entire world—even myself. Mom's story made it so easy to concentrate all my anger on Blaire. Not only that, I also pushed my other brothers away because my heart couldn't take another loss.

Trying to move on with my life without Blaire wasn't smart. All these years I've known, deep down, that I could never love anyone the way I loved her. And I wasn't interested in loving anyone but her.

It's late when Henry walks into the suite that we share.

"You're still awake?" he asks.

I check the time and respond with a question of my own. "It's late, and are you still working?"

He shrugs. "The hotel business never stops, you know. I'm sure you can relate, unless you're one of those fancy doctors who only works a couple of times a week."

I huff because I sure know the kind he's talking about—I'm not a fan of them. One of my practice partners is just like that. His waiting list is as long as mine but only because he sees patients on Tuesdays, and he operates on Fridays. Leaving the doctor on call in charge of any post-surgery emergencies that might arise. I don't work all week long in the practice, but the time I don't spend in the office, I am at the hospital.

And in just a few hours, I quit, and now I'm planning to walk on a different path.

"I'm selling my part of the practice," I announce, and saying it out loud makes it real. "I offered it to my partners first, but neither one of them wants it. However, they trust I'll sell it to the right doctor."

"Are you out of your fucking mind?" he asks, his eyes bulging. "You can't give up your life. Weren't you the one who said earlier that we'd adjust, not just quit?"

"I'm not quitting medicine. I'm rethinking my future," I explain in a calm, moderate voice.

"It's Blaire, isn't it?" he asks disgustedly. "What is it about her that everyone falls for her."

"Don't bring Blaire in this conversation," I say, in a low warning voice.

"She married your fucking brother."

"Our brother," I correct him. "It's not what you think."

"Your mother—"

"I spoke to her, and she told me the truth," I interrupt him and tell him the story, adding the part where Blaire uses his money to help others.

He looks at me dumbfounded and says, "I wish I had known. I would have been there for Carter. He was cool, you know."

Carter wasn't just cool. He was also friendly, supportive, and sometimes I think he was the one who kept us all together until the end. He called all of us on our birthdays and tried to organize trips, even when it wasn't father's weekend, and sometimes, he made them happen.

"Can Pierce reverse the trust stipulation, so she can access it at any time?" Henry asks, after a long silence.

I shrug.

"Send me the information about her foundation. I want to research it, if you don't mind," he requests. "Still, Blaire or not, you have a life in San Francisco."

I don't have a life, just like him. I have a job and a busy schedule. But we don't truly live.

"As I told you earlier, there are more important things to life than what I've built so far. It's sad to see that our father died with no one around him. I loved him, you know, when I was young. I don't want to end up like him."

He looks at me confused. "This is not *A Christmas Carol*. Dad isn't Marley, Blaire isn't your ghost of the past, and we're not your ghosts of the present. Life isn't a story told by Dickens."

I laugh at his stupid analogy, though, in all honesty, Dad could easily be Marley, giving us a warning on how things will end for all of us if we continue following in his footsteps. All my brothers are concerned about their careers and how they'll be affected because of the stipulations. None of them mentioned a loved one or their mothers. We really aren't that different from William, are we?

"Laugh all you want, Hayes, but I'm telling you, this charade shouldn't even be happening. I'm trying to wrap my head around it. However, I think you're the only one who is willing to stay. In thirty days, they'll walk out of here and will keep living their lives."

I don't have time to say anything because he marches to his room and locks the door. Is he actually going to walk away?

SIXTEEN

Blaire

THE NEXT MORNING, I wake up early, but stay in bed, replaying my dream. It felt real. Hayes' warmth, his strong arms holding me. His mouth devouring mine and his hands... I touch my lips because they're still tingling from the dream. The wetness between my legs is for him: the only man who makes my body tremble with one touch.

Don't judge me; I miss him, okay. It wasn't just love that we shared, we also had great sex. Yes, the ending was bitter and painful, but before that, we were so happy. If I can see past him abandoning me and the years apart... No, that's never going to happen.

We're over, and nothing he does or says will convince me to give him a second chance. Not even those hypnotizing eyes begging me to love him. I need to push away the teenage crush. Our past should stay behind us. The time we will spend together isn't a test or an opportunity to go back to who we were. It's a way to turn over a new leaf and let go of any feelings that we think we harbor for each other.

We both need to move on. As for what he said yesterday, he is either stuck in the past or just not willing to let anyone else into his life and his heart. Hayes is friendly, but not everyone can penetrate the big brick wall he places between him and everyone else.

I wasn't his first girlfriend, but I was the first person he said I love you to—maybe the only one he ever loved.

Me ... well, I haven't been dating because my life is hectic. Love is something no one can force to happen, and I'm always on the move. There's never a time for me to meet someone new or interesting. I won't force that part of my future. Maybe I'm meant to find someone when I'm older.

I trust fate. I'm in charge of a part of my life, but there are things I can't change. I believe in destiny and that there are things, like love and health, that you don't have much say in.

That's, yet, another one of the mottos I live by: *you have to have faith while doing your best to live.*

I lay down in bed until the sun finally shines through the drapes. After taking a shower, I get dressed and pack my stuff. I have to be in Portland by four to catch my flight, but I have a few hours to walk around town before I drive to the airport.

Before heading outside, I look at myself in the mirror and decide to put some lip gloss and mascara on as well as put my hair in a braid. Today, I put on a baseball cap to go with my outfit. I'm wearing a white tank top with a blouse on top, and a pair of denim shorts.

Heading outside, I realize the road is empty. The birds are singing and the tree leaves rustling. The breeze of the morning makes me shiver, but I choose not to head back to my room for a sweatshirt. It'll warm up soon.

I walk along the trail surrounded by azures, lavender, and baby blue eyes flowers. Soon I make it to Main Street and continue walking east until I find the coffee shop.

Love You a Latte hasn't changed much since the last time I was here. They have a few tables and several old couches. It's like being in the comfort of your living room—and now, they have wi-fi. The line isn't long, and toward the front, I spot Sophia, who waves at me.

"Hi, I'm glad to see you. I meant to ask you for your number last night, but Henry had me working until midnight," she says when I reach her. "Do you have time for a quick chat? Or... at what time are you heading to the big house?"

"You worked until midnight, and you're already awake looking like a model?" I ask, impressed because she's dressed in designer jeans, an elegant top, and a pair of high heel boots. Her face looks fresh, and she's smiling from ear to ear.

She's ready to take over the corporate world—with style.

"I work for Henry Aldridge. I have to be up way before the sun rises. I'm pretty sure he never sleeps and hopes that I'll join his cult of delusional droids." She laughs. "That's never going to happen. In any case, I'm going to live eighteen months free of him."

Yesterday, I thought I liked her. Today, I want her to be my best friend. Such a shame that she's not staying with us.

"Here, this is my number," I say, giving her my card. "Text me yours when you have the time."

She produces her phone out of the pocket of her jeans, and I receive a text almost immediately. Then, she turns to look at me. "Quick pointers, claim the master suite for yourself, if there is one. I'm not sure how many bedrooms they have but get the best room."

I nod. What I don't tell her is that I'm not going to live in the house. The lawyer mentioned that we have to reside on the property, he didn't specify that we have to live together under the same roof. I'd rather camp outside than share the same space with those guys.

Living with my older brothers while growing up was a nightmare. I can't imagine what it would be like to live with six guys. And not just any guys. The Aldridge boys.

We order our coffees. She offers to pay, handing a black credit card to the guy behind the register. "Merkel Resorts is paying," she announces.

"Then, we should visit My Cookie Jar and buy some pastries. They have the best blueberry muffins and the yummiest buttery croissants in the Pacific Northwest," I suggest, missing Carter more than usual.

Waking up early and getting pastries was his favorite thing, no matter where he lived or visited. Somedays, he'd buy a dozen croissants and eat them in one sitting. Carter liked to live life without reservations or limitations. That's something we had in common; we tried to live our best day, every day.

I look at Sophia, and I think he would have loved her. He'd be giving her pointers on how to tease Henry. It was one of his favorite hobbies. We wait for her coffee and my tea latte in silence. Then, we march next door to My Cookie Jar. When we push the door open, the bell above it rings.

The place hasn't changed much. The floor inside is a black and white checkerboard of tiles that show the wear of several decades' worth of customers, walking in and out of the shop. Bagels and muffins dominate the display, but my favorites are there waiting for me to buy them, the chocolate croissants.

The air is more delicious than I remember. Somehow, the aroma captures everything good in here. I wish I could stay all day trying all their pastries.

"These muffins better be good," Sophia says. "We should figure out a way to have them delivered to the hotel."

"Waiting for them is part of the experience," I tell her. "The line moves quickly, and they're still warm from the oven when they hand them to you. As you take your first bite, they melt in your mouth."

"Would you like me to leave you two alone?" she asks with a laugh. "You are eye-fucking the pastries."

"Wait until you taste them. They are orgasmically delicious," I say, licking my fingers while I imagine eating them.

"Try a vibrator or Tinder," she suggests. "They're much more effective than hot pastries, and this is coming from a Latina who loves her pan dulce."

I laugh and shake my head. Before I can talk, her phone buzzes, and she grunts. "Ugh, can he leave me alone for a few minutes?"

"The boss?"

She nods and asks, "What's the name of this place again?"

"My Cookie Jar," I tell her, while she's typing on her phone.

Henry has never been an easy person to deal with, and I imagine that, as a boss, he's even more difficult.

I'm about to say something when I hear the ladies in front of us speak. "William's funeral was yesterday, and no one was invited."

"Are you sure?" the one next to her asks.

"Yes, the reverend confirmed it earlier today. The only ones in attendance were his sons."

"They're just like William. We're not good enough to be invited to their celebrations," the other woman says.

Sophia and I look at each other. The sons didn't want to be at that funeral either. I'm glad I skipped it.

"Did you hear anything else?" one of them asks intrigued. "What's going to happen to the main house? The factory is still running, but I heard they're going to fire everyone before they sell it—or was it after?"

"There's a rumor that they're closing the resort and selling everything he owned. Those men are greedier than their father. They were always too good to be around town," the other answers. "What if they increase the rent or... I heard they almost fired Nick."

"No one cares much about him, but if his job is in jeopardy, what's going to happen with everyone else? He's been managing that hotel for five years on his own."

That explains why this Nick guy is such an arrogant asshole. He pretty much owns the place.

"It was the doctor who threatened to fire him. Apparently one of the brothers is part of a gang and came in all bloody. Nick also messed with the doctor's mistress."

Mistress? I mouth to Sophia, who is shaking in laughter.

A gang? Vance works for a security company ... or he owns it. I'm not sure since everything that has to do with him is classified.

"Yesterday, there was an uptight woman strolling around town with a baby. Someone said that's the baby mama of one of them. She didn't have a ring, though."

I turn to look at Sophia and mouth, *Hey, baby mama.* She rolls her eyes.

"I tweeted it. You have to get into Twitter."

Sophia arches an eyebrow and pulls out her phone. She starts typing until her face brightens and mouths, *This is ridiculous.*

She hands me the phone.

First look at the Aldridge family. New blood for the town, or will they tear it down?

I can't help but giggle along with Sophia. The two women turn around and look at us. One of them is tall and slender. Her hair is gray, her eyes are the bulging, staring kind that always seem about to jump from their sockets.

"Oh, you're the women who came with *them.*" She crosses her arms and gives me a glare. "So, what are you doing in town?"

The bell rings, announcing someone has arrived. I turn around, and it's Hayes. Next to him is Henry.

"Hey," Hayes greets me, as he reaches us. When I tilt my head toward the lady, he looks at her, and then lowers his voice, pressing his lips to my ear and making me shiver. "Is everything okay?"

"As okay as it can be when you're not welcome," I whisper, trying not to breathe him in but failing. I love that fresh, citrus scent mixed with sandalwood that's all Hayes.

"Don't pay them any attention," he says.

That's easy to do if you're here just for the weekend, but for more than a year... Baker's Creek is a very small town, and everyone knows your business. And apparently, they have Twitter.

"You two look a lot like William," gray hair, bulging eyes says. "Are you here to fire everyone?"

"Hayes Aldridge," he introduces himself. "This is my brother, Henry."

"Hayes," she repeats. "The doctor, and you're the hotel owner."

Well, she's been doing her homework. "I'm Anna Tattle, and this is Jane Heywood."

"Nice to meet you, Mrs. Tattle," he says.

Sophia and I look at each other, and before we both burst into laughter, Hayes and Henry grab us and pull us to them. I press my face against Hayes' solid chest, trying to control the laughter.

"Well, I heard you guys were in town to bury your father. It's such a shame that we couldn't attend his wake."

"He requested to have a family-only life celebration, Mrs. Tattle," Henry responds. When I turn back around, I notice that Sophia is gone, and it's just the three of us in the middle of an interrogation. "We tried our best to follow his last wishes."

"What's going to happen to the town?" she asks. "We keep hearing rumors about you tearing down the resort and building a brand-new one under the Merkel Hotels and Spas. We heard that you're selling the factory next month, but before it happens, you'll be firing all the employees."

Where did she hear the rumors? I'm astounded by the way she twisted everything, and yet, she's not too far from the truth.

Hayes is the first one to speak. "You can't possibly believe all those rumors. We're not sure how we're going to handle the transition from our father's administration to ours, but I assure you, it'll be done smoothly—or as smoothly as possible."

"Is it true that you're buying the medical practice?" the other lady asks. "We need a doctor in town. My husband had a stroke a few years back, and we've been driving to Portland to see the specialist. My granddaughter helped us, but not everyone is as lucky as we are to have someone like her."

"How is your husband doing?" I ask, wondering if he recovered, and if he's getting the medical attention that he needs. We should open a hospital here. "Is there something we can do? I can check his blood pressure, maybe—"

"Blaire," Hayes interrupts me, shaking his head. "We're looking into the needs of the town. As soon as we have a plan, we'll give you more details."

"I told you they weren't as bad as their father, Anna." Jane Heywood sighs with relief.

"Got the goodies," Sophia steps in, showing us two white paper bags with the logo of the bakery.

How and when did she do that?

"Let's head out. We have a meeting in twenty minutes, Mr. Aldridge," she says, pushing through the crowd, as if she owns the place.

"If you'll excuse us, we have to leave. It was nice to meet you, Mrs. Heywood and Mrs. Tattle," Hayes excuses us.

"I hope the others are single. My daughter could use a hunk like that one to marry," one of them says as we leave.

"The town girls are going to be hounding the new blood," says the other.

Sophia and I look at each other and grin. I'm not sure about her, but I can't wait to watch the parade of women trying to snatch themselves an Aldridge.

Once we're out and away from the townies, I say, "And the town gossip begins."

"What the fuck was that?" Henry asks.

"The welcoming committee?" I guess.

"And they have Twitter," Sophia says mockingly and shows him the phone.

"The fuck is this," he says angrily. "You're not Mills' baby mama. How did they get that picture? Fix this Sophia. If this gets in the wrong hands, we're going to have a PR nightmare on our hands."

"Stop exaggerating!" Sophia says, waving her hand. "They're harmless. Everything they have in there makes no sense."

Then Henry laughs. "Hayes, I didn't know you came back with the missus."

"What?" I ask, taking the phone.

Doctor Hayes Aldridge is setting up a medical practice, and his wife is lovely. There's already a picture of us that they must have just taken.

"Yeah, fix this, Sophia," I agree with Henry. "How do you even fix gossip?"

Sophia laughs. "That's not part of my duties." She hands over one of the white paper bags. I ordered muffins and croissants. "Here's your share. They better be worth the wait."

"Thank you," I say, sipping my latte. "I think it'll be safer if I head to the hotel."

"We have an appointment with the doctor," Hayes announces.

"Good luck with that. We have to head back to the resort," Henry tells Sophia, then turns to Hayes. "Keep me posted about the house. It has to be furnished in twenty-nine days, or we'll have to sleep on the floor according to Pierce."

They turn around and walk away.

"Where are you going?" Hayes asks, grabbing my elbow carefully. "You and I have work to do.

"As I said, you and I have an appointment with the good old doctor, and then we're going to the house. The contractor is going to meet us there. He said he'd be arriving at seven to see what he'll be working with."

"I'm sorry, but you're on your own, Hayes."

"You agreed to do this with me."

I blink a couple of times then glare at him. "When?"

"During the meeting," he explains, "since we both live in San Francisco."

"That's impossible. If that had been the case, I would have offered to take over the entire operation. Not work with you. Are you sure?"

He smirks and nods. "You nodded a couple of times and mumbled a few others. Knowing you, you were daydreaming and just nodding yes and no, so we wouldn't interrupt you."

Fuck, I knew some day that was going to bite me on the ass. Can I talk myself out of this one?

SEVENTEEN

Blaire

———————

"I REFUSE TO WORK WITH YOU," I state, handing him my latte and looking inside of the paper bag. The pastries are getting cold by the second. Sophia didn't order chocolate croissants. I have to tell her all about them, but I pull out a butter one.

Carefully, I break a corner, toss it into my mouth, and moan as it melts like fresh butter with vanilla flavoring.

Hayes is staring at me, and I'm not sure if he's in pain or in lust.

"What?" I ask, touching the corner of my mouth dusting the crumbles.

"You just made your sex face while eating that piece of bread," he says uncomfortably. "I'm trying not to drag you to the hotel and fuck you. It's been too long since I've had you, which is not how I want things to go between us. But if I could, I'd eat you right now."

"It's a good thing that I'm leaving, and we won't see each other for a month," I say, trying to claim back my latte.

He lifts his hand high, and I glare at him. "Stupid gigantic man, give me my drink."

"Listen, we don't have time for games, Blaire," he states, drinking from my latte and scrunching his face. "Tea?"

"Yeah, I'm trying to cut my caffeine intake," I inform him and grunt when he takes part of my croissant.

"Look," he says, talking with a mouth full. "Fuck, I forgot how much I loved these pastries."

"They are better than an orgasm," I state.

He bends over, his lips almost touching my ear. "I should refresh your memory, Love. Nothing is better than an orgasm."

"Stop," I order, taking a step back, before I'm the one pulling on his collar and kissing him mindlessly. "We should agree on a few things, like we don't talk about our past or sex. EVER."

"Sex is one of your favorite subjects, and we never talked about it, just acted—unless you mean the dirty talk," he mumbles, tracing his lips along my jaw and making me shiver.

"Hayes," I say, my voice quivering just like my insides.

"Fine, let's go," he says. "We have an appointment."

"You do that, I'll stay close to the bakery, so I can eat my weight in cookies and croissants," I say dismissing him.

"You can have another muffin tomorrow. Right now, we have to go, Blaire."

"Nope," I say, looking into the bag and pulling out a muffin. "My flight leaves later today. I have stuff to do."

"You can't leave. We have a lot to do. You heard those ladies. Everyone is worried about their future. You were the one who insisted that we needed to do this for them."

"So, what? Now I'm stuck with you until—"

"Dear, I forgot to ask. Are you two dating, or are you married?" Mrs. Tattle asks. "You know how much I hate to give the wrong information."

No, we don't. We just met you.

She's like a gossip journalist; we're lucky she doesn't snap a picture of us while asking questions. I work hard to hide the laugh as I picture her in the middle of the street in a few years asking, "Hayes, when are you marrying? Hayes, are you ever going to date one of the girls from this town?" But it's impossible not to laugh, so I end up coughing.

Hayes pats my back. "Are you okay?"

"Yeah, I'm perfectly fine," I say, gasping for air.

Jane Heywood says, "You two look adorable together. How long have you two been together?"

"Well, you know..." Hayes says, giving her a sly smile.

I could stay quiet, but if I'm going to be here, it'll be fun to see the single available women try to snatch an Aldridge.

"He's single," I state, and then add, "All the Aldridge boys are single."

Without saying another word, I head toward the doctor's office.

"Why did you do that?" Hayes asks, when he catches up to me. "I had a great way out. Didn't you hear the shit about the women parading and trying to catch the single guys?"

"Tell the truth?" I ask innocently. "It's a habit of mine."

"You did that on purpose, Blaire," he says in an accusatory tone.

"Oops, I forgot about your imaginary girlfriends. Please, tell me I didn't become one of them."

"It was only one, and it was necessary, but I stopped when I met you," he reminds me. "You could've let me have a buffer. Instead, you just put us *all*, not just me, on the spot."

"Did I?" I ask innocently.

He bends down, kissing the corner of my lips. "You know what you're doing, Babe. You're the sweetest, most giving person I know. Also, the most vindictive."

"Keep your lips away from me," I order flustered, trying to control my body that's zinging after his touch. "We're not a couple, and I don't plan on covering for you."

"You can't help your evil side. I can't help wanting just a little taste," he says. "If that sends a message to the town that I'm taken, well..."

"Are you taken?" I ask curiously, because I know the lawyer didn't mention a wife, but what if there's someone else?

"Wouldn't you like to know."

And I do, because, in another reality, he never left me. In that reality, our love never died. Today, though, in this reality, he's just a stranger I want to kiss.

Why is it that I've never been able to fight this attraction between us?

EIGHTEEN

Blaire

"DO you want to go to my brother's apartment?" Carter asks, as we walk back to our dorm after chem lab. "He has food, cable, and beer."

I haven't spoken to Hayes since our stargazing dinner, exactly a week ago. Though, I've seen him around at times, and when he notices me, he waves from afar and walks away.

Do I want to see him?

My heart thumps fast just thinking about him. I've been fantasizing about kissing him all week long. Each time I see him, I hope he'd walk *toward me and kiss me in the middle of the quad. If only... He's hot, sexy, and super smart. His presence melts me into a puddle of goo.*

I'm not sure if I want to see him because it's clear that I have a big crush on him, and he... well, he said a few heart stopping lines, but I doubt he's interested in me. He hasn't attempted to speak to me all week, and he's had the chance.

"Will he let us drink his beer?" I ask, wondering, because I've never tried beer in my life, and what if I get drunk at Hayes' apartment.

"Nah, he's fucking lame," he says. "But if he's in class or with his girlfriend, maybe we can steal a couple of them."

My stomach drops with the news that he has a girlfriend. Then what was last week? He seemed ... interested in me. At least I thought so. He was friendly, and I assumed ... but it's obvious that I misunderstood his intentions.

And here I've been thinking about his lips and wondering if he's a good kisser. I wanted him to be my first kiss, but...

He has a girlfriend.

I hear a crack inside my chest, but I try not to fixate on it. He's older. I'm just ... me.

"So, he's not there?"

Carter shakes his head. "I hope not, and if that's the case, we have the place to ourselves."

"Okay, let's raid his apartment." I try to joke, but sound more like a wounded animal.

He's not single and led me to believe we were soulmates. I swear that's what he said.

"That's the spirit," Carter says sarcastically. "You sound like you're going to the dentist."

"Ha! I'm just tired, okay?"

"Look, if you're concerned about us hooking up, I can tell you that you're not my type."

"Wow, way to let a girl down," I say and wink at him. "Listen, I know your type, and you're definitely not mine. I saw you flirting with Tiffany during Chem. And then making out with Darcy in the cafeteria—then there was the girl coming out of your bedroom last night fixing her clothes."

"Hey, I'm young. Remember, Carpe Diem."

"That's so nineties," I tell him with disdain. "As long as you use condoms, I won't judge you."

We walk across campus. This place is a maze of narrow winding streets and large groups of college students walking in different directions. Hayes' apartment is almost at the edge of town. It's a modern four-story building made of glass and steel. Carter unlocks the front door, and as we climb up the stairs, my hands begin to sweat. What if Hayes is in his apartment, with his girlfriend?

With every step, I regret accepting the invitation. I could be across town at the crepe place, ordering dessert before I buy a salad at the sandwich place. Instead, my heart thumps as Carter turns the door handle to the right and pushes open the door to the apartment.

When we enter, I spot Hayes, right away, wearing nothing but a towel around his waist. Liquid adrenaline runs through my bloodstream. My skin tingles, and I know I have to look away, but my eyes stay locked on him.

His chest is cut, layered with slabs of lean muscle. My eyes dart to his hips, remembering all the books I've read describing the defined v between them. His is well-defined, if not perfect, just as his chest and face. I itch to touch him. I want to feel him.

He has a girlfriend, I remind myself.

"Fuck, did we catch you with your girl?" Carter asks, and I feel as if all the air has been sucked out of my lungs.

Hayes looks at me and then at his brother, shaking his head. "No, I'm alone."

"We should go," I suggest. "You have a date, or something."

"Stay," Hayes orders with a bark. "I was planning on picking up some food and visiting you."

I'm not sure if he's talking to Carter or me.

"But your girlfriend," I say, and I'm not sure why I'm upset.

He grabs his wallet from the counter and throws it at Carter. "Go pick up some food while I get dressed."

"Seriously?" Carter asks, glaring at him. "I'm not your butler."

"Dude, you've been freeloading from me. Yesterday, I caught you *fucking a girl on my couch. The least you can do is pick up the food if you're going to be a mooch."*

Carter sighs, turns around but before he leaves, Hayes says, "Bring strawberry ice cream too."

"You only like chocolate," Carter points out.

"Just do what I asked, Cart!"

As I'm about to follow behind Carter, Hayes orders, "Stop, Blaire!"

I turn around and glare at him. "You're bossy today."

"Rough week," he exhales. "I don't have a girlfriend."

"Okay," I say and shrug. "Still is none of my business."

"It is your business," he presses, and his tone is less bossy when he says, "Please don't tell my brother."

"I'm confused. You don't have a girlfriend, but you want him to think you do? Or you do, and you want me to think you don't?"

"I. Don't. Have. A. Girlfriend," he repeats. "It's an excuse to avoid family reunions, holidays, and any other thing my mother wants me to attend. I want you to know the truth."

"Why?" I ask, without adding a snarky comment like I don't care, because then I'd be lying, and I don't like to lie.

I care if he has a girlfriend because I like him, a lot. Also, I'm curious about his confession. "Why would you care what I know or think?"

"Fuck if I know. I just know it's important to be frank with you," he says with earnest honesty, as he combs his wet hair with one hand. "I'm going to put some clothes on. I'll be right back."

I stare at his strong legs, firm ass and muscly back, as he walks away.

"Stop ogling me, Blaire," he reprimands, with a playful voice. He's not even turning around, so how does he know? "At least buy me dinner before you eye fuck me, Babe."

I laugh loudly and set my backpack down, looking around his apartment. It's not as small as I imagined. The living area has a large leather couch and a loveseat. There's a large television decorating the wall. He has a few frames on the bookcase. There's one of him with a woman, who I assume is his mother. There's a second one with Carter. Others with his brothers. The one that I love the most is the portrait of a young kid with a guy who looks a lot like Hayes but is at least 20 years older. Is this his father?

I want to know everything about him, his family, what he wants to do once he's done with med school.

"You haven't called me," he says with a loud, commanding voice. I like it, and I'm not one to take orders. He's dressed in a simple dark t-shirt and jeans. No shoes or socks. Why do I find even his feet attractive?

"You said, 'If you need me, call me,'" I reply, setting back the frame I hold.

He smirks, and I melt a little more.

"Why don't you give me your phone number?" he asks.

"So you can call me in case you need me?"

He winks at me. "Expect at least two calls a day and maybe a few texts to remind you of me."

After a moment of silence, I ask, "Are you flirting with me?"

"You're a very strange person, Blaire Wilson."

"You're a nerd, and I don't complain," I answer, and then add, "I don't do socializing or flirting very well. I was homeschooled for the past four years."

He examines my face and smiles. "Hey, I like to label myself as a science aficionado."

"So, you don't have a girlfriend?" I confirm.

"That's right," he answers. "The position is open in case you're interested."

"Why would you lie to your family?" I ask, because I've no idea how to flirt back. I feel like I'll say something stupid, and he'll lose interest.

Would he? Is he even interested?

"It's easier to say I'm going to Tahoe with my girlfriend than I'm ditching you for my friends because I hate dealing with family drama," he explains.

"It's still a lie."

"I never said I wasn't lying. How about you? Do you have a boyfriend waiting for you in San Francisco?" He's genuinely curious about my dating life. I'm sure I told him last week that I haven't dated. Maybe I just thought about it. That's right, I was daydreaming. "Your high school sweetheart is on the other side of the country, emailing you daily and telling you how much he misses you?"

"No," I say, looking at my hands, covered in small scars from the poking I've dealt with during my hospital stays and treatments.

He takes my hands and touches them. "What was it?" He sprinkles kisses on both hands. "Cancer?"

Trying to reclaim my hands, I say, "We don't talk about it, okay?"

I'm almost out of breath because no one has ever been so gentle with my scars or paid attention to them. I've never felt so much electricity flowing through my body because of such tender touches.

"Then tell me about your last boyfriend," he insists.

I swallow. "I was too busy doing other stuff to have one..." Or friends.

Most of the friends I made in the hospital moved on or ... died. My best friend from middle school stopped talking to me after she started high school. Everyone forgot me.

"So, you don't have a boyfriend?" he confirms.

"Nope, or crushes, or ... anything really. Ever. I was too busy being sick," I respond.

"Ever?" His green penetrating gaze holds mine. "Well then, we'll take this slow."

He bends and kisses my cheek, moving his mouth close to the corner of my lips, sending an electric surge that makes my entire body vibrate.

"Would you let me be your first kiss, Blaire?"

I can't speak, but I nod slightly, trying to control the fluttering happening inside me. I'm so excited, and the anticipation is killing me. The oxygen around me disappears.

His lips brush my forehead, his arm wraps around my waist, as he bends closer to me. Tenderly, he feathers some kisses along my face until he reaches my mouth. He teases my lips with his tongue, and my mouth parts for him. I shiver at the feel of his hand on the back of my neck.

When he brings his lips to mine, he presses them lightly, his tongue teasing me, and when I part my mouth to let him in, he moves slowly. He laps me, slowly. I follow his moves, tasting him. I melt in his arms as I feel the warmth of his body. I don't want this kiss to end, but after a long, breathtaking kiss, it does.

His eyes meet mine. "You taste better than I thought. I doubt I'll ever get enough of you."

I touch my lips and stare at him because I might not be in love, but I'm surely falling fast for him.

"Can we keep this between us?" he requests.

"What?"

"Us, dating. I want it to be our secret for now."

"Why?" I frown.

"Because I need to break up with my fake girlfriend before I get serious with you. I don't want to..." he shakes his head, "set a bad example for my brothers. Even though I'm really single. My father had a lot of affairs, and I don't want them to think it's right."

"I don't want to be your dirty secret."

"Give me a couple of weeks, okay?" His voice is low, and he takes me by the waist and kisses me. "It's going to be harder for me. I don't think I'll be able to live without your mouth after today."

NINETEEN

Hayes

IT'S obvious I can't try to act aloof with Blaire and pretend that I'm not interested in her. Ever since I met her, I've been clear about my intentions toward her. There's something about Blaire that disarms me and makes me act like myself.

The guy who compared everything with science, watched the Discovery Channel instead of cartoons, and read fantasy and sci-fi books instead of playing video games. She's known that guy since day one. I've never hidden myself or the way I felt about her.

Before, it wasn't a problem because she felt the same, but now... I hurt her, and I have to be cautious.

It's obvious that I pushed her too hard with that almost kiss. I have to keep my mouth away from her.

Fuck, what is wrong with me?

I'll tell you what is wrong. When I met her, it was so easy to fall in love with her. Falling for her was like entering into an amazing world that I could finally call home. Even when I stepped out of that world by breaking up with her, my mind still travels back to it and yearns to be let in again.

Every single day, I crave the closeness Blaire and I shared. The intimacy, our long talks and also, I'm starving for her. She's right here, and I can't reach, touch, or even taste her.

So far, I've said all the wrong things. I have to take a step back and rethink my strategy. This Blaire doubts my intentions. She doesn't trust me, and I have to convince her that, this time, I won't hurt her. I learned my lesson. But what should I do next?

She's clearly pissed at me because, as we walk to the doctor's office, she's quiet.

Too quiet.

That's never a good sign because she's most likely thinking about how to retaliate. As we walk side by side, my attention keeps moving to her lips. What would she have done if I hadn't stopped?

I shouldn't have gotten so close to her, but when I arrived at the bakery, she looked upset, and I hate when people bother her. I had to fix it, but just leaning closer and whispering in her ear had me wanting to grab her. Which I did when she almost laughed at the Tattle lady. Having her in my arms ... I came undone. It was impossible not to lose my mind and try to devour her with just one kiss.

"What's the plan?" She finally speaks, right before we're in front of the building.

"We buy him out, and we figure out how to run the practice. I researched where to get equipment, and maybe we hire a couple of new doctors," I explain. "We might need to hire more people. You're good with general medicine, and down the road, we can set up a clinic—maybe a hospital. It's part of what you do, right?"

"You don't know if I'm a good doctor. After all, I'm just a physician's assistant," she says, and there's a challenging tone in her voice.

"You're full of shit," I smirk, "Google told me everything you refuse to share, Blaire."

"Really? You cyberstalked me?" She crosses her arms, but there's humor in her eyes.

"You're going to tell me that you haven't googled me?"

She shakes her head. "Nope, it didn't even occur to me," she answers honestly. "I'm still recovering from my last trip, and I didn't even finish it. Thankfully, it was my third trip in less than a year to the same town, so I was there, mostly, to deliver medicines, to make sure my kids are doing well, and to check on the orphanage that we're building. Leaving didn't affect them—or me. But still, I'm tired."

"Maybe staying put will be good for you," I conclude, brushing a loose strand of her hair around her ear. "So, what do you say? We buy this place and run the practice together as partners."

"Aren't we going a little too fast, Mr. Aldridge?" she says in a flirtatious tone. "Partnership sounds like a big commitment."

"I can commit," I argue, wondering if she still has the pendant I gave her when I promised we'd be together forever. "But then I fucked everything up because I was scared that I wouldn't be able to follow through, that I'd be a shitty ... everything, like William."

"Trying not to be William, you followed his pattern," she says.

This feels like the conversation we avoided so many years ago, the one we need to have now in order to start anew. "It's okay. I just hope you stopped that pattern, and that you're happy."

I scratch my neck, looking at her. "What pattern?"

"Avoiding emotional entanglements," she says. "Have you fallen in love lately?"

"Have you?" I answer her question with my own, and my gut tightens, scared of the answer.

"Of course, with all my kids. It's hard not to love them, even when I know I might not see them often—if ever," she answers.

"How about another man?"

"You have no right to ask. You told me you didn't want to see me, hear from me, or even think about me again." Her voice is cracking. "My best friend had just died. I barely had the strength to keep it together, and you..."

Her words slam through me like a physical blow. My heart aches for her, for my brother, for myself.

"I was a cruel bastard." I admit my callousness. "I became emotionless and didn't think about my behavior toward anyone—not even you—the one person I've loved with all my being. My brother died, Blaire. I was in London, ignoring his calls, because I had a plan, and nothing could interrupt it. Not you, not him."

"Your priorities were pretty screwed up," she concludes. "It was a long time ago, Hayes. Carter loved you no matter what, and he was happy during his last days. I hope you moved on—just like I did."

"Moved on?" I ask, almost in shock and definitely hurt.

She doesn't love me anymore. It's expected, but painful, nonetheless. Is there someone else? She evaded the question, and I'm unsure where I stand. That doesn't deter me from continuing the conversation. She might be pissed, or even hate me, but she still has feelings for me. I have to hold onto that sliver of hope. I'm determined to see this through because, even if I'm not successful, at least this time, I'll know I did all I could to win her back and keep her forever. "As in stopped loving you?"

"You can't possibly still be in love with me, Hayes."

I run a hand through my hair and ask, "How can you expect me to stop loving you when you are the only person I've loved. Every day and every night, I think of you. I still remember our first kiss. Your lips are seared on mine, and the memory of that moment is branded in my heart and my soul. Do you remember how it felt like the world stopped, and everyone disappeared, leaving just the two of us to wander the earth? With every kiss I fell more in love with you."

"Stop!"

Blaire holds her head and closes her eyes briefly. When she opens them, she stares at me and says, "Why are you telling me all this nonsense? You put an end to our story. Those old feelings are just memories, and there's no point in reviving them."

"They are very much alive. You're just denying it," I assure her. "This is the first time I'm being honest since the day we broke up, Blaire.

I'm opening my heart to you again. What I said after Carter died was despicable, but hearing that you married him—"

"Because—"

"I now know why you did it, but..." I rub the bridge of my nose. "Those days were a blur. I was hurting. I lost my little brother."

"You had four other little brothers who you neglected, too," she says, with an anger I've never seen before. "Have you been there for any of them? No. You just walk away from everything and everyone, including those four guys."

Her eyes scan my face. "You're still the same guy who likes to avoid feelings and messy entanglements," she concludes. "It's sad, because, when you open yourself up, you're a great guy."

She looks toward the door we're supposed to enter then at me and says, "I'll be happy to work for you if you choose to buy this practice. However, I'm not sure if I can be a part of a partnership."

"Why?"

"Partners trust each other, and honestly, I don't think I know you well enough to say that I can rely on you. We're different from those kids who fell in love and believed they'd be together forever," she concludes. "That's what we are. We're two strangers."

We're not, but there's no way I can convince her that she's wrong, not after everything I did before. I could argue with her and tell her that I'm still me, the same man she fell in love with, but she's right. We're not the same people we were back then, but she can't deny who we are to each other, even now.

"Yet, it still feels like I've known you all my life," I say, pushing her against the wall, connecting our gazes, allowing me to get lost in her big blue eyes.

"Hayes," she whispers, and I feel as if every ounce of air is taken from my lungs. I need to kiss her in order to stay alive. My hand curls around her neck, and I bend, the sizzle between us increasing the moment I bring my lips to hers.

Softly, I kiss her. It's a slow injection of desire and love. Blaire's hands hold onto my biceps, grasping me hard, as if trying not to lose her balance. Her lips are like silk. She tastes like vanilla, butter, and Blaire.

So much for going slow. In an instant, I lost my mind and all the self-control I gathered during our walk to the office. How can I not kiss her like that, when I fucking missed her so much. I snake one arm around her waist, pulling her tightly to me and caress the nape of her neck with my other hand. I kiss her possessively, fiercely, with all the hunger that has built up during the past twelve years.

"Why are you doing this?" she asks, out of breath.

We're panting, our gazes locked. I can feel her heat searing my skin, see her hunger getting out of control, and the lust melting her determination. Knowing that I have an effect on her and that our connection still exists makes it feel like oxygen has returned to my body.

"I needed to remind you that deep down, it's still us," I answer, looking at her sparkly eyes filled with lust. "That my heart beats just for you. That we can't ignore what's between us."

"There's nothing between us," she insists.

"I thought you only like truths, Blaire," I say, challenging her.

"You're insufferable," she protests, serving me with an angry look. "I can't deal with you right now."

"We can't just pretend there's nothing between us, especially when we're going to be living together for almost two years."

"You go and buy your practice. I'll check with the contractor," she says, refusing to acknowledge what's happening between us. "I can't be around you right now."

TWENTY

Hayes

———————

MY MEETING with Dr. Garrison doesn't last long. He shakes my hand and is out the door after accepting my verbal offer. He told me to have my lawyer send the paperwork to get things rolling. So now, on my way to the big house, I call Pierce.

"Hey, I'm buying Dr. Garrison's practice. Can you draft me a contract?"

"Who is Dr. Garrison, and don't you have a lawyer?" he asks, a little put off. "I have work to do and shit to figure out before I pack and move.

Leyla will only agree to sign the divorce papers if I give her half of what my father left me, today."

"We won't receive anything until his last wish is completed."

"Exactly," he says angrily. "Look, I have money but not that much. She knows it, and she's just trying to see how not to give me the divorce."

I'm tempted to ask what happened between them, but I don't. Instead, I ask, "Does she know that she has to come here with you?"

"Yeah, and she's actually researching the area," he says frustrated. "She's fucking packing and making arrangements to move the animals. Even though she hates small towns. I think she's bluffing."

"What's your plan?"

"You know, I tried to look at the fucking silver lining like my mother told me, when we concluded that there's no fucking way to work around the testament. I'd be divorced and living in another town. Leyla just can't let me be happy," he complains. "I'm going to try to buy her out of the marriage."

"If you need money let me know," I offer.

"Thank you. I might have to ask everyone to pitch in. I'd pay you when this circus, that is our new life, is over," he says. "I'll send you an email with a questionnaire. Fill it out and then I'll get someone to work on that contract."

"I appreciate it, and sorry about your wife," I mutter, not sure if I should tell him that if he needs anyone to talk to, I'm here. Is it too soon? He said it the other day. We're not that kind of brothers.

"So, about Blaire..."

"She's keeping the money," I warn him.

"Actually, I was going to ask if it was cool with you that I donated money to her non-profit," he responds calmly. "I did some research, and the thing is legit."

"She'll be happy to have it, more so now, when she's not allowed to travel," I tell him.

"Sorry, I wish I could do something else for her." He sounds apologetic.

"We can figure out a way to help the foundation," I suggest.

"Sounds like a plan," he says. "Let me figure out what my role will be at the firm and then we can sit and talk about Carter's Kids Foundation."

"Your role?" I ask confused. "I assume you're going to have to make some drastic changes. What are your options?"

"I could take a long sabbatical or open a branch in Baker's Creek."

"Which one do you prefer?"

"I don't know yet," he states. "I could take a sabbatical and focus on the legal operation of father's businesses. We can save a whole lot of money on legal fees. There are a few things I still need to discuss with the senior partners—my grandfather and Mom—before I make a final decision."

"I'm at the house. The contractor is already talking with Blaire. Let's plan on meeting later tonight, so we can discuss the renovations, the resort, and whatever Henry feels is imperative to complain about before the day is over."

"Don't forget the home offices," he reminds me. "I'll check with Sophia to see when the best time would be to schedule the video conference."

"Now that you mention it, what if we convert a couple of the conference rooms at The Lodge into offices?" I suggest. "Adding any rooms to the house might not be wise."

"I hate to agree with you," he says. "Can you oversee that, too? Maybe get a couple of offices, so we don't work on top of each other."

"You got it," I say and hang up the phone.

The gate is open. I walk inside, and I notice Blaire is moving her hands around while speaking to the contractor.

"Hey, sorry I'm late," I apologize, as I approach them.

"Easton Rodin," he introduces himself, shakes my hand and gives me his business card. "As I was telling Ms. Wilson."

"You can call me, Blaire," she says in a friendly tone.

"Ms. Wilson is fine," I insist, glaring at him, because his eyes are focused on her toned legs.

She huffs at me and rolls her eyes.

"I'm new in town, too. I own a big construction company in Seattle. The one I'm starting here is like a hobby. I'm planning on just building custom homes or renovations. I don't have the manpower here to remodel under your timeline. However, I have it in Seattle, and with the right price, I can bring my people."

"You can assure me that this will be done in twenty-eight days," I confirm.

"Twenty-five," he guarantees. "I'll have to work around the clock, but I know how to tackle a job this big. As I was telling Blaire, you'll have to make a lot of decisions within the next couple of days, and you can't customize any of them."

"As long as the place can be occupied and nothing will break within the first two years, we can live with that."

"It'll last years," he promises, tilting his head toward the house and heading that way.

"I have measured everything, and I got the original blueprints of the house from the town center's archive."

"Imagine a mud room in here," Blaire says, as we step into the house. "The original wood is in great condition. Do you think you can just sand it and stain it?"

"That's easy to do, and you're right. It's old but in great condition. They don't make floors like this anymore," he concludes.

"He was telling me that as soon as we pick the style for the kitchen," Blaire explains as we walk through the damaged kitchen, "he can order the cabinets, and we can choose the slab for the counter."

"Well, you get to do that." I assign her the task.

"Why?" She crosses her arms, giving me a glare. "Because I'm a woman."

"No," I answer. "Because I have shitty taste and you know it. How about appliances?"

"This is how we're going to make this work quickly. I'm going to send you my catalog later today," he explains. "You can choose the style you'd like to have in the bedrooms, bathrooms, and kitchen. The reason I'm not allowing you to customize anything is because that takes time, and you need this to be done by the end of next month."

"But do you think you can deliver?" I ask again, making sure we're on the same page.

"Yes, as long as you don't make too many changes. The pictures I'll send you will be based on material availability. You have to send me your choices tonight, and you'll have to pay me fifty percent of what I quote you no later than tomorrow morning. There'll be an extra charge to rush everything. I'm hoping to receive some of the materials early next week. Tomorrow, I can start with the plumbing and the wiring. There'll be an option on my quote that includes internet, cable, and security. You can add them or not, but I need the decision to be made by tonight. Once the house is up to code, I'll continue with the walls and, probably, by next Tuesday, I'll be able to sand the floors. I will stain them before I paint the walls."

We walk through the eight rooms. Blaire is very specific about how she wants the master bedroom.

"I think I have the exact design for it," Easton assures her. "This is good. Tell me what else you have in mind."

We head into the smallest room, and she says, "This one needs some built in bookcases, one of those beds that are like forts, and security for the windows. I want it to be fun, yet safe."

"Who's going to be in that room?"

"Arden," she answers and looks at the time. "We have to plan on setting up a playground for him, too. Let's hurry because I promised to spend some time with him before I leave."

"You have to change your flight," I remind her.

She checks the time on her phone and sighs. "I can't anymore. I'm going to have to pay for a new ticket."

"Let's fly together," I offer, as we continue walking through the rest of the house.

Once we're out of the house, I tell the contractor about Beacon's studio. I don't have much information, but his answer is just what Beac would like to hear. "That should take me about two months. I'll send you the information of the one I built a few years back, and you can tell me if you need something bigger. It's soundproof, has a voice room and other features I can't remember at the moment. My brother uses it to compose and also to produce music for bands and other artists. Would that work?"

I nod and text Beacon, just to make sure it's something he'd like.

Beacon: *Who is his brother?*

Hayes: *Does it matter?*

Beacon: *Yes, it does. Maybe he is some shitty musician, and I don't want his studio.*

I grunt and show the text to Blaire; she chuckles and texts back.

Hayes: *This is Blaire. I assume his brother is Gage Rodin. Maybe I'm wrong.*

I want to ask who the fuck is Gage Rodin. Blaire might be traveling around the world to obscure locations where they don't have internet, but her pop culture knowledge is more extensive than mine.

Beacon: *Can you ask him? If it is him then I want it. I've been in that studio, and it's fucking impressive. Though, I'd want to make a few additions.*

"Is your brother Gage?" Blaire asks.

Easton arches an eyebrow and stares at her mindfully, as if trying to solve a mathematical problem—or letting her in on a secret that only a few share.

"Listen, this studio is for one of the guys of Too Far From Grace," I say, using a stern serious voice. "I texted asking if what you described could be an option. He's been in Gage's studio, and he's excited about building something similar with a few modifications. Only if it's that studio."

He looks at me and smiles. "You look like Beacon. I wasn't sure if I was right."

"We just don't tell people. He prefers to keep his private life to himself," I explain.

"Yeah, tell him that's the one, and we can do any modifications if he wants, but that'll delay the delivery," he answers.

"Can you start building the studio this week, too?" Blaire asks.

"If you need me to, I can get a crew to focus on that starting next Monday, but it might not be ready in a month or two. Is that okay?" He asks.

"Sure, that's better than nothing," I answer. "Let's also take a look at the barn and the garage. We're bringing animals and, of course, cars onto the property."

Both buildings need some repairs but nothing major. He includes them as part of the stuff he needs to work on for the next month.

"Anything else?" he asks.

"How long will it take you to build a brand-new house?" I inquire casually.

He cocks an eyebrow and gives me a curious look. "How big do you want it?"

I shrug. "Multilevel, four or five bedrooms," I say. "Right by the lake."

"We'll have to design it first. I won't have time for that until the house is done. I'd say six to eight months after breaking ground," he answers. "Unless you want a new house instead of fixing the old one, which I wouldn't recommend. It needs work, but the foundation is solid and the structure can last you another hundred years."

"It'd be a different project," I answer, looking at the lake.

"We can talk about it in a few weeks if that's okay with you," he says. "I should be emailing you the initial quote and the contracts shortly. Please make sure to send me everything I need by tonight. Any delays or big changes would affect the deadline."

I shake his hand before he leaves.

Once he's gone, Blaire walks to where I stand and gives me a suspicious look. "Why would you build another house?"

"The will says we have to live on the property,"

She smirks. "Not in the house. I thought the same. I'm planning on bringing my camping equipment."

"You still go camping?"

"Yeah, when I'm away from home. They don't have five-star hotels, if you know what I mean."

"Why would you want to sleep out here when we have the house?"

"Six men and a toddler?" She looks at me as if it's obvious and she doesn't comprehend why I can't understand the issue. "No, thank you. I have brothers, remember?"

"How are things with your family?"

"Weird, as usual. We never recovered after my illness," she answers, and there's sadness in her voice. "My parents are still afraid the cancer will come back, and they'll have to deal with me. My brothers blame me for our parents' divorce. All of them are scared that the cancer will come back. I'm over it, don't worry."

She's acting as if it doesn't matter, as if the fact that her family practically abandoned her when they said she was cancer free didn't hurt. So much happened after she went to college.

"It won't come back, and if it does, you're not alone," I assure her, and it's not an empty promise. I'm here to stay, either as a friend or, hopefully, as more. This time I'm not letting her go.

"After all these years, I've made peace with it. So, don't fret trying to make me feel better about what happened. People come into your life and then they leave. That's an unavoidable cycle. You have to live with it and keep what you learn from them."

Okay, she's gently dismissing me and telling me she doesn't expect much from me. I accept it, for now. At least we're talking, and that's a big step. Two weeks ago, I had no idea what to do with the emptiness in my chest.

Today, I have hope.

I have her.

"What do you think about flying back to San Francisco together?" I bring the subject back to a lighter topic.

"Nice change of subject." She looks at me, somehow pleased. Maybe she was wondering how to stop the conversation. It was getting heavy. Too heavy. "That'll be good. By then, I should be rested, and I can go into the office and get some work done. We received another big donation, this one from Pierce. We have a lot to plan. Tonight, we'll gather everyone in the conference room, and we'll choose everything we need for the house."

"What do you think about building a house by the lake?" I ask, because it's not just about letting me build a house, it's more about starting to build our future.

"You love the area, the view..." she pauses, looking around, and then continues, "Just make sure the master bedroom has a veranda that looks to the lake. Maybe even make it so it goes from one side of the house to the other, so you can see the sunrise and the sunset.

"Whoever moves in with you will appreciate the little details that you add. Maybe we can set up a beauty pageant and choose your future wife."

"Funny that you mention it, because after our kiss in front of the medical offices, they know I'm taken."

"You're not!" she says defensively.

"But I am," I correct her.

"It's always been you, Blaire," I whisper. "I'm here because my father lost his fucking mind, but I'm staying for you. I want to save the town, but I want to save myself, too. Recover the love I threw away years ago. I made a mistake, but I want to fulfill those promises I made when we were younger. We'll take it one moment at a time, and, hopefully, all of them will become your favorites."

I look into her eyes, and they reflect the same ache and longing I feel for her.

"Tell me no," I warn her, before taking her and kissing her.

TWENTY-ONE

Blaire

UNABLE TO FIND MY VOICE, I nod. I could've said no, but how can I say no to his kisses when I'm starving for them.

Starving for him.

Time seems to stand still for a bit, as he looks at me intensely before his lips are on mine. There's no gentleness to this kiss; it's one consuming movement after another. As his tongue invades my mouth, his thumb caresses my jaw. I'm turning into liquid, melting into him.

Every flick of his tongue reminds me, not only that he once owned me, but of our favorite moments. Those times when we'd be hiking and just talking about our future.

My mind screams, *don't let this happen, stop.* I shouldn't let our past, my wishes, and our dreams drag me into this nonsense.

The electricity shooting across my skin and traveling up and down my body isn't allowing me to think straight.

You know how the story ends, I coach myself.

It's a battle between my lust and my mind. Pleasure and desire are fighting for what's rightfully theirs, Hayes. The next year and a half is going to be a hell of a test to my self-control.

On second thought, we could make a deal. Ex-lovers with benefits. That could be a term, right? No, that's my starved body talking. I miss his touch.

If only... Use your head!

But how can I when my heart is thumping too fast and my soul is about to give itself to Hayes again. As much as I'm enjoying his lips and consuming him as he consumes me, I order myself to stop this nonsense.

Pushing him away, I try to recover from the world-shattering kiss, and I notice his blazing eyes filled with desire. I fight fire with ice and remember the cold words he said to me before he left me.

"You called it off. You said it was over," I say angrily, panting as I fight for oxygen and push away the desire.

I'm not that girl begging for his love, for someone to care for me. I'm a woman who loves herself above everyone and will only let herself love someone who is worthy of her heart.

"You said you stopped loving me," I insist, bringing back his words, not only to remind him of what he did, but to remind myself, too. "It's been years, and you can't just assume that because we have chemistry, you can just pick up where you left off. Yes, we could try to pass the time by fucking each other and then go our separate ways, but I loved you too much back then, and I'd be stupid to believe that I wouldn't fall for you again."

He studies me, crossing his arms. Whatever I said was not just interesting but something he could use for later. I wait for his next move, his next words.

"You won't be alone. We can fall together," he says with that low commanding voice that used to get me every time.

Damn it. What is his game?

"I won't allow it."

Yes, it's a childish answer, but what else can I say when I'm not sure about his intentions? I follow that up with, "I'm too old to fall for the same trick twice. In less than two years, you're going to say, 'I don't love you anymore'—if you ever did."

"I never said I didn't love you, Blaire," he says, taking a couple of steps closer to me. He's almost towering over me. "If you're going to hold on to the past, at least grab on to the right words."

It's not like him to play around with words and feelings. What is he saying? I feel like I missed something or... It doesn't matter. I can't deal with him right now.

"So, what now? You're saying that you twisted your words?" I'm fuming, and my fists are closed. If I could, I'd punch him in the gut, but nothing happens when you punch a brick of muscles.

"We should talk," he insists.

"Just stay away from me," I warn him, walking away from his tempting body and delicious mouth. Next time, I'll say no to the kiss.

I shouldn't allow there to be a next time, but I'm weak when it comes to him. In any case, if I'm ever tempted, I'll remember the moment he broke my heart. I'll remember his blank stare and dead expression. The void he left in my heart and soul the day he left me.

BY THE END of my freshman year, I move in with Hayes. My parents sold our family home when I moved on campus. Mom lives in a studio down in San Diego. Dad moved to Kansas with his new girlfriend. Living with Hayes makes sense since I practically stay at his place every night.

Our lives are hectic. I get a part-time job at the coffee shop and volunteer at the hospital a couple of times a week. And Hayes is always busy, but at the end of the day, we share dessert, eat dinner, and go out for a walk. At the end of his senior year, he chooses to go to med school in Palo Alto, so we can be together.

However, at the last minute, the Johns Hopkins program sends him an acceptance letter, and he chooses to leave. It's okay, I tell myself, as we make plans. During the few weeks we have left, we do some traveling. We camp near Baker's Creek—his family's hometown—during the fourth of July.

Hayes asks Carter to move in with me since I need a roommate, and he doesn't want me to be alone. Everything is going as plan, I worry about the distance. However, I trust Hayes.

"It's just two years," he says every night before I fall asleep in his arms.

The day comes, and I'm feeling uneasy. I wish I could go with him. At least drop him at his new apartment. Carter is downstairs waiting in the car to drive him. I wish someone had taken my shift at the hospital so I could at least go with them.

"I can't do this anymore, Blaire." He looks at me sternly. I worry, because he's never looked at me like that, as if I was a stranger. Not even when we met.

"This?" I ask confused.

"Us. We're already at different stages of our lives. Who knows what's going to happen with me while I'm away, and you have a couple of busy years ahead of you. I think it's best if we just go our separate ways."

My entire world blows into a million pieces. His words negate everything we talked about since he received his acceptance to Johns Hopkins. All the nights when we planned our schedules. Calls, texts, trips to see each other. I have a ticket to Baltimore. We're supposed to be spending my birthday in D.C., visiting the Smithsonian museums.

"Wait, you're joking right? We made plans. I'll be applying to Johns Hopkins. Maybe if we get married, they'd have to accept me."

He laughs, and it's like he's mocking me, as if saying, you poor, incredulous child, you can't possibly believe this can work.

"Blaire, the odds that we end up in the same city are low. Too low," he explains to me, as if I'm a stupid child who can't possibly understand the grown-up world. "I refuse to spend the next ten years of my life trying to make this work when we know it's impossible."

"You said we were meant to be together ... that we're soulmates." I'm *feeling hollow. He's stripping me of everything I've known since we met. From our future.* "We belong to each other."

"Well, things change. Love doesn't last, Blaire. It's a fact of life, and I'm going to be too busy to put any effort into..."

Me. He doesn't say it, but I know he's thinking.

"You're young. You haven't lived. This is a good thing," he assures me. "You'll meet people, fall in love with someone else, and find a different path. Life is always changing."

"But you love me."

He shakes his head. "I don't love you the same way I did when we met."

His words feel like a knife through my heart. My entire world disappears in an instant. Everything I built with him is gone. Blown away by his words. The ache in my chest is all-consuming.

"Take care of yourself, Blaire," he says and walks away.

When I close the door, I fall onto the floor and lose my composure. I gasp for air as the sobs continue. I don't know how long I'm on the floor crying because I'm drowning in sadness and pain, in the fact that he left me and doesn't love me anymore.

"Hey," I hear Carter's voice, and then he's holding me up. "I'm sorry, babe. He's an asshole, just like our fucking father. You're going to be okay. We'll get through this together. Okay? I'll find you a rebound guy and then we'll find you your forever. We Aldridges aren't meant for love, sweetheart. But when I saw him with you, I thought ... there was hope for the rest of us."

TWENTY-TWO

Hayes

———————

I WALK BEHIND BLAIRE, but I don't say a word. She's right. I said those exact words to convince her it was over. There were no lies; I just twisted the words. I don't love you the same way I did before meant, I love you even more. In fact, I love you so much that it scares the fuck out of me, and I have to run away.

It was so much easier to end what we had than be brave and stay with her. Here's one of the ways young people allow fear to ruin their lives. We think that we have time, that love is everywhere, that happiness will be waiting just around the corner, that everything will come together once we become adults.

We're so gullible.

When Blaire enters The Lodge, she turns around and looks at me. Her eyes are filled with moisture, and I want to reach out to her and tell her that I lied, but maybe she already knows and is disappointed in me. She exchanges a few words with Sophia and then walks to the elevator.

I stop by the check-in desk where Sophia is now chatting with a guy who is installing a new computer as she types away on her laptop.

"Where's your boss?"

"Either training Nick and his team or having Vance kill them and dispose of their bodies," she answers seriously, her attention still focused on her monitor. However, I detect a glint of humor in her expression. "It's hard to tell. You know how volatile he can be."

I laugh because, even though she's joking, Vance and Henry are the hot-headed ones of the family. They could be plotting the demise of Nick if he's being an asshole.

"Can you please book a flight for Blaire and myself to San Francisco?" I request, because Henry mentioned she could take care of it for us.

She finally looks up at me and narrows her eyes. "What's the story between you two?"

"It's a long story, and I'm not good at giving just the CliffsNotes version—or telling it at all for that matter," I answer.

Her suspicious gaze reminds me a little of my mother when I try to hide something from her.

"Is it really long?" she asks. "She's Carter's widow, yet you seem to be in love with each other."

"Not sure about the latter," I argue.

"Either way, this is better than a telenovela. I can't wait to see who wins. I really need to set up a board like the one they create for March Madness, but instead of NCAA teams, I'll add all of your names. I'd call it the Aldridge Madness board," she jokes.

Her excitement is contagious. Her working relationship with my brother intrigues me, so I decide to poke around Henry's business, too.

"I like you, and yet, I can't understand why you work for Henry. You're everything he hates."

She winks at me. "Maybe that's why we work so well together."

"What's the story?"

Sophia shrugs. "There isn't one."

"I don't believe you," I insist.

"Well, he used to fire every assistant he had before me," she answers. "If there's a story, I'm not privy to it. Anyway, send me your personal information, so I can book your flight. Do you need a helicopter to take you to Portland?"

"Yes, please." I thank her and head to my room.

I start my laptop and the email application notifies me that I've received an email from Pierce. Attached to it is the questionnaire he mentioned. It doesn't take me long to answer and then I email it back to him. I send another email to my practice partners and open the message Easton sent with his initial quote. A few minutes later, there's a knock on my door. When I open it, it's Blaire.

"What can I do for you, gorgeous girl?" I ask, wiggling my eyes.

I doubt she's here to have sex, but a guy can always hope. She gives me an unamused glare.

"Are you in a bad mood?"

"No, just..." *annoyed at me,* she doesn't say, but I can feel it in my bones. "Sophia texted me. We received a bunch of binders from the contractor. She put them in the conference room for us to review. The messenger said it was urgent."

"Let me grab my computer, and we can head downstairs together," I announce.

Once I pack my laptop in its bag, we leave the suite. She walks in front of me, and I can't help but stare at her delicious ass.

"Stop ogling," she orders, as she calls for the elevator.

"Can you blame me?" I ask. "You're not the only one allowed to eye fuck others, you know."

She looks at me with an angry expression, but her eyes, those cool ice blue eyes, sparkle with humor.

"We're great together, Love."

"Hayes," she says, and it's a bit of a warning or more like a 'let's not do this now' kind of tone.

"I received the initial quote," I mention, changing the subject, while we wait for the elevator. "It might be cheaper to buy a new house if we weren't pressed for time."

"Are you still building the house by the lake?"

I glance toward her and nod once.

"Why would you do it when you'll be going back to San Francisco after this is over."

"We're setting up a practice," I remind her. "There're a lot of things that can happen between now and then. I could demonstrate it with the laws of physics and show you how they can be directly responsible for the future. Which is why I need that house."

She smiles. "You're such a nerd."

And you used to love it, I think, but don't say.

"Is that an observation, or are you judging me?"

"I'm just bringing up the obvious," she declares. "You're telling me that you can foresee your future based on the laws of physics. That's not only judgment worthy but unbelievable."

"It's science."

"Everything can be explained with science according to you," she says and rolls her eyes. "Educate me, which laws apply to your life."

"As much as I'd like to impart my knowledge upon you about quantum physics, the laws of attraction and ... you and I," I say, stepping into the elevator, "I regret to inform you that, today, I'll have to leave you in the dark."

"Ha," she groans and crosses her arms. "Why are you denying me such an honor?"

"You've heard it before, for every action, there's a reaction," I explain. "Every time I bring up our past, present or future, you get upset. I'm smart enough to quit while I'm ahead, babe."

In that moment, the elevator arrives on the main floor and the doors slide open. Blaire is looking at me speechless, so I wave my hand for her to step outside first, and I smirk at her.

If Sophia had the Albridge Madness board like she joked, I'd be marking my win.

Hayes 1.

When I enter the conference room, Blaire frowns at me. I'm about to say something when Mills waltzes in with Arden in his arms.

"We found Aunt Skittles," he announces in a very excited voice.

"Kittos," Arden says and releases a sweet laugh, as if he just saw a rainbow.

"I don't carry Skittles anymore," Blaire corrects him. "Maybe we can just call me Blaire."

"Like Beyoncé or Madonna, *just Blaire*," I mock her, and she glares at me. "What? I'm just wondering if that's what you're going for."

"I'm watching you, Aldridge," she warns me. "You're up to something."

"What are you up to?" Mills asks, handing Arden to Blaire, who produces a lollipop out of her backpack.

"Nothing," I respond innocently and add, "So you went from Skittles to suckers?"

"I carry individually wrapped candy that's easy to store and share," she answers, then turns to Mills, "Are you here to help us design our dream home? At last, I can put to use all the hours I've spent watching HGTV."

Blaire opens her magical backpack, producing a coloring book and crayons.

"No," Mills answers, "I'm driving with Beacon and Henry to the factory. We're hoping Arden can stay with you while I'm gone."

Her face illuminates as she says, "Of course. It shouldn't take us long to choose the amenities for the house, and, after that we're going to the bookstore where we might find some cool books for Arden. Uncle Hayes is paying."

She gives me a mischievous smile, and I wink at her. She quickly composes herself, though. *That's right, baby, I'm not backing down.*

"Books!" Arden repeats.

"I'm sure we won't be back before lunch time," he announces. "Would you mind feeding him, too? I promise to bring ice cream in exchange for your babysitting services."

She grins and says, "I'll be more than happy to do it for free."

Mills gives her a list of what he eats and his schedule, along with a small backpack where he has snacks and toys.

"Any allergies or medications?" I ask.

They both give me a glare. "What? I always ask that when I receive patients in the ER."

"He's not a patient. He's your nephew," Blaire chides.

I shrug because I don't have an answer for them.

"Anyway, what is it that they produce in the factory?" Blaire asks.

"Ice cream among other sweets," I answer. "That's why he promised to bring you ice cream."

Blaire arches an eyebrow. Clearly, I withheld important information, and she's irritated. She says, "You have a factory that produces ice cream, and you never told me."

"It belonged to my family, not me," I remind her. "And did I mention it produces chocolates, too?"

She serves me with a face scrunch but doesn't say anything.

"In exchange for taking care of Arden, I'll bring you ice cream, Skittles," Mills reminds her.

"You don't need to bring me more sugar," she says initially and then amends, "But Sophia ordered cookies... Fine bring us some vanilla ice cream we'll have a party. What do you think Arden?"

Arden nods once and focuses on the coloring book Blaire gave him.

Mills leaves right away, and Blaire and I focus on the binders that Easton Rodin sent over. It doesn't take us long to choose the amenities for every bedroom and bathroom as well as the rest of the house.

TWENTY-THREE

Hayes

AROUND NOON, we're emailing everything to the contractor. I take Arden and Blaire to one of The Lodge's restaurants for lunch. We head to the bookstore where Arden chooses several books and Blaire buys a few knick-knacks. The place is more like a gift shop. We end our afternoon walking around the hotel grounds.

"He's such a sweet baby," Blaire says on our way back to her room, placing everything we bought him today on the couch.

Arden fell asleep in my arms during the walk. "You're still great with kids. What's your secret?"

"Mom was loving and patient with us," she explains. "I learned it from her, I guess, and it was helpful for a few months."

"How so?" I ask, wondering if she's been fostering children.

"Before I got sick, the moms around my neighborhood paid me good money to babysit their kids." She smirks. "They'd fight for me and pay me a little extra."

"Why did you stop?"

She shrugs and gathers some pillows and the comforter from her bed.

"Children carry germs," she says, and the rest is implied because I know that as soon as she was diagnosed, her parents isolated her to avoid any medical complications.

"What do they think about your job?" I ask, since they always tried to keep her in a bubble.

She sighs, setting everything she brought on the floor and creating a bed or something like that for Arden.

"Dad and I barely speak, and when we do, it is just a quick call to wish each other a happy birthday or a Merry Christmas. Mom pretends I don't travel or put myself in danger," she informs me. "I can't talk to her about any of it. After all the sacrifices they made for me, I'm throwing my life away."

I set Arden on top of the bed she made.

"You're really good with children," she suddenly says.

"I rotated in pediatrics a few times. You learn a trick or two while you work with children. They aren't as terrifying as I thought."

Blaire's gaze saddens, and she turns away, looking into Arden's magical backpack. She pulls out an orca that holds a hockey stick and sets it close to him. She disappears in her bedroom, and I pull out my computer to check my email. There's one from Easton with an updated quote and a contract. I sign the contract, copy the wiring instructions, and go to my online banking browser where I send the fifty percent and email the receipt to Easton and my brothers.

There are a couple of emails from Mom, one from my boss, and three from my practice partners. I grunt. None of the people I want to deal with right now.

"Everything okay?" Blaire asks, when she comes out of the room wearing leggings and a hoodie.

"Yeah, I just transferred the money to Easton. I hope we made the right call," I say out loud. "We didn't shop around."

I click on my boss's email, and it's painful to read it. Asshole.

"I liked Easton, and Rodin Construction has a great reputation in the Seattle area. You know I'm good at reading people. Which brings me to my next question. What's with the face?" she says.

"Nothing," I say, trying to brush away everything that I'm reading. Mom sent me two new blind dates or profiles. Didn't I tell her Blaire is back into my life?

Blaire takes a seat on the couch, and I notice she's holding yarn and her crochet hook. Before I can ask her about the beanies she used to make, she says, "Tell Blaire what's bugging you."

"My boss is giving me shit because I quit."

Her head snaps, her eyes looking at me with concern. "Why would you do that?"

"Because I'm moving out of the city."

"For eighteen months," she reminds me. "You should ask for a sabbatical or a leave of absence, whatever it is that you call it at the hospital. Quitting is too ... final."

"What would you say if I told you that I'm selling my share of the practice, too?"

"I'd again ask, why?"

Avoiding her question, I tell her about Henry's *A Christmas Carol* theory, minus the Blaire part.

She huffs and shakes her head. "Why did you choose orthopedics?"

"That question is a few years too late, isn't it?"

"At least it's not plastics. I'd be pretty pissed at you," she says, and I hear the disappointment in her voice. "It pays well, you make a lot of money, but are you meeting your goals? Perhaps that's why you're second guessing your life and making rash decisions."

"I get to reconstruct bones, repair major fractures... I don't know, Blaire. It seemed like the best choice at the time. Pediatrics was..."

She gives me a sad smile. "Ours," she finishes for me.

"Yes, and also, if I chose that, my mom would've expected me to take over her practice, and I didn't want to work with her," I explain. "I love her dearly, but the whole 'joining the family business' isn't for me."

Blaire can't contain her laughter. "Yet, here you are, having to deal with the Aldridge fiasco."

"He fucked me."

"It's okay to grieve," she says out of nowhere. "You guys are trying so hard to pretend this didn't affect any of you whatsoever."

"He turned our lives upside down. Of course, we're affected by it," I say, and my voice comes out a little too forceful.

"Not what I'm referring to," she amends. "You loved him. Even when he wasn't always there for you. You had a few good memories of him. I'm sure the little boy who adored his dad is sad about losing him."

"Mourned him twenty some years ago," I say. "It's over."

"You're completely changing your life, not because of the will, but because you aren't happy," she says, setting her knitting down and moving closer to me. "I hate to say this, but Henry is right. You're having an existential crisis. What is it?"

Are we in a place where I can tell her that my life seems incomplete? Meaningless, even.

The waiting list I have because I'm one of the best, the papers I publish every year, the respect from my colleagues, even my salary feels irrelevant. She can't possibly understand my problem, when everything she does makes the world a better place.

"I think, in a way, the six of us are afraid that we'll end up like our father," I finally let one of my thoughts out.

"Alone?"

"Loveless," I answer or maybe I add to what she said.

Either way, it's all the same.

"How pathetic is this moment?" I ask rhetorically. "I'm telling you, of all people, that I'm fucking alone."

"Does it bother you that it's me?"

"No," I answer honestly. "Once upon a time, you were my best friend. Are you with someone?"

She smiles and moves away. "I know where that question is heading..."

"That's a no," I assume. "Why?"

"Relationships need time, which I don't have," she responds. "Love isn't something you just plan or force. It just happens, and so far, it has eluded me. How about you? Have you even tried?"

I open one of my mom's dating emails and give her my computer.

"She's been doing that for the last couple of years," I explain.

"Camille is pretty, graduated from Texas A&M. She's just twenty-three," Blaire complains. "That's ... too young, isn't it?"

"She's set me up with a forty-three-year-old woman, too," I inform her. "She's tried everything: older, younger, blonde, brunette. I'm lucky she hasn't tried to set me up with a guy."

Blaire laughs and hands me the computer. "I can see how this is also pushing you to a crisis. Maybe the social pressure is what made you snap, and then your father dies..."

"You and my mother don't see eye-to-eye, do you?"

She looks at me and shrugs. "Words were said, insults exchanged—not by me. What can I say? I'm not a fan."

"What happened to Carter's remains?"

"Why do you want to know?"

"I want to know where he wanted to be laid to rest," I answer.

She smiles and goes to her room. When she comes back, she's holding a box wrapped with a knitted case.

"Please don't tell me that's Carter," I beg her, because what the ever-fucking fuck?

"I did carry his ashes for a few years," she confesses, taking a square book out of the case and handing it to me. "His list of requests is in the first pages."

"When did you stop carrying them?"

"Once I ran out of them. I have a small jar with what's left, but those are for me to keep forever. I promised," she informs me. "It's item number one off his list. Bring me with you and sprinkle joy—and my remains around."

"Isn't that illegal?"

She shrugs. "I only took a little with me, so no one ever asked what I carried in that container. Sprinkling them around was so easy because no one noticed."

"I wish I had been there for him—and for you," I say regretfully.

"You need to let the past go," she suggests, shaking her hands. "Shake it off and just like that, it's gone. Turn the page and start a new life. Maybe you're on the right path to move forward. You're being slightly radical, but that might be what you need to finally find your future."

"Did you shake everything off that easily?" I ask curiously. "Turn the page and start something new without any resentment."

Her pensive gaze fixes on me. After a long silence she says, "We don't have much time to hold onto anger and bitterness, do we? I ... I'm working on it myself. You know, keep the lessons I learned from the sour moments and just hold onto what is worth cherishing."

"I have a theory," I tell her, when there's a knock on the door.

"A theory?" she asks and watches me as I rise from my seat to open the door.

"Maybe I found my future too early, and I was too young to understand what I had ... who I had," I answer and walk away, hoping she understands the meaning and that she's open to giving me another chance.

TWENTY-FOUR

Blaire

HAYES TALKING about his future and how empty his life is plays in my head for the rest of the day—and the night. I can barely sleep. It's around five in the morning when my phone buzzes.

Sophia: *Text me when you wake up.*

Blaire: *I'm awake. What's happening?*

Sophia: *I got your clothes. Want to go for a run?*

I stare at the screen, impressed by her efficiency. Yesterday, when Beacon, Mills, and Henry came back from the factory, they called everyone into a meeting. As thrilling as the invitation was, I reminded them about Arden, and I volunteered to stay behind to take care of him. We spent the rest of the day together, and he fell asleep around eight.

Mills came to pick up his son around ten to take him back to his room. Hayes, Henry and Sophia were with him. They wanted to let me know that we'd be staying in Baker's Creek until Monday or Tuesday. I complained that I didn't have many clothes to wear, but it was an excuse so I could go home. Sophia pulled out her computer and began to order clothes for both of us, because she had the same issue. Complaining that I didn't have money to pay was irrelevant since she said that Merkel Resorts was paying, whatever that means.

I won't lie, I'm tempted to ask for an application to work for Henry. He pays for everything. Though, I think Sophia would fight me for the position with her life. Her boss might be demanding, but she has so many perks that it might be worth it to deal with Henry every day.

Blaire: *Who sent you clothing this early?*

Sophia: *I have my secrets. Do you want to go for a run?*

Blaire: *I'm afraid to say that I don't have tennis shoes because you might pull a pair from a hat.*

Sophia: *No, it's part of the wardrobe I purchased for you. I left the bags outside your room.*

I get out of bed, open the door to my room and find several shopping bags and shoe boxes. Vance steps out of his room, already dressed.

"Morning, Skittles," he greets me, pointing at the bags and giving me a questioning look. "Did you go shopping on Rodeo Drive, and I didn't notice?"

"Good morning," I greet him. "Are you going somewhere?"

"Yes, I got a call," he informs me. "They need me."

"Who is they?"

He smirks. "It's classified."

I roll my eyes and ask, "When are you coming back?"

He shrugs. "In a few weeks?"

"Vance, we need to take care of your stitches," I tell him.

"I'll find you next Friday," he replies. "Text me when you get back to San Francisco, and I'll meet you there."

"You're coming back, right?"

He stares at me and sighs. "Yeah, about that..."

"Vance, you can't just let these people down."

"I'm not saying no, but you need to understand that I have a commitment," he explains. "If I walk away, it's forever. I can't go back after I quit, Blaire. What if I give up everything, and these assholes leave me hanging—again?"

"They won't," I assure him.

"You can't possibly believe that they'll stick around," he argues. "Hayes did it to you. You believed in him, and one day, he was gone. Henry doesn't stick to anything. Pierce might come because he's trying to get rid of his wife, but what's going to happen once she finally divorces him? Mills was on the phone with his agent last night, and I'm not sure if he's coming back. And Beacon is a wild card."

His words make sense, and yet, I have hopes that each one of them is going to come through.

"Can you have a little faith in them?"

"Are you for real?" he asks, sounding disappointed. "It's not like you met them yesterday. You know how things are between us. They're never going to change. If Carter was here..."

"If he was here, I wouldn't be here," I answer. "So many things would be different. You can't change the past, nor hope for a different present. You can only change the future. Please help us do that."

Vance sighs and shakes his head. "What's happening between you and Hayes? He's going to hurt you again," he warns me.

I look at him and sigh. "You just sounded like your mom before you go on a mission. You might get killed. He can hurt me, but what if I take a leap and find my happiness? Those questions are valid. For now, I'm giving us a chance to see beyond the pain he inflicted and focus on the love we once shared. I still have feelings for him, and I can't shut that down too soon because I'm afraid he'll break my heart again. You have to have faith in others and in yourself."

He smirks, "Are you trying to use some kind of reverse psychology on me?"

I shrug. "Go on your mission. Come back to get those stitches off, and hopefully, by then, I'll show you that people can change."

He gives me a hug and leaves the room. I shouldn't be surprised by his reaction, but, out of all of them, I thought he'd be the one jumping into staying right away.

I grab the box with the running shoes as well as a pair of yoga pants and a sports bra from the bags. I change and head outside where Sophia is already waiting for me.

"Do you ever look like us commoners?" I ask.

She's wearing athletic clothes, but she looks stylish.

"If I didn't like you, I'd hate you," I say, as we head toward the stairs.

"I saw Vance leave the suite," she says, ignoring my question and my remark. "He mentioned that he's going back to work. Does that mean he's out of the race?"

"Again, this isn't a reality show," I explain, as we step out of the elevator. "We all have to stay. If anyone leaves, the town is fucked."

"Wouldn't it be more fun if the one who stays last is the one who gets to keep it all?"

"I think all of them would've left on Wednesday," I respond. "What's the deal with the factory?"

She shrugs, and we make our way toward the town. "I stayed behind to supervise Nick and the other employees. From what I overheard, they're in trouble, but I don't have all the information, yet. Thankfully, Hayes and Henry had a lot more to talk about last night, so he gave me the night off, or I'd be going through all the documents he brought from the factory."

We continue jogging through the town, go by the house, and then Sophia stops by the coffee place while I go to My Cookie Jar to buy pastries.

"Where are the coffees?" I ask, as we meet outside the shop.

"They're bringing them in twenty minutes," she answers. "I even got their phone number so I can have them deliver to the hotel every morning until we leave for New York."

"You should strike a deal like that with the bakery," I suggest.

When we make it back to the hotel, Henry is already in the lobby, pacing back and forth, while talking out loud.

"Yes, Mr. Parrish. I understand that according to the stipulations you can't do anything until we are all moved into the house, but this is an emergency," he says out loud. "Then, you should be the one solving the major issues that my father's companies have, at least until we take over."

He stops, pinches the bridge over his nose and exhales loudly. I look past him and spot Hayes next to Nick. He's wearing a pair of black slacks and a button-down shirt. He smiles at me when he notices my presence.

"Morning," he greets me as he walks to where I stand.

Henry's voice booms through the lobby when he says, "You don't understand the payroll process. It's pretty simple, the workers do their job, and you pay them as stipulated in their contract."

I open my eyes wide, and Hayes shakes his head.

"How bad is it?" I ask.

"Bad," he answers. "We could lose it."

How big of a mess did William leave? He left money, didn't he? The lawyer mentioned several accounts all with billions of dollars in each one.

Henry hangs up and shakes his head. "We're on our own until the seven of us are officially moved into the house."

"So, we don't have to take care of the factory until then?" Hayes asks.

"Mr. Parish just informed me that they're the executors of the will. In no way they are responsible for any of the assets, companies, or legal disputes that my father might've left. Those are transferred to his next of kin—us."

"Are we going to wait until everyone moves in?" I ask, followed by, "Is that even an option?"

"If we don't do something, no one is going to save the factory, fix this hotel, or manage Aldridge Enterprises," he answers.

Hayes sighs loudly. "What's the plan?"

"We're going to have to use our own money to save the factory—if it can be saved," Henry answers. "Call everyone. We have a lot of decisions to make."

This would be a great time to let me use my trust fund. I should ask Pierce to look into it. Maybe with the approval of the Aldridge brothers, I can access it and help them save the factory.

Henry looks at Sophia and says, "We need to go into the conference room. I need a human approach because, if it's me, I'd sell that place and wash my hands of it."

"Let me gather my things and I'll meet you there," Sophia says, pulling her phone out of her sports bra and typing furiously, before marching toward the elevator. Seconds later, I receive a text.

Sophia: *Emergency meeting. Meet us at the conference room if you're still here at ten. If not, I'll email you a link to connect via videoconference.*

"Tell them it's not optional," Henry yells.

Sophia: *This is a mandatory meeting.*

Henry puts away his phone and glances at us. "I'll meet you both at ten. Don't be late."

"Or else," Hayes says mockingly.

Henry flips him the finger but doesn't say anything.

Hayes finally moves his attention toward me and asks, "Do you want to get some breakfast?"

I nod because Sophia took away our pastries, and the coffee hasn't arrived.

On our way to the diner, I ask, "Can you tell me more about what's happening in the factory? If it's okay to tell me," I add quickly.

"It's fine. The factory isn't in great shape," he answers promptly. "None of us has experience with it. In all honesty, it'd be best if we sell it to some chain that can just absorb it. The security of the employees wouldn't be compromised, since we'd be selling it to someone who needs a factory to produce stuff. However, the will doesn't allow us to do anything but run it. As Henry just pointed out, we can't count on any funds until we're settled into this town."

"It's like The Lodge," I conclude. "That place needs more than some TLC. How about Aldridge Enterprises?"

"Pierce hired an auditor to go through the company to make sure there are no discrepancies. If William messed up with any of the accounts, we could lose everything—including our own money."

"If we walk away?"

"We're screwing even more people than we thought in the beginning, which is another big problem since Mills said, 'I don't need the aggravation, I'm out.'"

"No," I gasp.

He runs both hands through his hair and says, "We'll deal with him later. For now, we focus on what needs our immediate attention."

"Can I help you with anything?"

"Henry is going to brainstorm a few ideas with Sophia," he explains, then adds, "If we have to invest, we might not be able to afford the practice. I can't pull money out of my trust fund until June."

"Your birthday?" I ask.

He nods in confirmation.

I reach over and grab his hand, squeezing it. "Have faith, okay. Everything will work out the way it's supposed to."

He entwines our hands, and his shoulders relax. It's a simple gesture, but it makes my blood run hot and infuses it with a wild, reckless surge. It's not the hand holding; it's the realization that I soothe him.

"Have dinner with me tonight," he says.

"What?" I'm surprised by his question. "We're just about to have breakfast."

"This is just a meal. I want to have dinner with you. A date."

I glance at him, my eyes widening. "A date?" My voice comes out low and raspy.

"Dinner, tonight. Just the two of us." He stares at his shoes and blows out a breath. "I'm trying to slow down. Just give me a chance, Stardust."

He brings my hand to his lips and kisses it. "One date."

My body shivers from the contact of his mouth against my skin. It's a simple request, a simple gesture. The words *I'm trying to slow down* mean a lot to me. He understands that it's not that simple for me to catch up with him. Hayes swears he still loves me. I'm not sure if I want to open the door that he closed so many years ago, but I'm willing to give it a try.

I clear my throat. "Okay. I'd love to go out with you on a date," I say, before we enter the diner.

Unfortunately, our breakfast isn't uneventful. The hostess sits us in the middle of the diner. The waitress takes our order, and a few minutes later, the diner is buzzing with customers. We're surrounded by patrons who are staring at us. We don't speak much. I'm afraid that anything we say would be recorded. Anna Tattle arrives when we're halfway done with our food. A woman stands next to her. She waves at us and marches with determination to where we sit.

"Doctor, what a surprise," she says, then glances at me, giving me a fake smile. "I want you to meet my daughter, Nina."

Nina holds out a hand. "Nina Tattle, it's a pleasure to meet you, Hayes. I heard you're buying the medical practice. I currently work at the factory in Happy Springs, but if you need me, I can be your receptionist."

"It's a pleasure to meet you," he answers properly.

Seeing them holding hands makes my skin crawl, and I'm not the jealous kind. While we dated, I could care less when women flirted with him. He never responded to them. For some reason, I'm upset about Nina and her friendly handshake. I shouldn't care about this. He's not mine, but my blood is boiling.

"We could meet for lunch later today, if you'd like," she offers. "I can show you the town and tell you more about myself."

"Nina, meet Blaire," he says, claiming his hand back. "She's going to be my partner, and she'll be in charge of the hiring process."

"Well, I can still show you the town," she presses, eager to show him everything she can. I'm sure that includes her, naked.

"Maybe another time," he insists. "This weekend we're all pretty busy."

"Of course," she says blushing slightly and pulling out her cellphone. "If you want, I can program your phone number, so I can check with you."

He gives her a phone number—which isn't his own and waves at her.

I lean over and whisper in his ear, "She really wants to show you *the town*. Are you going to let her?"

"I'd rather discover it with you," he answers, kissing my temple. "Are you done?"

"Eating or teasing you?"

"Both, babe. I want to go back to The Lodge."

"Yes, please get me out of here. I feel like I'm part of a reality show, and everyone is waiting for me to do something embarrassing," I pause then whisper, "which we both know I might do."

It's almost eight when we step outside the diner. My phone rings, and it's Tori.

"Hi," I greet her, as I answer the phone.

"At what time are you arriving?" she asks. "I can pick you up at the airport."

"Sorry, I forgot to text you last night. I won't be going home until next week," I inform her.

"Hmm," she says.

"What's happening?"

"Do you know the Aldridge family?"

"Why?"

"We received six donations between Wednesday and today from six different members," she explains. "I only know of Hayes Aldridge. He's a doctor."

"You know him?" I ask a little concerned. "How well?"

"My mother set me up on a date with him. But I never met him. He stood me up. Maybe he's gay or he wasn't interested in me," she complains, and I laugh.

Hayes looks at me and frowns. I give him an innocent smile.

"He's not gay," I clarify, then agree, "You are a catch. He's just a very strange man."

"So you do know him," she confirms. "Who are the other five Aldridges who sent you money?"

I sigh. "It's all too complicated to explain over the phone. I gather that we have money in the account."

"Yes, that's why I called you. We have plenty, and we can start planning. I just need to know when you'll be back to start working."

"Things aren't going as I thought," I simplify the current event to just a few words. "Why don't you send me the applications we've received and our updated wish list. I'll start working on it, and when I have time, we can connect through FaceTime."

"Do you think you can ask Hayes to call me? I think we could make beautiful babies," she suggests.

"Sorry, Tori, I don't think I can persuade him to go out with you," I say, ending the call.

"Who was that?" he asks, as we step into The Lodge and march toward the elevator.

"Victoria, my assistant—and one of your blind dates," I tease him. "You've been busy."

His face turns red, and he scrunches his nose. "I never slept with the women Mom set me up with."

"Hey, I'm just kidding," I clarify. "You actually stood her up, but is this a sore subject?"

The doors of the elevator open, we step outside, and he lightly grabs my elbow, stopping me. Once I turn, he holds me gently by the shoulders. Our gazes connect, and his eyes have this light to them, a mix of concern and hope.

"If you want to know what I've been up to for the past twelve years, please ask *me*. I won't hide anything, and I won't lie to you," he states. "There's really not much to tell. I haven't had any serious relationships since you. I'm ready to fight for you, for your heart. Don't count me out just because of the string of dates I've had in the past couple of years—I already told you about them."

He kisses my nose, turns away and enters his room without another word. I'm left standing in the hallway confused about his behavior. It's so different from the old Hayes. Usually, he'd try to kiss me, to convince me that things with Tori and all those women don't matter. He'd have said something about Nina and her eagerness to catch the first Aldridge.

Is he changing his approach, or is there something that I'm missing?

I feel as if an imaginary ball has been given to me, and it's up to me what I want to do with it: pass it or stop the game.

I yawn, maybe I should take a nap before the next meeting. But as I try to lay on the bed, I only think of Hayes. It'd be too easy to stop the game, but that's not me. You can't miss the love of a lifetime. Yes, he hurt me, but he hurt himself even more. The kid I dated wasn't ready for a long-lasting relationship, and neither was I. Maybe it's time to take a leap of faith and believe in us again.

TWENTY-FIVE

Blaire

AT TEN, Sophia, Henry, Hayes, and I are in the conference room. The rest are somewhere in the world connected through videoconference. Henry starts immediately by saying, "William neglected the factory for years."

"Does that mean we're closing it?" Vance asks.

"No, we think we found a way to make it work and bring it back to its former glory," Henry announces.

"What part of 'I'm out' didn't you guys understand?" Mills

complains. "I can't jeopardize my kid's future. The factory is heading toward bankruptcy."

"It can be saved." Sophia is the one who jumps in. "It's all about rebranding, marketing the product correctly, and dedicating some of our time to the company. Chocolate sells itself, but with a campaign and a few additions, we can make the factory a profitable business. We're selling sweets."

She gives us a conspiratorial look. "I'm going to let you in on a little secret, most people love sugar. We just have to make it special, and everyone will be buying from us in no time."

"We all have to invest today," Henry continues. "I already transferred enough money to cover this week's payroll, but that's not enough."

"If I could give you money from the trust, I would," I add.

"Pierce, can you please tell Blaire what you found out," Henry directs our attention to him.

"I'm the executor of Carter's trust. In other words, I'm supposed to make sure that the trust is used the way he requested. I can adjust the amount you receive or withdraw, depending on each case. This emergency merits the necessity of taking a large amount out of the account. That said, we're about to ask each one of you to invest five hundred million dollars into the factory."

"I'd only agree if you give me the same amount to use at my discretion. That means, no questions asked nor restrictions added," I say with determination.

"Deal. And that's our first yes," Pierce says, without even asking me what I plan on doing with the money.

"Just so you know, we're not only investing money but time," Sophia intercedes. "Before you tell me that your career has nothing to do with the factory, I'll assign each of you something that you can do, so no worries."

"Send me the information on where to wire you the money," Hayes agrees.

"That's two, and I am obviously in the middle of the storm, so we have 1.5 billion so far," Henry states. "Beacon, Mills, and Vance. We don't have many options and if what you said about not having touched the ten billion dollars trust Dad left us is true, then you have the capital to invest. I guarantee that we will recover the money, or I'll pay you back from my own pocket."

Mills grunts but says, "I'm in then. It'll be sweet to see you fail and not lose a cent."

"This fucking issue is taking over my life," Beacon complains. "It's not the money. I can give you that without sweating. The question is how far is this going to go?"

"The auditors are going through Aldridge Enterprises already, and, so far, they haven't found any discrepancies," Pierce explains. "From what Dad's assistant told me earlier today, that's the only thing he paid attention to in the past couple of years."

"What's going to happen to The Lodge?" Hayes asks. "Are you absorbing it Henry?"

"I can't," he answers at the same time Pierce grunts, "Fucking William thought about that too, and he *forbid* it."

"That's yet another place where we might have to inject some money in," Henry adds. "But not as much as we have to invest in the factory, and there's no clause where it says that I can't use resources from Merkel Hotels & Spas."

"Woohoo, one point for us," I quip. "Are we opening The Lodge's restaurants?"

He closed them earlier today, claiming that they're not up to code. The food I've eaten there so far has been fine, but he's the expert.

Henry shakes his head. "No, I have to update the kitchens, the furniture and probably remodel all three places before we bring chefs into the place. I already contacted the contractor, who can't take on any new projects until the house is done."

"Easton Rodin is going to be rich by the time we're done," Hayes complains.

"Is there anything else we need to address?" Pierce asks, definitely not amused by us.

"Beacon, I haven't received your cut for the house," Hayes says.

"You're charging me more than the others, man," he protests.

"They're building you a studio and that bastard isn't cheap," Hayes answers. "You added a bunch of shit to it, too. Why do you need two extra rooms?"

He grins and says, "Fine. If that's why then I'm willing to pay. Maybe Pierce should pay for the repairs of the barn, too."

"I want to keep that as the family barn—just like the house. In case anyone decides to bring another animal," Hayes explains. "If Pierce or anyone else wants a barn of their own you have to contact Easton and handle the transaction on your own. Are you all settling your affairs?"

"Look, I'm still thinking about it," Mills answers. "My agent and I are trying to find a solution to this predicament. Pierce and his team could've missed something."

"It's not optional, fucker," Pierce tells him. "You don't have a choice —and they can't find what's not in there. Pack your fucking shit and move. With that, I'm out of here. I have real work to do."

After they all disconnect from the videoconference, Henry says, "They're going to leave us hanging."

"I'll make sure they show, *and* that they stay for the length of the stipulation," Hayes promises, before closing his laptop.

This time, I stay quiet, because asking if he's insane or delusional is out of the question. Science would agree that it's just him and Henry. Pierce might be on board, but the rest...

We're so screwed.

TWENTY-SIX

Blaire

"WHY DID I SAY YES?" I grunt, covering my face and sounding desperate.

"This isn't me." I look down at the dress I found among my new clothes.

I've never worn a little black dress. I'm a jeans, top, and hat wearing kind of gal. Sophia even bought me a pair of high heels, which I won't wear. Those things are like cars to me. They're beautiful, but I avoid them as much as possible.

"Do you want me to help you with your makeup?" Sophia asks as she steps into my room.

"Remind me why you moved into this suite?"

"You invited me," she answers.

"That was before I stopped liking you. I should be wearing something more comfortable. No, I should've said no to this date. It was that kiss."

"The one from yesterday in front of the medical practice?" she asks.

"How do you know about it?"

"Instagram," she answers, showing me her phone with a picture of Hayes's body almost swallowing my own as we kiss.

"You can't deny that it's a good picture," she continues. "This town's social media is pretty impressive. I'm tempted to hire whoever is in charge. You know, use their powers for good and not for gossip."

I study her and realize she is serious. "You think about work a lot more than you like to accept."

"Only when I'm starting a new project," she acknowledges. "Sorry for talking your ear off earlier. Hayes mentioned a couple of times that you have a sweet tooth. I needed to pitch you some ideas about the products that I'm planning on adding to the factory. Henry doesn't see beyond the hotel business."

"It was fun. I'd agree to do anything in the name of ice cream and confectioneries. We can call the boutiques Sweet Sexy Dreams."

"Whoa, I never said we'd be opening them. It's just an idea," she corrects me but then cocks her eyebrow and says, "That's a good name. I'll add it to my list. Just in case we end up setting something up. For now, I'm just rebranding the products. Later, we'll see if we can create an exclusive line. I'd have to hire someone to create the product before they mass produce it in the factory."

"We can do it," I assure her. "Medicine is my passion, but I am also great at creating desserts. When I was a teenager, I lived in the kitchen, and I'm pretty good at making truffles."

"Why are you looking through your clothes?" she asks.

"I need something different. This is too much for dinner at the diner," I explain.

"You're not going to the diner, and the dress is perfect. I have a gorgeous pair of red heels that I could lend you."

Where is he taking me? I ask curiously, and excitement takes over me. One thing about Hayes is that he makes everything special and perfect.

For my eighteenth birthday, he drove me to San Francisco. He made reservations at a swanky restaurant, and we dined in a private room. We finished the night at his apartment. That night is definitely in the top ten best moments of my entire life.

"Can you tell me where we're going?"

Sophia shakes her head. "Nope, I promised not to tell you. Also, I didn't help as much as I wanted to. He wanted to do everything himself, because it's for you."

She climbs up on my bed and suggests, "Leave a sock outside the door if you give up the goods on the first date. There's plenty of rooms where I can stay."

"Ha! We're not in college, and that's definitely not happening tonight." I check my reflection in the mirror, feeling self-conscious.

"You look delicious. If I liked women, I'd be asking you on a date myself. Bring that confidence back," she orders. "Hayes will be drooling the moment you open the door. Now, let me do your makeup and then you'll be ready."

"Thank you," I say, as I sit down on the bed.

"Don't thank me. I love this."

"Applying makeup?"

"No, watching people fall in love. Romance always gives me hope."

"Where's your Prince Charming?"

She gives me a sad smile. "Maybe that's why I love it. Those who can't do, teach. Or in my case, watch."

Before I can ask about her love life, there's a knock on the door.

"I'll open the door. Put some shoes on, and you're ready," she says excitedly.

My stomach is tied up in knots, but when I hear Henry's voice, I frown.

"Let's go," he commands.

"It's Friday night. I'm off the clock."

"We both have to have dinner, might as well do it together."

"I'm sure I can go to the diner by myself," Sophia answers.

"Why are you always this difficult? Get ready. I'm taking you to Happy Springs."

"Goody, I'm going to Happy Spring's diner," she claps.

"Don't get too excited. We're going to be talking about work."

"This is why you're single," she mumbles, walking toward her room.

A second later, there's another knock on the door. Henry opens it, and I spot Hayes. He's wearing a pair of jeans and a black button-down shirt. He winks at me and says, "You look gorgeous."

"I knew the color of the shirt would complement my ass," Henry answers.

"Your ass would look better in jeans" Sophia says. "I'm ready. Let's go and dine in the best place that Happy Springs has to offer."

Before she leaves, she marches to where I stand and says, "Relax and enjoy. The hardest part of a first date is getting to know each other, and you mastered that years ago. You two are past awkward conversations. If all goes wrong, I promise to have some cookies, ice cream, and a few romantic comedies ready to binge watch."

"Thank you," I say.

"Anytime. And good luck!"

"You need luck?" Hayes finally walks to me and takes my hands, kissing the back of both and then looking at me. "I'm going to kiss you, Blaire."

His words are a husky whisper. His hand holds the back of my head, and my pulse thuds in anticipation as our gazes connect with a sizzle, right before his mouth presses against mine. His silky lips move slowly and softly against mine. The kiss begins with reverence, and I feel my cells ignite because I know what happens when he starts like this. I open for him, anticipating the fire that's about to start. His tongue darts inside, and he groans pulling me tighter to him. One hand caresses my neck, as the other holds me by the waist.

My heart shutters as we devour each other. His hands move up and down my body, mine hold onto his neck. We become a soft melody of moans and grunts. My body is high from his touch, burning with the heat of his own body.

"God, I can never just give you a simple kiss," he growls, nipping my earlobe. "I wish we could skip dinner and just concentrate on my dessert."

"Let's not skip that many steps," I request. "We're not there yet."

He rests his forehead on top of mine. "Come on, Love. Let's get out of here before I lose my mind and yank that dress off your beautiful body."

A part of me thinks, *yeah, why not,* but I talk myself out of that and we leave the room. When we arrive at the lobby, I expect us to leave the hotel, but he walks to the opposite side of the building. We arrive at the west side of The Lodge, where the three restaurants connect. He pushes open the big wooden door of the old steakhouse, and I gasp when I see it illuminated with thousands of fairy lights.

There's only one table in the middle of the dining room with a lit candle in the center and a small arrangement of red roses. There's also a waiter on the side, waiting for us.

"How do you do it?"

"What?"

"Always make it special?"

He kisses me on the corner of my mouth. "You're what makes everything special."

TWENTY-SEVEN

Hayes

"DESSERT FIRST," she says, smiling at the crème brûlée.

"Life is too short. Why not start with the fun?"

"Yes," she agrees. "But I don't do it as often."

"What?"

"Eat dessert," she explains. "I only do it when I get back from a trip to celebrate the success of my mission."

"Why did you stop doing it?"

"So many reasons," she begins. "For starters, I visit villages where they serve you what they're eating. I guess I got rid of the bad habit by visiting and learning from other cultures."

"It's not a bad habit."

She leans back and smiles. "Probably not something you'd want to teach your children. Though, I understand why my parents let me do it. They weren't sure I'd make it, so why not make a few concessions as long as I didn't stop following the doctor's instructions."

"Well, for what it's worth, I loved our traditions. That's one of my favorites. No matter what, we always had dinner together and dessert was first—or sex."

Her face flushes slightly. She breaks through the sugar shell and takes a spoon full of the custard along with a raspberry.

"As I said, you always know how to make things special—even traditions." She speaks after giving me a taste of dessert. "I stopped eating them for several reasons. Another one is that it had become a thing we did, and I missed you too much."

I was a fucking idiot. How could I have left her when we had everything?

We should start with a light conversation, but I can't help myself and ask, "Why did you change your phone number?"

She licks her lips and clears her throat. "It was a year or two after I started traveling. It happened during my trip to Tanzania. I accidentally dropped it, and it smashed into a billion pieces. When I flew back home, I called Dad and told him to cancel the line and that I'd be responsible for my own phone."

"Pretty grown up of you," I state. "You could've just switched your number to the new account."

"Did you try to call me?"

I nod. "I drunk dialed a couple of times."

Maybe more than a couple and a handful of those I was sober. "I just needed to hear your voice. Getting through med school without you was difficult—it was so fucking painful. I hurt you, but I did some major damage to myself, too."

"What scared you the most? The baby or the long-distance relationship?"

Luckily, the waiter brings the corn chowder, one of her favorite soups. It gives me plenty of time to give her an answer.

"The idea of being a dad at twenty-two freaked me out," I confess. "It wasn't the reason, but it certainly made me think about the future. I thought I was a lot more like my mom than my dad. Doubts about what would happen once I left started nagging me every minute of the day. Thinking you'd find someone new and fun. A guy who would like to see the world with you."

"Instead of waiting for me to abandon you, like your father did. You ran away," she concludes.

I nod, so much for giving this the feel of a first date. Changing the conversation would be best, but also stupid. We have to discuss the past in order to move forward, so we might as well do it now.

"It seemed like the most logical thing to do at the time," I explain. "The best way to protect us both."

"You really hurt me. I didn't just care about you. You were my everything."

It's hard to hear those words expressed in such calm tone. I expect her to yell like she did a couple of days ago. Instead, we're having a rational conversation. My worry dissipates and I begin to relax because this moment feels like us. We listen, rationalize, and try to compromise.

"After all this time, it makes sense that you took off without looking back. You loved your father, and he was barely present. One day, he just left, abandoning your entire family. It's life altering to see your mom suffering the loss of the man she thought was her soulmate."

I stare at her, because she makes sense, but her words sound too well-thought out. "Have you been psychoanalyzing my family?"

"I've been thinking about it all day, after my early chat with Vance," she explains, reaching for my hand and giving it a squeeze. "Your dad was charming, like Carter. They were like flames that everyone followed. I assume that your father was as easy to love as your brother. None of you can deny that you loved him. All of you were neglected and abandoned by William—a man you adored. It hurt you, and since then, you can't trust anyone, not even each other. You live with the constant fear of getting hurt. Because of that perpetual feeling, you sabotage your relationships."

"You spoke with Vance?"

"That's all you got from what I just said?" Her annoyed voice carries throughout the empty room.

"Everything you said is true. I'm just astonished that you spoke to Vance. He doesn't speak. It's mind blowing to hear that you have a better relationship with him than any of us has ever had," I remind her. "It also makes me realize that I have to try harder. My relationships with all my brothers are terrible."

She gives me a shrug that means, *what can I say, people trust me.*

"Is he going to stay?" I dare to ask.

"He's not sure," she answers. "Unlike you guys, he can't just ask for some time off and then go back to what he does. If he quits, he's done. How can he make such a commitment when you guys have never shown any support for him?"

"He doesn't know that we won't come through this time," I protest.

"Well, he's basing his decision on past experience. What if he gives up his life and you guys walk away? If I stay and one of you quit before the eighteen months, it won't affect me. I'll go back to my life, and I have plenty of money. The same goes for all of you. He's worried about his future, not the inheritance."

"We're going to stay," I assure her.

She shakes her head. "You want to make this happen, but you can't force them to trust each other."

I scratch my chin. "Do you trust me?"

"Why are you asking that?"

"I need to know where I stand with you, Blaire. I have five other people who I need to show they can count on me. If they at least know I'm going to stay, they might give it a try, too."

"You quit your practice, your job, and you're investing your fortune on this town," she answers. "I trust that you'll stay. Do I trust you with my heart?"

She stares at me for several beats then says, "I'm working on it. It's not easy to erase the past. What we shared was unique and I miss it, but I can't go back to that. I'm a different person. As much as I keep saying that I moved on, it's clear that I still have feelings for you. We have to give this some time and be patient with each other. You lost your father, and you're making a lot of radical changes. I can't expect you to change nor would I want you to change for me."

Am I being radical? I'm definitely not the man I was when we met.

"We could talk about my changes for hours, but what's the point? Twelve years is a long time. I'm focused on showing you who I am and what I'm willing to do for love. For you. If my brothers don't stay, if they decide that this isn't worth it, I'll stay and try to help the people of this town the best I can."

"What about your future?"

"We founded this town," I explain. "Well, my ancestors did. We can't just abandon it. My future can happen in this town."

The waiter takes away our soup bowls and brings the steak and lobster tails.

"This date went from casual to life-altering before the entrée," Blaire says, attempting to lighten the mood.

I place my hands on the table and look at her. Her eyes glow with the reflection of the fairy lights. "The way I see it, I have a small window to convince you to give me a chance. Every day that passes that tiny opening closes more and more. Each time I try something, I feel like I fuck it up royally."

"Then it seems fair that I tell you a few things," she says, taking a sip of wine. "Once I can leave town, I'm planning on going back to work. It's my mission in life, and I'm passionate about what I do. You want to settle down here, and that's admirable. However, I'm leaving. I can't just quit my kids and my job forever."

She sighs. "I'm sorry, I'm trying to believe that this isn't some crisis you're going through and that you'll abandon your ideas once they fail or you succeed. That you'll stick around this time, no matter what happens during these eighteen months. I'm open to the possibilities and to see past what happened between us because what we had was unique and I loved you with an intensity that I doubt can be replicated."

"Look, I'm aware that in every scenario that you run, I come up like an asshole who shouldn't be trusted," I agree with her. "Why would you quit your job? That's something I'd never ask you to do. In fact, I hope that once this is over, I can travel with you. I'm sure you can use my skills."

"What about the practice you're planning to set up?"

"We're going to hire doctors, nurses, and enough staff to serve the town. It'll be equipped, so we can travel. I don't know how the future looks. All I know is that I want to be wherever you are, Blaire."

"You make it sound so easy."

"Our connection is more than skin deep. We didn't have a fling," I remind her. "Our relationship has always been easy because we've known each other forever. I don't see why we have to complicate it. You've always said it, 'Life isn't granted. You have to live it before it's taken away.'"

Suddenly, she changes the subject. "Remember my eighteenth birthday? It's the first time I was out on a date."

I frown, not understanding where she's going. "That's all you remember?"

Her face turns red. "Well, I ... never mind."

"Sorry, but the best part of your eighteenth birthday is unforgettable," I say, without adding that it was the first time we made love.

"I noticed you still use it as your password."

"It's important to me, too," I disclose, because it wasn't just making love but the fact that she trusted me to be not only her first kiss, but the first man she allowed to touch her body. "You're important to me."

"You had sex before that night," she points out the obvious.

"I had never made love before that night," I explain.

"My point is, I trusted you from the beginning. Every time you asked me to do something, I did it blindly because I knew you had a reason. I never lied to you, and I won't start doing it today. I still have feelings for you, but I'm old enough to keep my heart safe. That doesn't mean I won't give you a chance, it just means that you have to understand that I'm not going to have sex with you today—or any time soon. My heart is the last thing I'll give you, and I understand if you keep yours guarded."

"Well, you still have mine, so there's no point in giving it back," I retort. "Thank you, though."

"For?"

"Being open to giving me another chance," I state. "Maybe this wasn't the date I was planning, but everything you told me is helping me understand you and my brothers. Next time, though, I hope we can have a more romantic dinner."

"Sorry?"

"Don't be, I feel like I'm learning to roller skate. I keep falling, but at least I'm getting the hang of the skates while it happens."

She pushes her entree and sighs. "I'm full. Thank you for being honest and patient. I really want us to try, you know."

"You want to take a walk?"

"I'd love to," she answers. "Thank you again for dinner. It was perfect. All of it."

TWENTY-EIGHT

Blaire

LAST NIGHT, after our walk, we found Henry at the front desk, giving orders to the concierge. He switched us all to the presidential suite. It has three bedrooms and one of them has two queen beds where he and Hayes stayed. After Henry's dinner with Sophia, they decided that we should stay until next Friday. I swear, at this pace, he's going to keep us in Baker's Creek until the stupid stipulation is completed.

When I wake up, I feel rested. It's the first time in a long time that I slept through the night. As I step out of my bedroom, I find Hayes and

Henry already working. They're both sitting at the table, shirtless, looking at some documents. Looking sexy. Well, Hayes looks sexy and pretty edible. His corded back has a few tattoos that I want to explore in detail.

Sophia sits on the couch, drinking coffee and browsing through her iPad.

"I got you a tea," she says, pointing at the cup on top of the coffee table. "There's a chocolate croissant on the table. Hayes is guarding it for you with his life."

I chuckle and grab my tea, sitting next to her. "How long have they been up?"

"I don't know," she answers, staring at the brothers.

They both look like freaking models. My fingertips itch to touch Hayes's well-defined muscles. I am craving the chocolate croissant and his kisses. Not in that order, but I don't give into the uncontrollable urge. Not when we have Henry and Sophia right in front of us.

"I woke up an hour ago. I went for a run, ordered our morning drinks and pastries, and now, I'm enjoying the view while keeping up with my family." She tilts her head toward the brothers.

"You're texting your parents?"

She glances at me, opens her mouth, closes it and sighs. "No, I'm just reading their posts on social media. It's easier and I don't have to interact with them."

I give her a confused look, and she says, "Don't ask. How was your date?"

"Don't ask," I answer back. "Way better than your working dinner, though. What is it now?"

"The Lodge," she answers. "He's moving people from his other hotels to this location. I have to find housing for those who relocate. All kinds of fun stuff. I'm ready to quit."

"You have to give me a two-year notice," Henry grunts.

"That's not even legal," she complains. "I thought you said I wouldn't have to work today."

"How about if we drag them out of the room and into town," I propose. "We can have breakfast at the diner."

"I could use a heavier breakfast," Hayes says, stretching before standing up from his seat and walking to me. "Did you sleep well?"

I take a good look at him. He looks tired. His hair is all ruffled and askew, and there are bags under his eyes.

"You need more sleep," I state the obvious.

"Tell that to Henry who thinks we're machines," he groans then bends and gives me a peck on the lips. "We should've camped or paid for our own room."

"As I mentioned earlier, we have guests coming in today," Henry says annoyed. "We're already losing money since the restaurants are closed."

"You are the one who said they weren't up to code," Hayes reminds him. "When are we going to open them?"

"I'm working on that," Henry answers. "Sophia, I need you to work a deal with the diner, the coffee place, and the bakery."

She stares at him. "What are you talking about?"

"Well, I was thinking that our guests are going to complain when they realize that the restaurants are closed. What if we have a special discount for guests at those establishments."

She groans. "I don't see that happening this weekend, but I can try to get that done early next week. We could try to work the same deal with the restaurants in Happy Springs, too. We could email each guest a coupon, a free night for the inconvenience for their next stay," she suggests.

Henry looks at her pleased. "Good thinking. When are the cars arriving?"

"I'm off duty," she protests.

"Get dressed, Hayes," I suggest. "I'll take you to eat something. My treat."

"We have work to do. You can't just take off," Henry protests.

"You're like a grumpy bear," I complain. "Eat something. Enjoy the day. You can get some blood flowing through your body and maybe your mood will change."

Henry makes a grunting noise. "Exercise keeps my blood flowing. We should go to the gym later. I'll accept your invitation to breakfast, but only if we work during that time."

They both make their way to their room. Henry slams the door shut. Sophia rolls her eyes and says, "I'm going to change."

"Me too," I answer and add, "Try to dress like a civilian."

She laughs. "You're cute."

Ten minutes later, we are all ready to go into town. Henry dragged his tablet with him. At almost seven in the morning, the road headed to town is silent. The sky is already illuminated. I sigh in appreciation, and Hayes grabs my hand, squeezing it.

"You love it, don't you?" he mumbles, and I nod in agreement.

Honestly, I want to enjoy the singing of the birds and the view, but it's hard when Henry is still talking about work. Can he not take a break?

By the time we reach Main Street, there are already dozens of people walking on the sidewalks. Others are setting up tents.

"What's today festival?" I ask out loud.

"Baby Blue Eyes Flowers." Sophia answers enthusiastically. "I can't wait to see what they do during this colorful day."

"You're here to work, Ms. Aragon."

We both glare at Henry and continue walking to the diner.

AFTER BREAKFAST AND THE MEETING, Henry and Hayes agree to walk around town. Henry scrunches his nose at the group of vendors and tents set-up

"This looks like those farmer markets you like to frequent, Sophia." Henry mentions as we stroll around. "How many do they have a year?"

"I remember someone mentioning they did them every weekend," Hayes answers.

"You should know," Sophia says confused. "This is your hometown."

"It's our father's," Hayes answers. "We each were born in different cities, and we only visited a few times. Dad didn't allow us to go around town."

"Why not?"

"Our grandmother didn't like townies," Henry answers, matter-of-factly. He's not bitter nor talking about the people of the town badly.

"We visited once a year and stayed at the big house with Dad—if he came—and my grandmother. It was one week where we spent most of our time on the property fishing, taking care of gram's animals, or doing chores for her."

"The way you describe it makes me feel like free labor," Hayes chuckles. "But it was fun to hang out with you. The young ones were our responsibility. It was a fucking imposition to watch after Beacon. He was a daredevil. Looking back, I'm impressed we kept him alive."

Henry nods. "Who leaves the care of young kids to two irresponsible teenagers?"

"Our grandma couldn't be bothered with them, so someone had to," Hayes answers and then looks at me.

I wish I could tell what he's thinking, but he stays quiet.

"We should figure out more about the festivals. We could tailor the weekends at The Lodge to attract more visitors," I suggest to Sophia, changing the subject completely. "Maybe we can partner with the vendors. We can talk to whoever organizes the festivals and see how we can work together."

She nods, her eyes squinting as if she's thinking. Without asking, she takes Henry's tablet and taps it.

"You know my password?" he protests.

She smirks. "Yes, and I just need to send an email so I can research more about these festivals. Blaire is right. We can bring in a lot more revenue if we market this well."

"If we're renovating the hotel, we should add some ballrooms," I suggest. "We could have weddings too."

"Do you know they used to have yoga and other classes at The Lodge?" she asks.

"No. When did they stop?"

"Mrs. Heywood, the woman who owns the bookstore, said they stopped a couple of years ago because Nick increased the rent of gym use for the instructors."

"Nick should be fired," I state.

"It'll happen soon," Henry confirms. "I can't deal with his arrogant attitude, and the way he treats his employees is deplorable. That's why I'm transferring some of my best employees to this town."

"Since we're starting with new management, we can try to reconnect with those instructors," I suggest. "Maybe I can run a health program that includes nutrition, exercise, and physicals."

Sophia and I stop at the first booth where they have handmade jewelry. We notice the vendor comes from Idaho. I grab their card, and Sophia buys a couple of bracelets for her niece. Not every piece is blue or has blue eyes flowers, but all the booths are decorated with the same blue, white, and yellow colors.

"Look, that guy handcrafts furniture," Sophia announces. "What kind of furniture are you guys buying for the house?"

I grunt.

Hayes snorts with laughter. "You're asking the wrong person. When we moved in together, I decided to buy an apartment. Furnishing the place was..."

I roll my eyes. "A nightmare."

"She wanted to buy antiques. I just wanted to get it done."

"Well, this time, there's no choice," I remind him. "We have to order everything soon. Do you think Easton knows anyone who can give us a discount and deliver fast?"

"I don't care about the discount. All I care is that they deliver everything before we move into the damn house," Henry barks. "You're in charge, Hayes."

Hayes doesn't bother to answer, however he does grab my hand and pull me into the next booth where they have a gorgeous antique armoire. Honestly, I'm not sure if I like antiques, but, at eighteen, I thought it was cool to visit flea markets and antique shops."

"We can't buy furniture right now."

"Why not?" He frowns.

"Where are we going to store it?" I question. "The house is off-limits while they're renovating it."

He gets a card and places it in his wallet. "For later then."

I smile, thinking of the possibilities of later and maybe that house by the lake. Our house.

TWENTY-NINE

Hayes

WE SPEND the rest of the morning with Henry who teaches us how to check in guests, how to look up reservations, and every other task that might be necessary in case his people need help. Needless to say, we end up working the front desk for the rest of the day.

At midnight, Sophia excuses herself, and Blaire is already asleep on the couch. I move her to her bedroom and close the door. Henry has a bottle of single malt, and I'm not in the mood to go to sleep just yet.

"That was fast," he says.

"What?"

"The honeymoon period is over, and you two are already fighting," he explains.

"We're not fighting. You put us to work the whole freaking day."

"I've never been in love, so I can't give you advice, but I would be careful because we have to stick together for eighteen fucking months. This isn't a crazy reality show like Sophia keeps saying. No one can be voted out of the house."

"You'd vote yourself out first if that was the case." I finish the amber liquid and pour some more. "So, why are you still single?"

"My parents fucked me up," he answers. "I don't see the point of having messy feelings."

"What would happen if you put yourself out there?" I ask. Has he even tried to date or fall in love?

"Fucked up shit," he answers. "People are willing to do a lot of messed up shit just to marry a guy like me or you."

I wonder what happened to him or if maybe something happened to one of his rich friends. Henry was the kid who avoided adventures but learned from watching others.

"Would you do it again?" he asks. "Knowing how much it'd hurt both of you."

"There's no going back in time to fix what you fucked up in your life," I answer. "If time travel existed, just by changing one thing, you could create a ripple effect through time that might affect the present and the lives of not only one but maybe millions of people."

He stares at me and laughs. "Fuck, I always forget you're a fucking nerd. It's a yes or no question. I didn't ask you to recite some quantum dynamic theory or for you to quote Einstein."

"You're wrong in both instances."

"And yet, I don't give a fucking shit about that," he answers with a grin. "If you can't change it in the past, what makes you think that you can change it now?"

"That's where you're wrong. I'm not trying to change anything."

"You are," he says. "You're trying to make us a family. It never worked before. It won't work now. You're trying to convince Blaire that you're not your father. Yet, we are just like William. No matter what we do, we carry his fucking genes. One day you'll cheat on your woman with someone new, and then, you'll find another one because none of them satisfy you. He might've married your mom, but she wasn't enough to keep his dick out of some other woman."

I spring from my seat and push him against the couch where he sits. "Do not bring my mother into this conversation."

"This isn't about your mom." His voice is as loud as mine. "It's about knowing that I'm fucking right. If you really love Blaire, like you say, leave her alone."

"Hayes, you're choking your brother."

I turn around to look at Blaire, and Henry hits me on the jaw and kicks me in the stomach.

"Stop it you two!" she orders and puts herself in the middle. "Are you two drunk?"

"No. Your boy here doesn't like to hear truths."

"Shut the fuck up," I warn him.

"You'll never be loyal to her. Let her go now. I can't stomach seeing you together for eighteen months when we all know what's going to happen after that..." he chuckles. "Maybe I'm wrong. She'll leave you just like William did when baby Beacon appeared."

"Do you always have to be this cruel?" Blaire asks. "Is this the only way you can feel satisfaction, by wounding others?"

"Tell me I'm wrong, Blaire," he almost screams. "Are you staying to play house with the Doc? Even his mother left. Look at us, the Aldridges are cursed."

"My relationship with Hayes is not up for discussion. No, I'm not staying with him to play house. We're working together to forge a future because we once had a meaningful connection. I'm giving *myself* a chance to know Hayes and fall for him all over again."

"You're just setting up yourself to failure," he tells her bitterly.

Blaire walks to him and gives him a hug. "It's okay, Henry. He left, and you were never able to tell him how you felt about him or how it felt to be abandoned by him. However, Hayes isn't your dad, and he's not your enemy either."

Henry stays frigid under her embrace for a couple of minutes, before stepping away and leaving the room. Blaire looks at me and says, "Go after him."

"What about us?"

"As long as there's still fear in your heart, I don't think there can be an us, can there?" she answers.

"Blaire, I..."

"You got upset because he hit a nerve. Me. You're still afraid that I'll leave you. Hell, you already left me once for that very reason. Is this time any different?"

I stare at her, dumbfounded by her question. "It ... of course *it is*."

"The answer came a second too late. You don't trust me—or yourself. Fix yourself from the inside out. I'm not the answer to your midlife crisis, Hayes. I can't be. God knows I love you, even after all the years and all the pain, but before we can be an *us* ... you need to start with yourself. I'll stay with you in spite of your flaws, but I need you to confront your fears."

"Blaire..."

"Go have a long talk with Henry. You have to learn to get along and be brothers. He lost his dad. He feels like he doesn't have any family left."

I stare at her because what am I supposed to say?

"Prove him wrong," she says with a smile. "He thinks he can push all of us away because we don't care. I think we need to show him he's wrong. He'll hate that more than anything."

"Have I mentioned I love that you can be good and yet pretty evil?"

"A few times."

"I SEE YOU'RE STILL PREDICTABLE," I say, when I find him on the roof of The Lodge.

"Grandma hated when we came here," he reminds me, taking a swig from a bottle of wine. He didn't bother to bring glasses.

"We were usually drinking or smoking pot and were caught by the sheriff. Of course, she hated it. She had to pay money to everyone who knew that we were bad so the Aldridge name would stay clean." I chuckle.

He laughs and hands me one of the bottles of wine he brought with him. "I stole them from the restaurant."

"Dad barely visited us," I say out loud and then tell him the story of what happened just before the Beacon fiasco came to light.

"I was almost okay with the way things were in our family because he wasn't any different from my friends' fathers. I lived in a boarding school since I was eight for fuck's sake," he says. "Then, I met you guys and ... your mothers actually gave a shit. Mine was too busy running a company, charities. I didn't want your dad. I wanted your families."

"You had us."

"Did I? Because I haven't heard from you in years."

"You never reached out when my brother died."

"My brother died, too, Hayes."

It's true, *our* brother died. Carter was always mine, but he became theirs. My little brother was the glue. Mom used to say he had one of those personalities that everyone loved. He was the life of the party. Losing him hurt, and it was easier to push everyone away rather than having to face the same pain if anything like that happened to these guys.

"Blaire is not going to stay," I confirm. "No matter what I do, she's getting out of this town when we meet the stipulations of the will."

"You're already giving up?" He punches me on the arm. "You're so fucking lucky. No one has ever seen me the way she sees you. Let alone love. Every fucking woman—or girl when I was younger—just looked at me as their ticket to popularity or to a lavish life. I am, Henry Lloyd Merkel Aldridge."

I look at him, and I finally understand what happened with my parents. Dad didn't follow Mom. He dropped her in Baltimore to do her thing, and he moved to New York to start a new life. He never cared enough to be a part of anyone's life, just lived in the moment. Blaire isn't just a moment in time; she's a lifetime. My stardust is everywhere, and like a star, I can follow her no matter where she is. This time, I have to be smart. I can't lose her.

"No, I'm going to pack and ask her where we're going next," I say.

"Sorry for ... being just like William, I guess. He couldn't hold onto a relationship. Not even to a blood relative, could he?"

He takes a swig of wine and stares at the horizon.

"Blaire says that I have to grieve." I fill the silence. "What is it that I'm supposed to grieve? The man I wish he had been or the guy who gave me life?"

"Fuck if I know," he answers with anger, "You at least have Cassandra."

"I'm lucky to have her, and she loves you guys, too, in case you ever want to reach out to her," I mention. "Listen, I know you don't believe me when I say we can do this. It's hard to trust someone when you've been alone for so long, but for the few good times that we shared, please have faith in me. Help me get through these eighteen months."

"You fail me, and I swear I'll get Vance to finish you," he jokes. "I miss this. We didn't do it often, but you were my only friend. I thought you had my back, but then you were gone, too."

My chest constricts because he's right. We did have a lot in common back in the day. Even when I had Carter, Henry understood me more because he was older.

"I'm sorry," I repeat. "No matter what happens, I won't leave you again. We're a family. I'm not sure what that will look like, but I'll make sure it includes Christmas and all that shit."

We continue drinking and talking. I feel like I have one brother on board, but fuck, there are still four more, and I don't know how to reach out to them. Henry and I understood each other because we were the oldest. Pierce sometimes played along. The other four ... Carter was our link to the age gap. Now, it's not that big, but I feel like the gap is the size of the Grand Canyon.

THIRTY

Blaire

I SPEND the next two weeks working on the house, approving fixtures, appliances, and buying furniture. When I have a chance, Sophia and I go to the bookstore. Jane Heywood, the owner, knows everyone and everything we need to know, and she's discreet. She introduces us to the festival committee and the mayor; and she even invites us to her book club.

The festivals happen almost every weekend and the out of town vendors can register to participate a year in advance. We have a list of the events, and the organizers are more than happy that The Lodge and the Aldridge family will be participating in the festivities.

"Isn't it weird that the founders of the town aren't a part of it?" I ask Sophia, as we sit in the conference room, trying to see how we can fit the ice cream and chocolates into the festival.

She hired a marketing team to help rebrand the products, and we convinced the bakery to carry a few pints of ice cream.

"It's just as ridiculous as not having an ice cream shop," she quips and looks at me seriously. "Why do I feel like Henry dumped the factory's responsibilities on us?"

"Because he did," I confirm. "I would complain if I wasn't having so much fun. Are you going to visit us after today?"

We're all leaving Baker's Creek as soon as Hayes and Henry finish their meetings with the factory's manager.

"I like you, and I'm sure the rest of the brothers are lovely, but I am Henry-free for eighteen months," she says with so much excitement I want to hug and congratulate her. "You can call me. I might have to check on the factory a few times. However, I'll stay away as much as possible."

"If we're lucky, maybe he'll meet some innocent soul in this town, and the bitterness goes away," I joke.

She laughs. "As long as I don't have to clean his mess, he can date the entire town."

I don't have time to ask what that means because Hayes and Henry enter the conference room.

"We're set," Hayes says. "Ready to go?"

"Honestly, I was expecting you to tell me we were staying another week," I answer, closing my new laptop.

Hayes got it for me when Henry told me that he needed me to stay a few more days—two weeks ago. He keeps prolonging our stay because there are too many problems he needs to fix. Since Easton Rodin couldn't fit the renovation of the restaurants in his schedule anytime soon, he brought in some of the people who've worked for him in the past. He's hoping that we'll be able to open at least the main restaurant in just a couple of weeks.

During this time, I've been able to work with Tori too. We have a few candidates I want to interview for the next project. We also were able to add a few amenities to the orphanage we're building in Brazil.

Going home is important, since I only have two weeks to hire new doctors. Once we open the practice, I'll be dedicating most of my time to it. Hayes signed the papers and transferred the money yesterday. Dr. Garrison won't hand it over until we move in so the locals can have healthcare. Not that I think opening twice a week for only a few hours helps the town, but I kept my thoughts to myself while we finished the transaction.

"Here." Hayes gives a paper bag from the bakery to Sophia. "Paige, the owner of My Cookie Jar brought you this, since you're leaving."

"I'm going to miss my daily pastry," she whines.

"Don't worry. I'll send you a care package every week," I promise.

Henry looks at his watch and says, "We need to go. The jets should be ready to take off when we arrive at the airport. If we take any longer, they're going to charge us extra."

THIRTY-ONE

Blaire

"WE'RE GOING in separate cars, aren't we?" I ask Henry because all the cars he had shipped from home are two-seaters.

"No, I'm giving you a ride to Portland, Princess," he says, looking at me with a guarded expression.

I jingle the keys of the rental. "No, I have a car waiting for me."

Henry rolls his eyes and wiggles his fingers. "Hand them over," he orders. "I'll have one of the new guys drive it back to Portland. Your plane leaves in a couple of hours. It's easier to fly you."

"What are you? The Flash?" I cock an eyebrow and cross my arms.

Hayes explains, "Henry is flying us in his helicopter. Let's move, or we won't make it on time."

"So, this is how I die," I joke. "Angry brothers push me out of the helicopter in mid-air."

"You're ridiculous," Hayes declares, but there's a smile playing on the edge of his lips, and impulsively, I kiss him.

"Stop the PDA," Henry orders.

"What's the matter? Human contact gives you hives," I mock him.

"No, it's just you two." Henry states, glancing at us and then walking away.

"I might sound crazy, but I'm going to miss this place," Sophia states, as we walk toward the helipad that sits on the back of the hotel property.

"We should get this repaired, maybe build a shed for a helicopter," Hayes says.

"Add it to the things we need to do," Henry requests. "Vance could be in charge of the security and maintenance of the factory and lodge."

I'm tempted to ask if they've heard from their brothers. We all need to be here in two weeks, and I don't see anyone but Henry, Hayes, and Pierce working their asses off to make this happen. Sophia might be Henry's assistant, but she's doing a lot more for the town than she should be doing.

"We'll talk to him once we settled in the house."

"How's that project going?" Henry inquires.

"The kitchen and bathrooms are almost ready. I think Easton is going to finish by next week," I answer. "The furniture doesn't start coming in until next weekend, but if anything arrives before the house is ready, they're going to store it in the garage."

"You can't possibly think that the furniture is going to be right next to my cars," Henry complains.

"It's not your garage," Hayes protests. "We all agreed that we can't have more than five cars each."

He gives me conspiratorial look because I already promised to give him my five spots.

"Then we have to ask Easton to expand the garage," Henry protests.

"And so it starts," I complain. "The quest to show who has the best toys."

"And the bigger dick," Sophia adds, and we both laugh. Both men give us an unamused glare.

The flight is uneventful. When we arrive at the airport, Sophia and I say our goodbyes. I'm going to miss her a lot, but we promise to text every day and Facetime as often as work allows her to do it.

"Listen," I say, as we board the jet, "not to sound ungrateful, but ... this is a jet. I was already counting my spare change to pay you for the plane ticket, but now what am I supposed to do?"

"You can always pay me in kind." Hayes winks and throws that sexy smirk that shows off his kissable dimples.

"You're impossible," I say, standing close to him, unable to move to my seat.

He caresses my face with the back of his hand, warmth shimmering from his touch. I shiver, aware of the seductiveness of that simple touch. I push myself onto my tiptoes and my lips touch his. He takes my mouth and kisses me deeply until the captain announces that we're ready for takeoff and we have to take our seats.

"I COULD'VE CALLED a Lyft or an Uber," I say, as Hayes drives us through the already crowded streets of San Francisco.

"Is everything okay?" he asks. "I thought we were past awkwardness, and we trusted each other."

"We do, but I know you have things to do. You're selling the shares of your practice and you have to meet with your partners."

"That's tomorrow," he reminds me. "Unless the deal falls through."

"Do you think that'll happen?"

"Nah, it's going to be fine. That means I have some free time to be with you. I wish you'd stay with me." He suggested that earlier when we were landing.

"We're going to get sick of each other before we even have to move in together," I say. "Really, I appreciate the ride, but I feel like I'm taking advantage of you"

"I can think of many ways you can thank me for ... today," he says flirtatiously as he parks the car.

I squirm under his smoldering gaze. I'm only seconds away from unbuttoning his pants and either taking him in my mouth or climbing him and...

Rushing, I take off my seatbelt and jump out of the car. This isn't happening here, in a car, in the middle of the day.

"Where's the fire?" he asks.

"I just don't want to take any more of your time," I say, trying to sound cool, but I'm pretty sure I'm failing.

"Lead the way," he says, carrying my stuff.

"Just hand it over, I'll take it from here," I say.

"Are you feeling okay?"

Nope, I'm losing my self-control, and if Tori is home, I won't be able to push you down on my bed and...

"You can just leave me here," I insist, walking to the front door and inputting the code. We head up the stairs, and I unlock the door to my apartment and look at him. "Really, you don't want to go inside."

"Unless you have a dead body inside, I don't see any reason to send me on my way," he says, giving me a suspicious look. "Everything okay, Blaire?"

I exhale in a whoosh and send a quick prayer, *please don't be home, Tori.* "I'm fine, let's go into the unknown. Just be aware that my roommate doesn't believe in housekeeping."

"How long have you lived here?"

"Six or seven years," I explain, checking the tray where Tori sets my mail. There's just junk mail, so I place it on the 'to shred' bin, which is overflowing.

"This is a nice area," he says. "How did you get it? I tried to buy an apartment around here, and it was impossible."

"Tori's family owns the building. She was already living here when she started working with me. Six months after I hired her, I lost my studio," I explain.

"How can you lose your studio?"

"Funny that you ask. Apparently, when you forget to pay the rent, because you're out of the country, landlords don't give a shit, and they kick you out," I explain, a little embarrassed. "If I say I was young and stupid, does that count?"

"I guess at twenty-five I did do a lot of stupid things," he agrees. "Forgetting to pay the rent wasn't one of them, though."

"Well, I was in a remote area of Mongolia, and there was no wi-fi." I give him a shrug. "My phone back then was still the flip phone my parents gave me. There's no data on that thing."

His eyes watch me with humor, and I'm glad he's not laughing at me.

"Let me put my things in my room," I say, and he follows me, carrying them.

When I open the door, I gasp and can't help but yell, "Oh fucking hell!" I jump back after I close the door again and grab my phone.

Hayes frowns, opens the door, and enters. His jaw twitches when he asks, "Boyfriend?"

"Nine-one-one, what is your emergency?"

"There's a man in my bed," I tell the operator. "A naked man sprawled in my bed."

"Were you drunk last night, ma'am?"

"Drunk, why would you ask that? I'm telling you there's a naked—"

"What's with all the noise?" Tori comes out of her room stretching. "Oh, it's you."

"There's a man in my bed," I tell her, wondering why she's still asleep at noon.

She looks at Hayes and grins. "Dude, if you don't want him, I can bring him to my bed." She wiggles her eyebrows. "Hello there, cutie."

"Victoria, I'm serious. There's a stranger in my bed."

"Ma'am, are you still there?" the operator asks.

"Yes, and as I told you, someone broke into my room, and he's in my bed—naked."

"That's Samson," Tori says, as if I should know who the fuck Samson is. "Now, who is this?"

"You have a man in my room?" I don't answer her question and apologize to the operator for the call.

"I told you two weeks ago that I was renting the room. However, I'm sure you were daydreaming. Thank fuck I didn't get a call saying that you were in a car accident."

"She shouldn't be allowed to drive," Hayes says, and then asks, "So, who the fuck is Samson?"

"My new roommate," Tori informs us.

"What happened to my stuff?"

She points at the boxes in the corner. "I'm not kicking you out, just making sure I receive an income. This city is too damn expensive and working for you doesn't pay that well. The couch is all yours, though."

"I have a guest room," Hayes says, and in that moment, the guy, who has claimed my bed, comes out, wearing a pair of shorts.

"What the fuck, Victoria? I just arrived two hours ago, and you are—"

He snaps his mouth shut and looks at Hayes with bulging eyes. "Dr. Aldridge, I ... did something happen?"

"You two know each other?" I ask curiously.

Samson looks at me and grins. "Well, you're more beautiful in person. Samson Kirk." He holds out his hand. I shake it, and he holds it a second too long for Mr. Alpha's taste. He's going to realize that Hayes might be quiet and peaceful, but he can also fight like his brothers.

"Kirk, take your paw off her right now," Hayes orders.

Samson releases me and moves a few steps back.

"Again, how do you know him?" I ask, looking at them both.

Samson looks a couple of years younger than me, late twenties or thirty, at most. He's a couple of inches shorter than Hayes and okay looking. I can see Tori banging her roommate soon.

"He's one of the residents at the hospital where I worked," Hayes informs me. "We have a lot to do, Love. Can I send someone to pick up your boxes later?"

"What?" I ask, confused about this whole 'let's take your stuff' and 'let me mark my territory' while I'm at it.

"It's obvious that you need a place to stay," he explains, as if it's just that simple. "As I mentioned, I have a guest room. It's just temporary, since we're leaving soon."

"Kirk, help me with the boxes," Hayes orders.

"These hands are made for patients," the good doctor excuses himself.

"Get the fucking boxes, now." Hayes doesn't take his bullshit. "We can move you out in a couple of trips and just take whatever you need to Baker's. We can have the movers bring the rest with my things."

Tori looks at me, and I give her a don't ask look, hoping she actually listens to me for once.

"Who is that hunk, and why are you moving out?" Tori asks, once Hayes and Samson leave with the boxes.

"You kicked me out of your apartment," I remind her.

"No, you can stay on the couch, I just ... my family and I are having issues. Don't ask."

I adore Tori. We're best friends, but there are some things about her life that she never talks about, like her family and how she supports herself. I don't pay her much, and she's fine with that—unless she has issues with whoever gives her money. Then she tries to find different ways to make fast cash. This isn't the first time she's rented my room.

"What about the hunk?" she insists.

"Hayes Aldridge," I answer.

She frowns and looks at the main door. "No, that's not Hayes. Is it?"

"You know him?"

"I told you my mother tried to set me up with him. She's been trying to marry me off to one of the most eligible men in San Francisco. Guys who move in my circle. The hot billionaires who make it to the list of 'must lick, must fuck, and I shall get his ring.'"

"Which circles are those?"

"Shhh," she says and covers my ears. "That's not information a person with a kind soul should ever hear about."

"I'm sure I can handle it." I chuckle. "So, which list does he belong to?"

She looks again toward the door and then back. "All of them. Everyone wants to lick the elusive Hayes Benjamin Aldridge. Fuck ... have you seen that body? The ring ... well, wouldn't you want to have his babies?"

Before I can ask her more about the lists or how many women have been licking or fucking his delicious body, he's back, and I noticed they took all the boxes at once.

"Stardust, ready to go?"

Tori frowns and studies me. "Would you like to share anything with me?"

"Not really," I respond. "Let's set up the interviews for next Monday. I want to assemble the team before I have to leave for Baker's Creek."

Tori and I agree on doing a videoconference once I'm settled at Hayes's place. There's more to the 'let's talk' phrase that she says at the end. I know she wants the dirt on why I'm hanging out with the most desirable bachelor in San Fran.

There's nothing elusive about him, is there?

"Why are you looking at me like that?" he asks during the drive to his place.

"Do you know you are on the list of most fuckable billionaires in San Francisco?"

He glances at me and chuckles. "Is there such a thing?"

"Who knows? Tori said it's not something for me—that's code for, 'It's a San Francisco socialite' thing, and let's be honest, I'm ... me."

"I had no idea that existed," he says.

"How many women have you screwed this year?" I ask curiously, and not jealous at all. Okay, maybe a little.

"None," he answers.

"It's May. You want me to believe that you haven't slept with anyone in the past five months, even when there's a parade of women outside your home?"

He laughs, but quickly sobers up. "I haven't slept with anyone in a couple of years. Are you upset because you don't believe me, or because you don't like the idea of me sleeping with other women?"

"Don't..." I close my mouth.

"So, you had no idea Kirk was sleeping in your bed?" he asks.

"I don't know the guy," I assure him. "He's not a fan of yours."

"No one is a fan of mine. It's a teaching hospital, and I'm pretty strict, so ... I don't have as many friends," he concludes as he pulls into an underground garage. His gaze connects with mine, and he gives me that heart stopping smile that has always been just for me.

The second he turns off the engine, the air thickens. The intensity in his eyes makes me burst into flames, at least that's how my entire body feels, like it's burning me alive, filling me up with desire. When I glance at him, his green eyes are looking at me with lust. I'm melting just with the thoughts of what can happen, the hopes that it'll happen. I'm hungry for him.

THIRTY-TWO

Hayes

IT'S BEEN A LONG MONTH, and we're only halfway through it. William left. Thankfully, there were no discrepancies at Aldridge Enterprises. The auditors Pierce hired assured us that we're in good shape. Henry's going to spend a couple of weeks with the interim CEO. We don't know if he's going to stay or if we'll hire someone new. Ultimately, Henry is the one who was groomed to run a business.

These past two weeks interacting with Henry were necessary to convince him that the risk of moving to Baker's Creek is worth it. He's getting a kick out of bossing me around, and I'm letting him because, as long as he believes he's in control, he'll stick around. Pretending to be just another one of his minions for this period of time is easier than making him see reason.

The offer to stay with me because I have a spare room was misleading. I want Blaire in my bed. I should've been more direct. I show her the place. I start with the kitchen, take her to the home office, and finally, the living room that faces the Bay Bridge.

She's quiet. Is she studying the apartment, daydreaming, or is there something she doesn't like about the place?

"Is it too soon to say that I miss the trees, the fresh air, and the sounds of nature?" Blaire asks, as she stares at the window longingly. "Don't get me wrong. You have a beautiful view, and the place is gorgeous. However, there's something about being close to nature that I miss. Not traveling..."

"I'm sorry, Stardust. Will you be okay at Baker's Creek? What are you going to do about the positions you need to fill? I can help you hire doctors." God, I'm talking like an anxious teenager. What is wrong with me?

She laughs softly, and while the sound shouldn't affect me, the fantasies of all the things I can do to her so she can make more of those noises pop in my mind.

I could make her moan, beg, scream my name. All of those hot sounds I could get out of her with just the right touch of my hands or mouth.

If there's one thing I know by heart, it's what she likes when we're making love.

"Adapting to a different place is easy. I just miss certain things, but never the city."

"Yet, you live here," I remind her.

"Barely," she discloses. "If I didn't need a real address for people to believe that I head a non-profit, I wouldn't bother to have the skeleton office."

"We could move the foundation to Baker's Creek," I suggest. "You and I can—"

She gives me *the look*. The one where she wants me to stop talking about a certain subject because it's a hard limit.

"What is it?" I ask.

She arches an eyebrow, tilting her head.

"Talking about the foundation, moving to Baker's Creek, or us?" I throw out the question because we also hate to walk on eggshells. I wouldn't do it to her, and I won't allow her to do it to me either. However, I don't let her answer, because the response is right there in her eyes. "You're afraid of me."

"Not at all."

"You're not?" I confirm.

"No, I'm just making sure that we're ready for this step. Once we take it, we know we're not going back."

"Have I mentioned you're strange?"

"A few times, and yet, you love that I'm everything but ordinary." She smirks playfully. "Have you reached out to your brothers yet?"

"No. Why do I feel like you're looking for an excuse to write me off?"

"Don't misunderstand. I want you, and it hurts so bad, as bad as it hurts not to have you," she whispers. "I know this is going to sound ridiculous, and it won't make sense, but I feel like unless you resolve all your personal issues, there's still a possibility that you might walk away, too. But I'm definitely not writing you off at all."

I groan. "Henry said the same earlier today. It's like the two of you have faith in me, yet you're not ready to go all in and bet on me.

"Your heart is what matters to me the most," I say. "Though I'd be lying if I say that my mind isn't filled with thoughts about devouring every inch of your delicious body. I want to torment you with neck kisses and light touches."

"Hayes," she whispers my name with a raspy voice filled with lust.

Something changes in the air. There's a radical shift, and I feel it echoing inside me. It's not her words, not her voice; it's the hunger in her eyes.

I walk to her and take her hand. If I could, I'd pick her up, take her to my bed and remind her exactly what we are. I lost the right to do that, but I have to try my best to convince her that we're great together and that if she opens up to me again, I won't let her down. Never again.

So, I lean in to kiss her. My hands slide up her body, and I grab her neck.

Soft.

Gentle.

My lips are like feathers caressing her precious skin. I'm not hesitant, just cautious. I want to reel her in slowly, until we can both agree that there's a lot more than this *old attraction.* Convince her that this new us is stronger than before and that we are going to be together—forever. She opens her mouth and the tip of her tongue slides across the tip of mine. They touch tentatively, like two estranged lovers who remember they're bonded. They embrace, twirl, and make love to each other.

All I want is to kiss her forever. Become her oxygen. Beat at the rhythm of her heart.

Fill her up and beg her to make me whole again.

Her hands curl around my neck, and she's as worked up as I am. I should stop because ... my brain is completely frozen. I can't think of why we have to take it slow. She's kissing me with the same hunger I carry, and I just give in to the passion. We consume each other. She moans and groans as my hands fidget with her clothes. I can't stop myself. The urgency in her movements tells me that she can't either.

Blaire's trembling hands stroke the hard ridge in my pants. I don't expect her to pull the zipper and release my hard as fuck length, but that's exactly what she does. Her small palm grabs my heavy cock, and she rubs it, tugging at it. Just the way I like it. She wants me to lose control.

Fighting my desire, I grasp the single drop of self-control I have left and stop kissing her. My heart kicks into a fast pounding tempo, as I stare at her lustful eyes. She's lost in a trance and tapping into reason is going to bring her back. But even though I'm going to lose the moment, I have to do the right thing.

"Stardust, if we do this, there's no going back," I rasp, regretting my words, but knowing it is the right thing to say.

"Why are you being sensible?" she asks, with a rough and smoky voice. Her lips part as both hands wrap around the head of my shaft.

The heat between us surges, once again, as she pulls me down to her, deepening the kiss, drawing me closer, and making me forget reason and the rest of the world. We're good at this, letting everything dissolve when it's just the two of us. Nothing matters but her. In her case, only me.

Moving my lips toward her jaw and then her neck, I repeat, "If you're trying to stop me, you're doing a shitty job."

She laughs and looks at me with so much lust.

"Who told you I wanted to wait?" she whispers, sucking the lobe of my ear, right before she drops to her knees. As she opens her mouth, her eyes find mine.

Fuck. I'm not sure if this is heaven or hell, but I don't care once her lips part and her hands bring the head of my cock to her mouth. She laps the tip, and her tongue plays with the head right before she adjusts her jaw and swallows me slowly. Her eyes are two puddles of desire. The ice in them melts as her tongue runs along the crest.

Stroking, sweeping, sucking. Her mouth brings me to my knees every time. I groan and can't help but move my hips forward, fucking her mouth. As I'm about to come, I realize that this isn't what I want.

I want her.

Just her. I want to claim her. Just as she claimed me.

Her mouth continues sliding up and down my shaft, taking me deep. My fingers are tangled in her long hair, gripping her. This isn't enough. I need more. I need to be inside her.

"Stop," I beg her, pulling out of her mouth and lifting her from the floor. "You fucking own me—always. You don't have to show me who has the power, but before I lose all sense of control... Please say no if you don't want us to continue."

"Make love to me, Doc."

Her words unleash me. I pull down her leggings, push her against the couch, and thrust myself inside her tight entrance. It sucks me in, and so I begin to fuck her softly, gently.

"You're mine," I whisper the words so low that maybe she doesn't hear me. "Please, let me back in. It hurts like hell not being with you—not being a part of you."

I'm burning inside. Knowing I won't last long, I reach between her legs and begin to quickly stroke and rub her clit with my fingers as I pump inside her faster and harder. When the pressure starts building at the base of my spine, I start breaking into a million pieces. We're both becoming brighter, shinier like stars. The same way we were created. Her walls squeeze my length. She's begging me not to stop, to push deeper. The moment we explode, we become stardust, fusing together into one large, newer star.

Our bodies tremble. We're both moaning nonsense as we come down from the high. She closes her eyes, breathing deeply. Is she regretting it? Mother fucker, I knew that we should've stopped, but how could I when her mouth was on me?

"Forgive me," I beg her. "I ... I was desperate for you. I missed you so fucking much."

Her eyes open, and she places a kiss on my chin.

"I wanted it, too."

"Then what is it?"

"We didn't use birth control."

"You're not on the pill?" I ask, calmly.

She shakes her head. "No. As I said, it's been years, and I really didn't see the point of it."

"What do you want to do?"

She looks at me suspiciously. "Why are you so calm?"

"I'm not twenty-two, and I'm not scared of a seven-pound baby girl who might look like you," I confess. "In fact, I'd love to have one of those one day—with you."

"Are we even ready for that?" she says, both confused and alarmed.

"Plan B?" I suggest. "Do you want me to go to the pharmacy and get you one?"

She looks at me, and her answer doesn't surprise me. "I'm not sure what the future will bring, but I want to see what the odds give me."

"Odds?"

"There's only a fifty percent chance that I can get pregnant," she answers. "If it's meant to be."

"Fate," I say and kiss her deeply.

THIRTY-THREE

Blaire

WE SPEND the rest of the day making love and snacking on whatever he has in his cupboards. Around eight at night, he orders food, and I step into the shower. As the warm water hits my skin, I realize too much is happening at once. I'm not talking about having unprotected sex—but that was a huge deal too.

That's not what's really bothering me; it's the possibility of me being pregnant. The odds are against me, a woman who went through almost four years of chemotherapy and radiation. The probability of getting pregnant is pretty slim.

The odds are against me, the woman who craves a baby. The realization only made me sad, and I don't want to have a heart to heart conversation just yet. Not after what just happened between us. He's not afraid of a little girl. He said he wants to have one with me, but I doubt I can give him that. Would that be an obstacle between us?

I jolt when I hear his gravelly voice asking, "You okay?" He steps into the shower, and honestly, I'd be better if he pushes me against the shower and thrusts himself inside me.

"Regrets?" he asks, embracing me with his strong arms.

"What?" I ask.

"Us. Do you regret what happened?" he asks. "I thought we were on the same page, but if I overstepped."

This is the part where I could lie, but lies are useless. They take too much time and energy from you. Life is too short to be spreading that shit. Lies are toxic and keeping up with them is useless.

"I love you, Blaire. This didn't happen just because I need to touch you, but because I..." He cups my chin with his hand and lifts my face, kissing me lightly. "Talk to me, Baby."

"There's nothing wrong," I insist.

"Blaire, I know you. What happened?"

"I went through years of chemotherapy and radiation," I say out loud and hug his waist, feeling vulnerable and needing him close. "So really, the odds of having a baby are—"

"You were young when it happened," he reminds me. "*Our odds* are as good as any other thirty-some year-old couple. If we can't make it happen, we'll harvest your eggs and fertilize the ones that aren't damaged."

"Fixing my sadness with science?" I joke.

He kisses the top of my head. "Always. Adoption is also an alternative," he adds. "If you're ready to have a baby we can start looking into it."

My bottom lip quivers. "You'd do that for me?"

He nods and kisses me. "Anything for you, Blaire."

"Let's wait. I'm in no hurry, but if it happens the baby will be welcomed."

"And loved," he adds.

WE'RE in the dining room eating pizza while he's in a videoconference with Henry.

"Listen, we have to work with people we trust, and I don't trust Dad's interim CEO," Henry says. "He worked for Merkel Hotels and Spas a few years ago, and as I mentioned earlier, I fired him."

"Can we replace him?"

He nods. "Yes, I already have a couple of guys in mind. We just need the approval from the majority."

"Have you spoken to Pierce?"

"He's my next call," Henry says. "Are you going to talk to the others?"

Hayes bobs his head a couple of times. "Yes. I'll be heading out this Wednesday. Can we take care of the CEO now, or do you need their input?"

"We need the majority to vote. We're lucky that our father didn't have a board, or this would be a fucking mess. As long as we have four votes, we can change the CEO. Blaire, what do you think?"

"Go for it," I approve. "You got my vote."

"I just need Pierce's vote, and we're golden," he continues. "That's all I need for now. Call if you need anything from me."

After he hangs up, Hayes looks at me and says, "Henry texted me earlier to tell me that Vance is unreachable. We don't know if he's in or out."

He's unsure, I don't say out loud. Instead, I ask, "What are you planning on doing?"

Vance needs him to reach out, to show him that they care about him.

"I'm going to Atlanta to visit Addison," he answers. "She should be able to find him for us."

"Why the sudden urge to look for him?"

"I want to talk to him, explain to him that we're all in."

"But you're not," I remind him. "Three, maybe four of us if you count Pierce are in. What about the others?"

"What do you want me to do? Wait until the last minute when everyone is in and see if he magically appears?"

"Yes," I answer. "Once everyone is there. If you call him, I'm sure he'll be there."

"I doubt it," Hayes groans. "He always ignores my calls."

"I would approach the other three," I suggest and show him my phone. "He always answers my calls."

"How often do you call him?"

"Only when I have an emergency. We usually text. As I told you before, we aren't that close, but he'll respond if I call. I won't make that call until I can promise that everyone is invested."

He runs a hand through his hair. "Okay. I trust you."

"I love you," I say.

He peppers kisses on my hands. "Thank you for today. I missed you so fucking much."

There's something about his statement that doesn't sit well in the pit of my stomach. It's probably my own insecurities, and I should let it go, but I can't.

"Just so we're on the same page, what was today?"

Hayes

"SERIOUSLY, BLAIRE?" I cock an eyebrow.

"Yes, I want to know. We don't play games, and it's important for me to know if you're recalling—"

"When I'm remembering our past, it's normally at three in the morning while I jerk off because you're not there," I say in a low firm voice. "Today, it was me loving you.

"It's always me loving you," I repeat.

She's about to speak when I interrupt her. "And before you tell me that I don't love you, I do. We know each other so well we can still read what the other is thinking without words. It's just a matter of catching up, Blaire."

Blaire purses her lips, far from satisfied, which is understandable. We need to talk everything through. That's the way she operates. "You make it sound so simple."

"It's that simple, Blaire. Love isn't as complicated as people make it—I complicated *us* by being stupid," I explain.

"This is happening too fast, and I know what you're going to tell me. That's who we are, still ... I have this nagging feeling that this is a summer fling. It's like your dad is playing puppet master," she declares, and she's right about that part.

William might be dead, but he is still playing with our lives.

"My father tried to fuck us up, but, in reality, he gave me a gift," I intercede. "I was getting restless, desperate. I'm sure that I was days or maybe weeks away from saying fuck my pride and looking for you."

"I saw my picture in your office. It was turned around."

God, this woman never misses any detail. She could be a detective or part of a forensic team.

"It hurt to see you and not to have you," I explain. "Some days, I'd turn it around, and others I would look at you for hours and talk to it, the way we used to talk at night."

"I talked to you through my blog," she answers.

"I read it," I say, reaching for her hand and kissing her knuckles. "Look, I'm making a lot of changes in my life, but it's not just for you. It's for me, too. You're..."

The first good thing I allowed myself to have—and to love. Since the first time I met her, I wanted her all to myself. To love her and never share her with anyone because she made me happy.

Ever since my father fucked up our lives, I worked hard to make Mom and Carter happy. It was like a penance I had to do for pushing Dad away. Obviously, I was delusional. That notion disappeared years ago when I realized I had nothing to do with his poor choices. However, as a kid, I believed my father had gotten himself a new family because I yelled at him.

He missed my science fair and Carter's baseball game.

"I hate you," I yelled. "I wish you weren't my father."

And then, it was on the news. William Aldridge had a new kid with a famous starlet and left us for good. So, I had to be a good brother and a good son to make up for what I did wrong. Then it was just required by Carter and Mom to cater to them because I was the dutiful son.

Blaire has always been the one person who I can be myself with, who I can keep for myself, who I can have without worrying about anything. We understand each other.

She's the person who I'd steal the sun for, who I'd want to build an entire universe with. I wouldn't promise her the stars because I want to create them with her. And once we have enough stars, we'd form entire constellations.

"You're the one person who makes me believe that there's more to science," I say.

"Like magic and fate?" she prompts. "They are real. Not everything needs a scientific explanation."

"Only you make me believe," I repeat.

It's true. Blaire is the one thing I could never explain. Like why I was so enthralled with her from the first moment I touched her. Something about her has always felt right.

"We just reconnected. We've been apart for years, but I think you're smart, interesting, and I like you. I can't wait to discover more. I look forward to working with you. From everything that I've read, you're a pretty knowledgeable doctor and caregiver."

She tilts her head to one side. "Stroking my ego, Aldridge, or fishing for a few compliments?"

"I don't need compliments."

"Good, because I still haven't googled you. I feel like a terrible ex-girlfriend." She smiles, and her words and posture lighten the mood.

"Well, consider yourself my girlfriend, and you get to learn all about me firsthand." I wink at her.

"Have you done any sightseeing while you work in foreign countries?"

"Not really. My schedule only allows me to browse for souvenirs around the airport, but most of the special things that I have from each visit are handmade objects by the kids or women who live in the villages I visit. Drawings are my favorites."

"What do you love the most about your job?"

She shrugs. "It's safe to say everything. The only thing I don't like is not having the money to fund more projects."

"If I could, I'd get you out of Dad's mess and make sure the financial piece was never a problem. I feel like among all of us, you're the most affected. Well, not you, but the work that you do."

"It's okay. I'm making things work, and Baker's Creek isn't bad. I like the town. It's quirky. I can run the foundation from any place as long as I put together a good team to work on each project. It's happened in the past. I stayed in Atlanta for a year."

"After the kidnapping?"

She nods.

"Is it okay to ask what happened?"

"Wrong place and wrong time," she announces. "I was buying some supplies for the village. One moment I'm paying and the next, there's a guy pointing a gun and shoving me into a car with three other women. Fortunately, I was able to send a text to Vance before they dragged me to their warehouse."

I don't understand how she says it so casually. "Are you okay?" I ask worried.

"Yes, I'm fine," she assures me.

"I mean, *kidnapping?*" I say, my stomach tied into knots just imagining it.

"It was scary, but lucky for us, Vance found us quickly," she explains. "He took me to Atlanta with Addison. She cared for me while I was going to a therapist. Again, I'm fine, but that's because I got help."

"You are brushing the subject, discussing it so casually."

"No, it was four years ago. I've had a lot of time to process it and a lot of therapy. I was lucky. Somehow, I believe Carter was looking out for me that day. He wouldn't let anything bad happen to me."

"He wouldn't," I agree. He loved her like a sister.

"We did it again, made this heavy. It's like every time we take an important step forward, we end up bringing up the past."

"Sorry, I'm just trying to—"

"Learn everything about me," she answers. "I know, everyone has their thing. Yours is learning. Discovering new things, and with me ... knowing me from the outside in and the inside out."

"You're a very strange person, Blaire Noelle Wilson," I remind her. "You like to learn, too. I remember teaching you a lot about yourself."

I wink at her, and when I spot a red hue staining her lovely face and her pupils dilated, I know she understands my meaning. This would be a great time to drag her back to the bedroom, but I don't.

"So tell me, Doc, what's been happening with you?" she asks. "I might not get to stalk you until later next week. Have you published any papers?"

"A few," I explain. "I love science. I'm good at what I do, and I get a lot of referrals from other states and countries."

"Then closing your practice is extreme. Are you sure you don't want to take a sabbatical?"

"It's fine because *we* are going to do a lot of good with our new practice."

"You're an orthopedic surgeon," she repeats. "You can't just drop it and forget about it. Unless you have a backup plan, and you know I don't like to be kept in the dark."

She looks at me expectantly. The woman knows me. She's actually proving me right.

"Not a backup plan, but ..." Her face actually brightens as she listens to me. "Once our practice is running and we expand, we can add some equipment and even have ambulatory surgery. Again, I haven't worked everything out in my head—"

"It's brilliant because the patients and their families can stay at The Lodge to recover, concierge service could be added to it, and we can have that covered by their insurance. If there are any injuries during ski season, you are right there, too."

"Marry me," I say, because this woman understands me like no other person in the entire world.

"Let's not get carried away, Aldridge." Her words and her eyes have an edge. "I like the idea to expand the practice, but proposing to me is moving too fast."

I wink at her. "Technically, we're moving in together."

She laughs. "We're just back to dating. Let's change the subject."

"Vance isn't in the Army. What does he do? You have to know."

She grins.

"We don't talk often," she responds. "I talk to Addison, his mother. We're good friends, and she likes to check on me. As I mentioned, I lived with her for almost a year."

"Is she married?"

"Yeah, and she has two other children—teens. Your family fascinates me. Your mothers responded differently after they figured out William was a scumbag."

"You've always been fascinated by us. We can barely stand each other," I say with a sigh. "If Carter was here, he'd have convinced all of them to stay."

"No," she answers. "You never understood how you seven worked. They look up to you—because Carter did. That's why Henry is an asshole, because he's the oldest and couldn't get the admiration you got. Yet, you always relied on Henry to make decisions, and sometimes you added Pierce. Stick to what you've done before. Make them see that they matter to you, that you guys are a team."

"I hope it works because if not..."

"Have faith," she presses. "It's time for bed. We can pick up this mess tomorrow morning."

THIRTY-FOUR

Hayes

THE NEXT MORNING, I sign the paperwork and sell my part of the practice. Blaire asks me to help her interview the doctors who might be going on the next mission. We hire a couple on the spot and agree to wait to interview more applicants before we fill the last three spots. The team she's assembling for her next trip should be leaving in three weeks.

We discuss the possibility of moving Carter's Kids Foundation to Baker's Creek. It would be a lot easier to help her manage it. Tori could still do her part from San Francisco, while the rest of us could help her with planning, executing, and even organizing a charity event to raise funds. Pierce even offered his legal services, pro bono.

We hire a moving company that'll be picking up my boxes on Monday. The rest of the weekend Blaire and I pack my belongings. We separate the stuff I want to keep at the house from what's going to storage. I decide to donate my furniture. Blaire calls a friend of hers who runs a safe haven home.

On Sunday, the company I hired to move my cars arrives. I only keep the car I'm using to drive to Baker's Creek.

Everything is moving too quickly, and yet, not fast enough. I'm ready to start this stage of my life. After the moving company picks up the boxes, Blaire and I drive to Baker's Creek. We arrive at midnight. Since we're too tired to deal with the new house, we stay at The Lodge.

"I missed this," Blaire says the next morning, as we jog through the town. "The birds, the people greeting you as you make your way through the town, and, of course, the pastries."

"Do you want to check on the house before we go to the bakery?"

"That's a good idea," she agrees.

"They changed the gate?" Blaire asks.

"It looks newer. Maybe they repaired it, painted it, or did something so it looks as new as the house."

There are a few workers around the area. Some are painting the barn while others are working on Beacon's studio. I spot Easton close to the main house, speaking with a man holding a blueprint.

"Good morning, Easton," Blaire greets him.

"Blaire, Hayes, I wasn't expecting you this early."

"Is the house almost ready?" I ask.

He nods. "I've had crews working around the clock. There are only a few details we have to fix, but you can start moving the furniture in that has arrived as early as tomorrow."

"Thank you for making this happen," I say, shaking his hand.

He scrubs his face and says, "I just hope it was worth it. We all know you have to be here by the end of next week."

"What do you mean you all know?" I ask concerned.

"You don't have to hide it," Easton continues. "Everyone in town knows that the only way to save the town is if the seven of you move in here and dedicate your time to the factory and The Lodge."

"Where did you hear that?"

He shrugs. "Everyone is talking about it, and let me tell you, the town is concerned because all of you suddenly disappeared without a word."

I look at Blaire who shrugs.

"It's nothing like that," I try to assure him, but Blaire is the one who speaks with such conviction that even I believe her.

"William Aldridge was sick for a long time, and he never asked for help. Unfortunately, we didn't realize things around town were bad until we came to the funeral. We're going to stay for as long as the town needs us. No one should be basing the future of the town on rumors."

"So, it's just the two of you," he confirms.

"No. Everyone will be here because all of us care," Blaire continues. "Thank you for doing your part. I'll come by tomorrow to start unpacking the boxes and setting the furniture where it belongs."

"We'll be here. I'll help you if you need me."

I want to say that she won't need help, but, in fact, she will because I have to leave her tomorrow. On our way back to the hotel, I ask her, "Who do you think told them?"

"We weren't discreet enough," she responds. "They're always studying us and trying to listen to our conversations while we were walking around town. At The Lodge, Henry always talked loudly. The workers never missed his outbursts. People are smart enough to piece things together. I'm surprised they aren't at the house demanding answers."

"Text Vance. Ask him for an address, a place to meet him," I request.

"No," she answers.

"Blaire, I need to speak to him first. I don't want him to feel like I reached out to him last because he's not important. Please, help me find him."

She puffs some air and pulls out her phone. When we arrive at our room, I ask her, "Can you handle everything on your own?"

"You mean make sure that the house is ready for next week?" she asks.

I nod.

"You're leaving," she states and doesn't look very happy. "Isn't this a little too late?"

"No. I have to make sure they'll be here. Did you get me the address?"

She shakes her head. "Not yet, but I will."

I kiss her. "I wanted to stay for another day, but you heard Easton. The town is concerned. The sooner we're here the better."

"Be careful," she mumbles, giving me a long kiss. "I'll text you the details as soon as he sends them."

FIVE HOURS after I leave Baker's Creek, I make it safely to Seattle. According to the address that I have, Beacon lives in Medina, Washington, which is just a twenty-minute drive from downtown Seattle.

I ring the doorbell that is also a camera. In just a few seconds, I hear his voice, "What do you want?"

"What do you think?"

"I'm not buying what you're selling," he says. "The last time you contacted me, you wanted to drag my ass to some hell hole and ruin my career."

"Beacon, open the door."

"No. You want to talk, talk."

Before I speak, the door opens, a young woman carrying a cat glares at me, her gray eyes look threatening. "Why are you here?"

"G, stay away from this."

"I need to speak to Beacon," I explain.

She shoots me a poisonous look. "Listen, you can't just show up after all these years and tell him he has to bail you out when you, in fact, have never cared about his wellbeing. Where were you for the past twelve years? He needed you when his grandfather was sick. Were you there when his grandmother died? No. So don't expect him to just drop his entire life and fix yours."

I rub the back of my neck and say, "Nothing I say will fix what I've done, Beacon. I'm a shitty brother. There's no fucking way I can fix the past. However, I'm trying to redeem myself. I'm really fucking trying, kid. I wish I had been there for you, but I wasn't even there for myself. This isn't about being there for me, but for a bunch of people who can lose their entire livelihoods if we don't step up. I didn't do this; it was William. All my life I tried to make Carter and Mom happy, you know," I chuckle. "I blamed myself for what he did—abandoning us."

"Everyone blames me," he says through the intercom. "I was a toddler."

I close my eyes because, of all of us, he's the one who got it the roughest. "Not me, Beac. I never thought it was your fault. He did a fucking number on us, but you know what else he did? He gave me brothers, and I hope it's not too late for us to become a family. If you decide that joining us isn't for you, that's okay. I'm working on a plan to save at least the town. Not sure about the rest of his assets and businesses, but I'll try my fucking best. As for you, I hope that we can get together often. I want us to be a family."

"Fuck off," he says. "I don't need you. I never did."

His friend gives me a sad smile. "When does he have to be there?"

"Next Friday," I answer. "This isn't about me, but I understand why he doesn't want to have anything to do with us—or William. Please, help me."

"I'll try, but if you hurt him again, you're going to regret it." This woman is intimidating, I wouldn't want to cross her.

"You have my word," I say.

"God, G. You make me sound like a fucking wimp," he says from the inside of the house. "Come on, let's go make some music. I'm need to shake this fucking mood."

She sighs. "As long as I get to play the cello," she says, before turning around and closing the door behind her.

THIRTY-FIVE

Hayes

———————

AFTER I LEAVE Beacon's place, I receive a text from Blaire. Vance will meet me in Atlanta on Thursday. I decide to visit Pierce next. Instead of driving, I leave my car at the airport. Henry promises to get someone to transport it back to Baker's Creek.

It's just past seven when I arrive at his house. He lives almost an hour drive west from Denver, right in the foothills. The place is stunning. Blaire would love it. I snap a picture and text it to her.

Blaire: That's a spectacular view. Where are you?

Hayes: Pierce's place.

Blaire: We should score an invite to visit him once we can leave Baker's. Call me when you're done with him.

When I pull up to the gate, the iron doors open automatically. Approaching the driveway, I notice a woman throwing a ball to two dogs. She turns around and frowns. As I leave the rental, she approaches me and smirks. "It is true. There are more like *him* around the world."

I extend my hand. "Hayes Aldridge."

"Leyla," she answers, shaking my hand, her brown eyes focused on me. "The resemblance is uncanny. If it wasn't for the hair color, you two could be twins."

Pierce clears his throat; I didn't notice he was there. When I look toward the house, I see the glass doors of the main entrance are open. He walks toward us. Looking at his wife he says, "I didn't know you were here."

She doesn't even look at him. "I was just about to leave."

"The papers are on top of the table," he informs. "You could just sign them and be done with it."

"Do you have the money?" she asks, her voice laced with irritation.

"For fuck's sake, Leyla, I already told you that I won't receive the inheritance until next year," he says frustrated. "Either you sign, or you have to move with me to Baker's Creek."

"My price is half of the assets—deposited in my account."

"You know I don't have that much money, but I'll sign the trust over to you. Ten billion dollars plus whatever the trust has made in interest. If not, you have to join us—or we all lose everything."

"I don't want to interrupt you guys, but I came to discuss the move. Someone tipped the town off, and they know what's at stake. They're concerned about their future and what's going to happen since none of us are there yet," I announce, hoping to stop their sparring match.

"Small towns, they are always getting into your business."

"If you hate them, why don't you just give me the fucking divorce."

"Maybe I won't go," she says.

"Listen, I don't know anything about your relationship. I'm sorry things are rocky between the two of you. I really hope you can come to some amicable agreement soon. In the meantime, I need you two to work together. Leyla, our father added you into the stipulations. You have to live with us for eighteen months. If one of us doesn't move in by next week or moves out before the eighteen-month period, a lot of people are going to suffer. It's not about us, but the future of the town and the people who worked for my father and still depend on his companies. My father wasn't a very nice person; he's toying with us, and if we were the only ones affected, I wouldn't be uprooting my life or begging you to rethink your position. I'm hoping that you could get past your differences and help the town."

"Ha, you're just like daddy. And here I thought you were like all the Bryants," she says, grinding her teeth.

"The bottom line is that if we don't move, thousands of people will lose their jobs and their homes. We can prevent it. If you give him the divorce, you don't have to come, but if you don't, I beg you to join us."

"So, it's true?"

Pierce nods.

"Okay, I'll do it," she says.

"You're signing the divorce papers?" Pierce asks, swallowing hard. "That's good."

"No. I told you that if I do it, it'll be when I'm ready."

"What the fuck do you need from me?" He pulls his hair with both hands. "Take everything. Just give me my freedom."

She focuses her attention on me. "When can I move the animals? I already chose a company who can do it and scheduled it in case this wasn't some scheme he cooked up to get rid of me."

"I think the barn is ready. Let me give you my girlfriend's number. You can text her, and she'll give you all the details."

"Make sure that whoever you hire sends the bills to my office," Pierce says. "Do you want me to hire the moving truck?"

"You should if you need to move your things. I have everything I need with me," she answers. "What's your girlfriend's name?"

Leyla saves Blaire's number in her phone and leaves us.

"She seems nice," I say sarcastically.

"Actually, if I'm not around, she is lovely."

"What happened between you two?"

He's staring at the horizon. "She was hot, I was infatuated, and now

I can't get rid of her. Do you want to stay for dinner? I was about to grill a steak."

"Yes," I say, following him.

"So, you kept the house?" I ask curiously.

He nods. "I offered it to her, but she didn't want it. One day she's demanding money to give me the divorce, and the next, she wants nothing to do with me. She comes around to take care of the animals after work."

Looking at me he asks, "Why are you here?"

"As I mentioned, there's a rumor around town that if we don't move in next week, they're going to lose everything."

"It's not a rumor."

"Focus, Pierce. They shouldn't know what's really happening. They're going to start pressuring us and making our lives a living hell. But that really doesn't matter. I want to assure them that we're going to be there for them. Blaire gave the contractor another version of the events. Hopefully, they'll settle with that and we can do our thing. I'm here to make sure you and your wife are heading to Oregon soon."

"Seems like we are," he answers. "You heard the missus. She knows how she's moving the kids. I already quit the law firm. I'm flying tomorrow to New York to take over the legal department at Aldridge. Dad's lawyers aren't happy about our decision."

"Why did you quit?"

"I'm not coming back. Maybe after the shit show is over, I'll set up a practice in Portland."

"That's extreme."

He grins. "My big brother set the example."

"If it's okay with you, I'll book a ticket to fly to New York with you."

"I hired a jet. We can share it. Are you harassing Henry?"

"Just making sure he won't bail on me."

PIERCE CONVINCES me to stay in the guest room. Around eleven, we call it a night. Once I'm ready to sleep, I call Blaire.

"Where are you?" she answers.

"At Pierce's house. Are you already in bed?" I ask with a husky voice.

"No, I was doing some yoga with Sophia," she answers. "Who does yoga at one in the morning?"

"Your friend," I answer. "You miss her."

"Yes, but that's okay. Pierce's wife is going to be here soon. She's adorable."

I roll my shoulders to ease the tension in the back of my neck before I speak. "Are you being sarcastic?"

"Not at all, she's really nice," she says enthusiastically. "She's going to let me ride her horses once they settle in. We discussed the possibility of buying a few more animals and... We had a long conversation and made a lot of plans. Why do you ask?"

"I met her, and she was everything but adorable and accommodating."

"Well, she was very pleasant with me. She's driving to Baker's Creek and arriving this Friday, at the latest. I'm so excited about the chicken coop I get to build tomorrow. Easton already got me the materials for it."

"Wait what?"

"She needs a chicken coop, and I'm going to build it."

"Do you know how to do that?"

"Yes. I've done construction during my travels. Do you think I just practice medicine?"

"I guess not. You're a woman of many talents," I declare. "Can't wait to see what else you've learned."

She chuckles. "Ooh, I'm sure we can arrange a little demonstration, Dr. Aldridge."

"I miss you, babe."

"Miss you, too," she answers. "Now tell me what happened when you visited Beacon?"

"I couldn't see him. This girl, woman ... I don't know how old she is, but she looked young, tall, willowy but strong, and pretty intimidating. Anyway, she opened the door and gave me this threatening look and lectured me. Afterward, she said she'd talk to him. Did you know his grandparents died?"

"He's alone," she sighs.

"I feel like a failure," I state.

There's a long silence, so I say in a pitched tone, trying to sound like her, "No, Hayes, you're not a failure. You made some mistakes, but we all do, and I love you."

"Wow. Do I sound that whiney?" she asks. "Babe, I wish I could tell you that, but you fucked up with Beacon. I'm a little upset at myself too for not calling him, and angry at you because he's your baby brother. You should've tried harder."

"I feel like an asshole."

"You're making amends, and even if he doesn't come to Baker's Creek, you plan on being a part of his life. That's all that matters."

"Are you giving up on me?"

"No, but I'm thinking worst case scenario. I trust you, but if we have to face this alone, it'll be fine."

Knowing that she's with me no matter what happens means the world to me. "Have I told you lately that I love you?"

"I love you, too. Overall, are you okay? This can't possibly be easy for you."

"What do you mean?"

"It is the first time you're visiting your brothers where they live and opening up to them," she says. "I know you had to do this on your own, but I wish I was there with you."

"That means a lot to me," I say. "You mean the world to me."

We spend a couple of hours talking about her day, and, at some point, all I hear is that cute snore she makes when she falls asleep in a weird position. I hang up the phone and send a text.

Hayes: *Call me when you wake up. Love you, Stardust.*

THIRTY-SIX

Hayes

THE NEXT MORNING, I wake up to the sound of someone banging on the door. I wish Pierce mentioned that the 'guest room' was his couch in the living room. The upstairs rooms don't have any furniture.

"Alexa, turn on living room one," Pierce orders, and the lamp right above me lights up.

"You suck as a host," I complain, sitting down and looking toward the door.

Pierce opens the door, and outside is Vance.

"Why are you here so early in the morning?" Pierce asks with a sleepy voice.

"It's five," he answers and marches toward me. "I was in the neighborhood and thought I'd drop by to see what you guys want from me."

"Hey, kid," I greet him. "I thought we were meeting tomorrow in Atlanta."

"Change of plans, I have to leave for a mission. What do you want?"

"We didn't have a chance to talk while you were in Baker's Creek," I say. "Listen, I'm sorry that I wasn't there for you in the past twelve years. I understand that you're hesitant about changing your life radically, but if there's anything I can do or say to convince you to join us..."

"Is everyone going?"

"I'm going to be there," Pierce confirms.

"What about Mills and Henry?"

"Henry has been working his ass off. There's no doubt that he'll be there to make sure everything runs smoothly," I say. "He might not be busting his butt to save the town, but he's doing it because he likes to win. For him, getting through this challenge is a win against our father."

"Beacon?"

"I spoke to him yesterday. He's pissed at me—like everyone else—but I'm going to tell you what I told him. If you decide not to go that's okay. I have a plan to help the town if you decide not to join us and Father's properties are sold. Maybe not all, but as many people as I can. Blaire is staying too, no matter what happens. However, things will work out a lot better for everyone if we stay together as a family."

"So, if I don't go, you don't care. You'll still send me a Christmas card every year," he semi-jokes.

"I hope it's more than sporadic calls and holiday cards. Blaire and I would love to see you often, even if it's just to patch you up."

I look at his arm. "What happened with the stitches?"

"They're gone. I know how to pull those suckers out." He grins. "Skittles is not going to be happy, but I had shit to do."

"Can we count on you?"

"You're asking me to leave my brothers-in-arms for a group of assholes who have never given a fuck about me. What would you do?"

I scratch my head. "Honestly, I wouldn't quit. I failed you—all of you," I pause, rephrasing because this isn't just on me. "No, we failed each other because a relationship is a two-way street. Can we get past that and try to build a future as a family? We deserve a chance to become brothers and friends."

He stares at me.

"Don't do it for me. Do it for yourself."

"Let me think about it," he answers.

"I'm sorry, too," Pierce says. "This family thing is hard to do when your family is so screwed up, ya know?"

We both look at Pierce, puzzled by the comment.

"Mom's family isn't easy. I don't have brothers, but my cousins are a bunch of fucking losers, and I'd rather be alone than have to interact with them—or you for that matter. I just lumped everyone in one pile and ignored them."

Vance nods a couple of times. I give him a hug before he leaves, and Pierce does the same. Instead of going back to bed, we head to Pierce's home gym. I swim a few laps in his pool. After breakfast, we load the rental, but he stops when we spot his wife by the barn. There are a couple of trailers, and she's helping load the animals.

"It'd be so much easier if we just split."

"Offer her the house," I suggest.

"I already did. She could have the house, the animals, and enough money to live comfortably for the rest of her life," Pierce says as he watches her helping the animals into the trailers. "Nothing is enough. Then some days, she tells me she doesn't want anything."

"What does she do for a living?"

"She's a veterinarian," he answers. "I don't even know what she's going to do in Baker's Creek."

"Does she own a practice?"

He shakes his head. "No. She works for an animal shelter. At least she did while she lived with me. Let me go and see if she needs money for the plane."

While I wait, I lean on the car, observing Pierce and his wife. She gestures a few times toward an old truck, then to the dogs that are running around them in circles. Leyla crosses her arms while Pierce speaks. He points at the side of the house and then at the old truck. She shakes her head. He tosses his hands up in the air and looks up at the sky.

This would be funny if it wasn't uncomfortable, and it hits me that this is going to be my life. Watching them fight every single day. I stare at the ground and say, "I hope you're burning in hell, William."

After a few minutes, Pierce jogs toward the me. "Fuck, I swear she's impossible."

"What happened?"

"She wants to drive to Baker's Creek," he says. "Because according to her fucking phone, it's only a nineteen-hour drive. I swear she doesn't have a sense of self-preservation, and worse, she wants to drive that fucking piece of shit."

He points toward the garage. "I bought her a truck a couple of years ago. She refuses to use it, so it's been collecting dust. But you know what, we're taking it to Baker's Creek. Damn, why are women so stubborn? No, it's not all women. It's just *her*."

"What about New York?" I ask him.

He looks at me. "You don't expect me to let her drive to Baker's Creek with two dogs all by herself, do you?"

"No, of course not."

"This is the right thing to do. She has to be there because of me," he rambles, looking toward the trailers where they are loading the animals. "It's a nineteen-hour drive. She has to take a few breaks so the dogs can walk around and have some release. Then, she has to stop for the night. Maybe I'll book two rooms either at Twin Falls or in Boise. If she goes alone, she's risking herself and the dogs. As I mentioned, she has no sense of self-preservation."

I almost tell him that he doesn't have to justify himself with me. It makes total sense that he wants to ensure her safety. After all, she's his wife. However, I do ask the obvious question, "What about the meetings you scheduled in New York?"

He rubs the back of his neck with one hand. "Fuck. I'll see if Sophia can reschedule them for next week."

"You're going to cut it too close," I say, trying to hide the panic.

"Trust me, I'll make everything happen."

I pat his back. "Drive safely and don't kill each other." I climb in the car and leave.

AT FIVE O'CLOCK, I arrive at Henry's office. Sophia is by her desk. The last time I was here, I hadn't notice that there were at least five other desks in the area.

"How many minions does he have?" I ask when I arrive at her desk.

She looks up and smiles at me. "Hayes!" She stands and gives me a hug. "I wish you had brought Blaire with you."

"Sorry, sweetheart. She's getting the house ready."

"And building a chicken coop," she adds. "He's in a meeting, but you can go in. It'll irritate him to see that we don't respect his conference calls."

"You're going to miss him when he's gone," I tease her.

"Nope, I'm already planning all kinds of parties in his office," she answers with a wide smirk. "Go ahead. I made reservations at a restaurant close to his penthouse. Hopefully, you can get him out of the office. He likes to bitch, but I notice he'll do whatever you say."

I enter Henry's office. He's sitting by his desk, looking at the monitor. Without losing focus, he waves at me to enter.

"This transition needs to happen by Friday," he says. "I'm heading to Baker's Creek next Tuesday and from that point forward, you'll have to travel to us."

"You're fucking me," the guy who speaking to Henry says.

"Nope, I'm dead serious. That's why I want you to be the interim CEO. It's a twenty-four-month contract. You don't like permanent positions, which is why I think this is the perfect job for you."

"Who is taking over after I leave?"

"That's a great question. We're going to start looking for your replacement six months before the contract ends."

I take a seat on the leather couch and text Blaire that I'm at Henry's.

Blaire: *Sophia texted me already. She even sent me a picture.*

Hayes: *How's the chicken coop?"*

She sends me a picture of the coop.

Blaire: *It's done!*

Hayes: *You are good with your hands.*

Blaire: *When you're back, I'll remind you just how good :wink face:*

Hayes: *How about if I call you later tonight. You can try them on yourself while I watch.*

Blaire: *I'm busy working the front desk. Let's talk later.*

When Henry ends his call, he says, "Fuck, we have a mess. Pierce called. The wife is heading to Baker's Creek, and he has to drive her."

"No, he offered to drive her," I correct him.

He gives me an inquisitive look, and I shrug. "What's the plan now?" I ask, because Pierce's life is not up for discussion.

"Sophia set up a few videoconferences for Friday. I'm going to be there in his absence. You should stick around. Maybe we can both leave that evening and head to Baker's. What's happening with the others?"

I recount my conversations with Beacon and Vance. His frown deepens as I speak. When I finish, his face is crimson.

"You're fucking kidding me. You told them it's all good if they don't show."

"Yeah, because I want them to know that above everything, they are my brothers."

"You mean I can cancel everything I've done, and you try to fuck my life seven ways till Sunday for failing you."

"That's right, but I know you wouldn't just quit because you've invested too much of your money and time to abandon everything."

He glares at me. "What are we going to do if they bail on us?"

"They won't. You have to trust them," I explain. "Give them the time to think about their choices. We're offering them a family, something none of us were offered before. Our mothers forced us to interact. This is different."

He scratches his head. "All I hear is philosophical crap and that I might get screwed. Lucky me. But as a consolation prize, you'll be inviting me to your first child's christening."

"I might even make you the godfather," I joke.

"You have to get them to Baker's Creek, Hayes. You swore you'd do it."

"Trust me," I insist.

He walks around his office taking several breaths.

"I understand your need to be in control," I try to ease his irritation. "The frustration that's eating at you because you can't do anything but wait."

"No, you don't," he says with a loud voice. "You're asking me to leave all I know and what I own for something that might fall through as early as next week. To trust you and those guys who have only been inconvenient to my future."

"Inconvenient?" I repeat, confused by the word.

"That's what my mother called all of you. If it wasn't for you, she'd have merged with Aldridge Enterprises. She didn't give a fuck about your father not being faithful. She was angry because she couldn't close a fucking deal. William had other kids, and they were inconvenient since I wasn't his only heir. I was a fucking transaction to her."

I blink a few times, surprised by his confession. Debra was cold, but I had no idea she was this heartless. He's just as alone as Beacon, but at least Beac has G and maybe his bandmates. He's not jaded or bitter. This guy ... his parents screwed him over royally.

"All I can say is that I'm going to do my best to make sure that by the end of this ordeal, you have what you always wanted."

"See, that's a fucked-up promise because I don't even know what I want anymore."

I grin. "Then we'll discover it together. Gather your things. We're going out to dinner."

"It's not even six."

"Who cares, Henry? You're your own boss."

He agrees, grabbing his jacket, and we march outside his office.

"You're slacking, Mr. Aldridge," Sophia teases him while typing on her laptop.

I notice she's the only one left in the office.

"Sophia, why don't you join us?"

She doesn't acknowledge me, and it's Henry who speaks. "You can use some food, Ms. Aragon. Join us."

"I have a few more things to do, but thank you for the invitation."

"You can leave that for later," Henry insists. "Gather your things and join us."

Looking at him I say, "I'm impressed. You're starting to act like a human."

"Shut the fuck up," he grunts.

THIRTY-SEVEN

Blaire

ON FRIDAY, Sophia calls me around seven in the morning while I'm jogging around town.

"According to Twitter, you inherited the town," she says, when I answer the phone. "I didn't even know the town was property of the Aldridges."

"Good lord, I don't know what's worse, their tweets or your obsession with their social media. Stop reading trash," I quip. "Is your boss going to yell at you for using his time for personal calls?"

"No. When I'm on the phone with you, I tell him we're discussing the factory."

"Which we're not. Just remember I don't lie," I say, stopping by the house where I spot two trailers and a dark SUV with Colorado plates right outside the gate. "Pierce and his wife have arrived."

"Goodie! Hayes said she isn't very nice."

"That's a big lie. I was on the phone with her for almost an hour, and we hit it off."

"You'd hit it off with a phonebooth."

"Those don't even exist," I complain. "I bet you'd like her."

"Are you going to greet them?"

"Yeah. Don't hang up, okay."

I wait until the trailers and the truck pull inside the property and park by the barn before I make my way inside. Pierce waves at me when he climbs down from the SUV and heads to talk with Easton.

When I reach the car, I see a woman getting out of the truck. She prances toward the trunk and opens it. Two dogs jump out of the back and start jumping around her. I look at her closer. She's about my height, dark auburn hair, green eyes and a beautiful face. She wears a pair of jeans, a long sleeve shirt and a vest.

"You can only stay around this area," she tells the dogs who begin to sniff around the car and then walk toward Pierce.

"She's cute," I state.

"Maleficent cute or Snow White cute?" Sophia asks.

"Ariel beautiful," I answer.

"Hey," I greet her. "You must be Leyla."

She gives me a guarded smile. "Yes, and you are?"

"Blaire. We spoke over the phone a couple of nights ago," I answer, hugging her. "It's nice to finally meet you."

Her eyes open wide when I release her. "Sorry, I'm not great with strangers."

"Well, she's meeting just the right person," Sophia says on the other line. "You're going to make her an extrovert before the end of the week."

I roll my eyes. "Soph, I'll call you later."

"No. I want to know everything about her. Fuck, I hate that I'm missing all the fun."

"Again, this is not a reality show. And you're definitely not the host of this circus," I say, before hanging up.

"Sorry. That was Sophia. You'll meet her soon," I tell Leyla, putting away my earbuds. "How can I help?"

"Pierce is checking the barn to make sure it's ready for the kids," she explains to me.

In that moment, Easton and Pierce approach us.

"It's ready," Pierce announces. "We're going to unload the horses first. Do you want to do it, Leyla?"

She nods and waves at me, running toward the trailers.

"Is the house ready?" he asks me.

"Not just yet. The beds should be arriving today," I inform him. "Dishes, small appliances, glassware, and all that stuff should be here tomorrow. I can get you a couple of rooms at The Lodge. We can move in on Saturday."

"That sounds good." He looks toward Leyla. "I'm heading to The Lodge so I can join a conference call. After that, I have to fly back to Colorado. I'm leaving the truck and taking one of the cars that we have in the garage. Could you keep her company? She's pretty independent, but this town is new to her."

I give him a reassuring smile. "She'll be fine."

A couple of hours later, there's a truck from Happy Springs delivering hay and food for the animals. Leyla sets the chickens in the coop, which she loves. Her dogs stay in the barn, and before Pierce leaves, he gets Easton to quote him an indoor and an outdoor arena.

"Thank you for everything you did. I should've come sooner to make sure everything was ready for my kids." Leyla's gratitude is apparent, and it makes me like her even more.

"Hey, they're settling, and you're here. That's all that matters. Not to be nosy, but what exactly do you do with them? Are you a therapist?"

"No, I'm a veterinarian." She looks around the street and says, "I don't even know what I'm going to do while I'm here. I used to work at a shelter."

"We can look at the building where we have our medical practice. Maybe there's enough space to set up a practice or even some kennels where you can offer boarding," I suggest.

"I could just apply for a job at the veterinary hospital," she replies, her attention everywhere. "This is a pretty place."

"It is, but we're going to make it better. Sophia and I have been toying with the idea of opening a few new stores, making this town cozier. We could use some help."

"I would like that very much."

FRIDAY EVENING, Mr. Parrish arrives at The Lodge, and he summons me to one of the conference rooms.

"I wasn't expecting you until next Friday," I declare, taking a seat. "What can I do for you?"

"Good evening, Ms. Wilson. As I said, I'd be here when the thirty days were over."

"Which is next week," I point out.

"Well, my partners found a discrepancy," he explains, pulling some papers out of his briefcase. "You see, we have to count from the moment you received the news. I let it slide and added a note that we couldn't find you—until four weeks ago."

He gives me a strange look and says, "twenty-nine days to be exact."

"What does that mean? We have a week to move into the town."

"Everyone should be in the house by tomorrow," he says. "It was thirty days from the moment the last of the seven of you learned that William died. Not from when I read the will."

"That's tomorrow?" I almost stutter, my breath quickens and my body freezes.

We're not ready.

Pierce won't be here until next Tuesday. Hayes is going to see Mills tonight, but I don't know if he'll be back tomorrow.

Vance and Beacon are still unsure on what to do.

"We'll be liquidating all the assets this Monday," he informs me. "We both know they won't show up by tomorrow."

"Why didn't you call us?"

"My assistant called the law offices of Bryant LLP. No one

responded to our messages." He hands me a call log with all the messages they left and the people they talked to each time. One of them is Sarah, Pierce's mom.

"We will be here," I assure him, my voice coming out desperate. My stomach is tied in knots.

"You and I know that's impossible," he assures me. "They never cared about it. The good news is that all the money goes to you."

"What do you mean?" I ask confused.

"Well, to Carter's Kids Foundation," he answers. "But you can do whatever you want with it. So in short, the money is yours."

That's a lot of money and the things I could do with it are infinite, but there's no way I can accept that in exchange of screwing an entire town. The Aldridge brothers are going to help me with the foundation. As tempting as this offer can be, I can't accept it.

"You can't do this."

"It's my job," he says and gives me a document. "I just need you to sign this accepting the donation from Mr. Aldridge and another one on this document confirming that none of the brothers are present."

"Wait, this isn't true," I cry out.

"This helps you. Wouldn't you want to have all that money?"

"No, I don't care about the money. If you're too lazy to be here tomorrow at midnight, it's not my problem. There won't be any witnesses to sign this piece of paper for you. If you try to get someone else to sign, I'll make sure we sue you, and they disbar you."

"Think about all the people you can save with what I'm offering you."

I rise from my seat and say, "We'll see you at the house, tomorrow at midnight. There's a bed and breakfast in Happy Springs. You're not welcome at The Lodge."

On my way to my room, I call Hayes, but it goes directly to voice-mail. Then I try Beacon, Henry, and Mills, but the same occurs.

Vance picks up on the first ring. "I already said that I'm thinking about it. You're too pushy."

"The lawyer is here," I tell him. "He said they made a mistake, and we have to be living at the house by tomorrow."

"Fuck. You're kidding me?" he grunts.

"No, and I can't find anyone."

"Who is in town?"

"Only me," I answer, but when I enter the suite and spot Leyla, I say, "Well, and Pierce's wife."

"Fuck, I knew they wouldn't do it."

"Vance, don't judge them so fast. They don't know what's happening."

"Did the lawyer try to contact us at all?"

"He said they called Bryant LLP, but that no one responded. I saw the call log. Even his mother talked to them."

Leyla snorts and gives me a look. I frown. "Would you mind sharing something with us?"

"Sarah loves to manipulate her son. She might pretend to be 'supportive,' but I bet she's not happy that her baby is leaving town," she answers. "I've no doubt that she did this on purpose, maybe his cousins are doing something, so he loses the money. The possibilities are endless."

"Fuck," Vance grunts. "I believe her. Pierce mentioned something along those lines when I was at his place."

"Well, we ran out of time. Vance, we need you," I beg him.

"Blaire, I can't do it."

"Please, I beg you."

"What if they don't follow through?"

"It's a leap of faith, and if they aren't here on time, a few of us will stay behind, trying to save the town. You can be here with us."

"Sorry, Skittles. That's a huge leap, and I'm not wearing a parachute. Those assholes aren't going to catch me." He hangs up, and my heart slows down.

"I can't believe he's not coming," I say out loud, closing my eyes taking a few deep breaths before I open them again. "Hayes is going to be devastated. I don't even know if we can have them all by tomorrow."

"Deep breaths," Leyla says. "Calm down."

"This is a clusterfuck," I respond to her calm down. "My zen flew out the window when the lawyer said tomorrow is the deadline. My anxiety is having a panic attack because Vance might not come."

Leyla gives me a look. "What do you want to do?"

"Save the town. Do you think we can get them here?"

She pulls out her phone and smirks. "Let me piss him off first. He'll be here, though. Keep trying to get in touch with the rest."

THIRTY-EIGHT

Hayes

I CONVINCE Henry to go back to Baker's Creek with me, but before that, we make a stop in Vancouver to visit Mills. When we ring the bell, Beacon's the one who opens the door.

"Great. We have not just one but two assholes visiting this humble home," he mocks as he steps aside so we can enter.

"I see that you and Mills are close."

"Very close," Beacon states. "So close that when you learn that your brother knocked up a puck bunny, you fly to check on him and visit him often to help him with his son. And when you learn that your brother's grandparents died, you go to their funeral."

"I had no idea that your grandparents died," I apologize.

"Sorry, Beacon," Henry says. "You were not the only who lost a grandparent or has a shitty life. We all did. It is our role as older brothers to keep an eye on you, but don't think that you're the only one who needed that brother to stick with you. At least you had Mills."

"You're no different than William," he says. "Both of you."

"A few weeks back, I would have agreed, but after these few weeks, I discovered that I am nothing like William. By trying to avoid messy feelings and becoming him, I failed myself. We missed a lot of years. Fuck, I lost twelve years with my girlfriend."

"That was pretty fucked up. I hope she doesn't forgive you. She deserves better than you."

"I agree. She deserves the best, but she forgave me."

"You two are back together?"

I nod.

He grunts and glares at me not believing me.

"Where is Mills?"

"He should be back soon. He had a meeting with his people."

"Why are you here?"

"He needed a babysitter, and I volunteered. Again, that's what you do for your family."

"As a family, can you move to Baker's Creek with us?"

He glares at me. "Are you sure Skittles forgave you?"

"You can call her to confirm."

He pulls out his phone and dials her number and sets her on speaker.

"Did you forgive his fucking ass?"

"What do you mean we need to be there by tomorrow?" He frowns, looking concerned. "No, he said next Friday. I was there."

He looks at me and gives me the phone. "She needs to talk to whoever is in charge. I assume that's you."

"What happened?" I ask concerned.

"Hayes?"

"Yes, Stardust. Is everything okay?"

"No, nothing is okay. I've been calling you, and your voicemail keeps picking up."

I check my phone, the roaming isn't working, so I'm not receiving any calls. "Henry, are you getting calls on your phone?"

He looks at it and starts tapping it. "Fuck, I forgot to have Sophia turn on the international plan."

"Look, it doesn't matter why you can't get calls. The point is that you have to be here tomorrow by midnight."

"Calm down, and tell me what happened, please."

My blood boils as she tells me about her conversation with Mr. Parrish. My anger spikes when I learn that he tried to reach us, but Pierce's law firm didn't forward the messages.

"Are you okay?"

"I'm worried and upset," she answers. "Pierce is on his way. Vance isn't sure if he'll join us, and well, you guys are in Vancouver."

"If I can get Mills on board, we should be out of here..." I check the time. "Listen, if we can't get out of here tonight, we'll be there tomorrow morning. Henry's flying us in. Can you try to talk to Vance again?"

"Uh-huh," she confirms. "I'll try again tomorrow once everyone is here."

"It's going to be okay," I assure her.

"He wanted me to sign an affidavit where I confirm that you weren't here," she pauses. "Also, he told me that after they sell everything, the money goes to Carter's Kids Foundation."

I chuckle. "Of course, father would donate everything to you. He thought we'd be pissed with you or maybe that you'll try to play us so you can keep the money. Fucking William, he put on some crazy ass show!"

"It's almost over," she assures me.

"Love you," I tell her, not adding that it's not over.

We're just beginning. Mills, Vance, and Beacon aren't on board yet, and then we have to live with each other for eighteen months. This is going to be a fucking freak show.

"I love you more," she says and hangs up.

"She really forgave you," Beacon confirms. "So, we have to be there tomorrow then?"

"Yes," I answer, surprised by his reaction. Maybe I shouldn't be; he adores Blaire and most of all, he trusts her.

"What happened?" Henry asks, so I bring him up to date. Once I finish my story, he calls Pierce and puts him on speaker.

"I'm on my way," Pierce answers annoyed.

"Did your family try to fuck us over?"

He sighs. "Mom insists it was a mistake because they're all busy."

"And you believe her?"

"She doesn't win anything if I stay or go," he answers. "Why would I believe Mr. Parrish?"

"Because if she's like my mother, she's still pissed at William and at us, his children," Henry answers. "Listen, I don't want you to fight with your mother, but I want you to be aware that Merkel Hotels and Spas is firing them. I don't feel comfortable doing business with people who can't pass a simple message, especially one that almost makes me lose a deal. With that said, make sure you help Blaire with tomorrow's deliveries."

"If that's all, I have a plane to catch," he says, and the line goes dead.

"What's the plan?" Beacon asks. "I could fly back to Oregon with you. I'm not sure about Mills though. Is Vance in?"

I rake my hair with my fingers and tell them what Blaire said. They look at each other, but we stop talking because Mills enters the apartment.

"Why are you all here?"

"We need to be there tomorrow," I answer.

"No, I'm not going," he says.

Beacon gives Mills a worried look. "What happened during the meeting?"

"They're releasing me from my contract," he says, closing his eyes. "The doctor isn't sure if I can skate again."

"You can," I reassure him. "I can make that happen."

"Only if I move in with you."

"No, you don't have to move to Baker's Creek. We're setting a practice and you can visit us often. We'll treat you until you're ready to go back," I promise him.

A shadow of emotion covers Henry's face, but he doesn't say a word.

"Just give the guy a chance and pack your things. Arden could use a break from the hockey life," Beacon says. "Hayes needs us. Skittles already forgave him."

"She did?"

Beacon nods.

"It's not just me. Henry and Pierce need you, too," I correct. "We've been working our asses off to ensure that everything runs smoothly. There's a lot we have to figure out, but we have plenty of time, and hopefully, you two will help."

Mills rubs the back of his neck. "Fine, you're going to have to help me pack because I can't leave Arden's stuff behind."

"Let's take the essentials," Henry says. "We'll have Sophia come back for the rest next week. She's the only one of us who can travel around."

"How about you, Beac?" I ask.

"Don't worry about my shit. I can borrow clothes from all of you, and my bandmates can move my stuff when the studio is ready."

My shoulders relax, knowing that these two agreed. I feel more confident that we'll pull through this first step. That we will be at the house by tomorrow night. If only Vance could just take me out of my misery.

THE NEXT MORNING, we arrive in Baker's Creek around nine. By eleven, we're organizing the kitchen, assigning rooms, and trying to reach Vance because he's not answering our calls or responding to our texts.

Our first official dispute begins when Pierce tries to claim two rooms, one for him and another one for Leyla.

"The stipulation says that you two must stay in the same room," I remind him.

"You are crazy if you think I'm going to share a room with him," Leyla argues, her voice loud enough that I'm sure the entire town can hear her. "I need my space, and if you want me to stay, you have to accommodate the one thing I'm requesting."

"Listen, I wouldn't mind sending him to the barn with the animals," I tell her. "However, Dad specified that you two need to share a room."

She huffs. Pierce looks at her and says, "You can sign the divorce papers."

"The master bedroom is big enough for the two of you, and there's an en suite where we can fit a bed," Blaire explains, taking them both by the hand. "See, this room is almost as big as an apartment."

"When can we order the bed?" Leyla asks.

"I'll do it today," Blaire answers.

"That was your room," I tell her, when we begin to take her stuff out of the master suite.

She shrugs, "That's okay."

"Hey, in six months, your room is going to be bigger than that."

"What?" she asks confused.

"We're building our dream house. They are breaking ground in a couple of weeks," I inform her. "We need to go to Easton's office to approve the design."

"That's a big step," she says with a mischievous smirk. "Are you sure you want to take it?"

I close and lock the door of the bedroom. Walking toward her, I say, "I missed you, Love."

"It's the middle of the day, and the house is full of people," she warns me. "Arden is in the room across the hall taking a nap."

"Then you have to be very quiet, Stardust," I whisper, taking her lips and kissing her hard, before I move my mouth along her neck.

She smells like vanilla, flowers, and my favorite, Blaire. I'm grateful that she's only wearing a tank top, so I can run my mouth along her shoulders and plant kisses behind her ear, making her shiver.

"Missed you," she moans, lacing her fingers in my hair. "I've been aching for you."

I scoop her into my arms, setting her on top of the freshly made bed. I crawl over her and stare at her beautiful face. "Do you have any idea how much I love you?"

"Feel free to show me, Dr. Aldridge," she answers in a low, sultry voice.

I drink in every part of her body as I undress her slowly and kiss every inch of her skin. My cock pulses when I nip her breast, and she gasps.

"Shh, you're going to give us away," I whisper, sliding my hand up her thigh and brushing her swollen clit with my thumb.

Blaire pushes her hips up, seeking friction. "Please," she begs.

Spreading her legs, I open her folds with my fingers. Bending down, I lick her pussy from the top all the way down to her sweet entrance. I do it twice and then suck on her clit. She puts a pillow over her face, muffling a moan. I slide two fingers inside her and lap at her slit. It doesn't take long for me to find a rhythm, stroking deeper, sucking her harder.

She squirms beneath me, saying nonsense against the pillow. I lazily circle her sensitive bud with my tongue, adding another finger as I anticipate her orgasm. Her body jolts, her legs thrust up in the air, and she grinds against my face when she reaches her climax. I slide up her body, kissing my way as I go. She moves the pillow from her flushed face, and I take her mouth and give her a hungry kiss.

She wraps her legs around my waist and pulls me close. Her thighs cradle me, and I reach for my shaft and caress her tight, wet entrance with it. I shudder as she lifts her hips, and I thrust inside her. I place my hands on her hips and pull out, plunging back in. She cries out as my cock fills her again, and I kiss her. There's nothing more life altering than making love to this woman. My woman.

Her arms tighten around me as she arches beneath me while I continue filling her up. I pound into her fast and hard.

"Hayes," she moans. "I'm so close."

She buckles around me. I muffle her screams with my mouth, drinking her orgasm and controlling my own urge to scream as I'm coming.

There's a bang on the wall. "Dude, it's too early to be fucking."

"Beacon, I already told you to stop cussing around my kid."

Blaire and I laugh, and she kisses my jaw. "I love you."

"I love you more, and I hope you don't leave my ass because you have to live with my family."

"It's going to be interesting, that's for sure."

IT'S ALMOST midnight when Mr. Parrish arrives at the house. He's like a vulture waiting for us to fail and pick at our bowels, feeding from our fiasco.

"Where is everyone?" he asks.

"Arden is in bed already," Mills answers. "You don't expect me to wake him up just to satiate your stupid curiosity, do you?"

"Can you show me his passport?" He asks. "I want to have physical proof that he's in the country."

Mills rolls his eyes but heads to the staircase.

"Where's Vance?" the lawyer asks.

"He should be here soon," I answer, and I'm not sure if I'm hopeful or delusional.

Blaire pulls out her phone, her eyes find mine, and she shakes her head. A few hours ago, I felt on top of the world. Everything was working out perfectly. We received the proposal from the advertising company for the new branding of our ice cream line. The renovations of The Lodge began yesterday. We had a pleasant dinner. I found the box that I thought I had lost during the move. I was planning on ending the day with a big gesture. Now, I'm not sure what's going to happen next.

The hope that Vance will arrive disappears as the minutes pass. Mills spoke with him last night. He said he couldn't promise anything.

Henry is watching me, and I can feel his words. *You failed me again.*

Vance not showing is going to break our relationship, and I'm sure, this time, there's no hope that he'll come around. Blaire grabs my hand and squeezes it. I kiss the top of her head. Pierce gives me a look that says, *we're in this together, we'll start from scratch.*

"It's going to be okay," Blaire assures me.

"We can buy some land to build a Merkel Resort," Henry proposes. "We can rent a couple of houses. I'm not sure who is going to stick around, but we can try to save this."

"Gentlemen," the lawyer says.

Henry and I nod. This might not be what we planned, but we still can try to get something accomplished.

"How long until we have to leave the house?" I ask him, but he can't answer, because there's a loud noise—blades cutting through the wind.

Henry frowns. "Do you think someone is stealing my helicopter?"

We go outside, and there's a man jumping off a helicopter, and a second guy hands him a body. Blaire closes her eyes and yells, "Find me towels. I swear I'm going to kill him if he doesn't die."

Pierce and I run toward the two men.

"I can walk," Vance protests.

When he enters the house, Beacon says, "Just another Saturday night in Vance's life. Sweet."

"What happened?"

"He has a bullet in his leg," the other guy says, as we set him on the dining table. "Where's the doctor?"

Blaire is coming downstairs with her medical kit. She hands me a bottle of alcohol and says, "Get ready to open him." She gives him a pill that's going to make him sleep and then applies the local anesthesia.

"We don't have blood," I tell her. "We should fly him to Portland."

"I have everything to do a transfusion if we need it," she announces. "Who has B negative blood type?"

We all raise our hands.

"Goodie, we have enough supply in case he needs it."

"Can I help?" Leyla asks. "I usually handle small animals, but I know a thing or two."

Blaire accepts, gives her some instructions, and then glares at the lawyer. "We're all here. You can leave now."

Mr. Parrish gives her a slight nod. "I guess the stipulation has been honored—for now. But I'll come around to check that things are in place, and I have a few people watching to ensure you don't leave the town—unless it's to go to Happy Springs."

Pierce and Henry are the ones who shove him out the door. In the meantime, Blaire, Leyla and I get to work on Vance. I remove the bullet that fortunately didn't break any bones. When we're done, Blaire goes to the garage and comes back with an IV bag and a hook to hang the tubes.

"Where did you get that?"

"Since we're setting up the practice, I ordered some medical equipment. You can't blame me for hoping that we'll be open on Monday," she responds.

Mills and the guy who came with Vance carry him to his room. Blaire settles him in and gives some instructions to his friend.

"Thank you for bringing him," I say, before I leave the bedroom.

"Thank you for taking care of him."

"Call us when he wakes up or when the IV finishes. I put antibiotics in it, but once it's done, I need to take out the needles," Blaire instructs, checking his wound one last time.

The guy nods, and we close the door.

"You need to teach me how to stich, Aldridge," Blaire says as we walk out of Vance's room.

"Ready to spend the next eighteen months with this crazy family?" I ask Blaire.

"I've been ready for this all my life."

Epilogue

Hayes

WE DON'T OPEN the practice the following Monday because Easton has to bring the building up to code. That also delays my plans to start building our home. However, not having an office doesn't stop Blaire from getting to know her future patients. She starts doing house calls. It's been two weeks, and she keeps dragging me around town because we're a team.

"You're getting them used to it and then they're all going to expect you to be there," I warn her.

"Which is fine by me," she declares, entering the house.

"You got a box," Sophia says from the kitchen.

"You're here!" Blaire runs to meet Sophia and gives her a hug. "That's what I call the best delivery service."

"Hey, I have to know before everyone."

"Not before him," Blaire looks at me and crooks her finger. "Let's go upstairs, Aldridge."

"Where are we going?" I ask, following right behind her.

We enter her room and step into her bathroom. She opens the box and takes out a pregnancy test. My eyes open wide. "Do you think you are?"

"I'm two weeks late," she announces, as she pees on the stick.

"Why didn't you buy that at the pharmacy or the convenience store?"

"Would you like that on Twitter or Instagram?"

"They'll probably post it in the Facebook group, and most likely, they'll add a poll for people to guess if it's going to be a girl or a boy," I answer.

She chuckles, sets the stick on top of the empty box, and washes her hands. Then, looking at me she asks, "Are you okay with this?"

"With the town posting my picture every time I'm around town?" I shake my head. "Not at all, but I guess it is better than my brothers who have women dropping off casseroles and baking goods every day."

"I'm talking about the baby," she says, her voice carrying some worry.

Before she can see the result, I pull out the box I've been carrying for a couple of weeks and go down on one knee.

"Blaire Noelle Wilson, I told you years ago that we had been created from the same stars. We were born soulmates. My heart has been filled with you ever since I met you. You are my dream come true, my future rolled into one beautiful woman who I want to spend the rest of my life with.

"You're the stars of my night, the sun of my days. I want to spend the next one hundred years with you, placing sweet lingering kisses on every inch of your body. Show you every day how much I love you.

"Nothing in this life scares me more than not being with you. I want to spend my life with you, and if there's a life after that, I want to spend it with you—loving you. Blaire, would you spend the next eternity with me?"

She places her hands on the sides of my face and kisses me. "Yes, of course, I would love to marry you."

We kiss long and deep until there's a knock on the door. "So, what's the result?"

Blaire's gaze locks with mine, and she asks, "What do you want?"

"Your happiness, to be with you no matter what happens along the way, and if it's time for us to have a little one, I'll be the happiest man alive."

I kiss the top of her head and reach for the stick where the word pregnant appears.

"We're going to be parents," she whispers, hugging me tightly.

"Thank you," I say before I kiss her, our bodies melting into each other.

"Favorite moment?" I ask, absorbing her heat.

"This is my favorite moment of all my life."

Dear Reader,

Thank you so much for picking up a copy of Loved You Once. I am so grateful to have you as my reader and if you are new to me, I hope this is the beginning of our journey.

Loves You Once, the story of Hayes and Blaire is only the beginning of the Aldridge brotherhood. I can't wait to share their bromances, along with their happily ever afters.

This series continues with Henry and Sophia's story, releasing August 13, 2020. You can pre-order here. I can't wait to go back to Baker's Creek and hangout with these guys.

If you loved it as much as I do, please leave a review and spread the word about it among your friends.

Sending all my love,

Claudia xoxo

Acknowledgments

First and foremost, I'd like to thank God because he's the one who allows me to be here and who gifts me the time, the creativity, and the tools to do what I love. Thank you for all the blessings in my life.

Thank you to my readers. I'm so grateful to have you in my life.

Special thanks to my husband for his continued support. I love creating those special moments with him.

Thank you to my beta readers, Sandy, Yolanda, Patricia, and Karen.

Hang Le, for always knowing what my books need.

Becky Barney, who has become a key element to my writing.

Becca Mysoor, for spending hours with me talking about this book and helping me plot the beginning. To Paulina for listening to my ideas. Thanks to these two amazing people, I was able to structure the town, and the main characters.

My amazing ARC team, girls you are an essential part of my team. Thank you for always being there for me. My Bookstagrammers, you rock!

To my Chicas! Thank you so much for your continuous support and for being there for me every day!

Casie, thank you so much for taking over so many things while I tried to finish this book.

Thank you to all the bloggers who help me spread the word about my books. Thank you never cuts it just right, but I hope it's enough.

To the readers, you guys are everything. Thank you so much for taking the time to read my words, spreading the word, and sending me messages about how much you love my characters or how the stories have touched your lives. It's because of you that I can continue doing what I love.

Thank you for everything.

All my love,

Claudia xoxo

About the Author

Claudia is an award-winning, *USA Today* bestselling author. She writes alluring, thrilling stories about complicated women and the men who take their breath away. She lives in Denver, Colorado with her husband and her youngest two children. She has a sweet Bichon, Macey, who thinks she's the ruler of the house. She's only partially right.
When Claudia is not writing, you can find her reading, knitting, or just hanging out with her family. At night, I like to binge-watch shows with his equal geek husband.
To find more about Claudia:
www.claudiayburgoa.com

Also By Claudia Burgoa

Back to You

Printed in Great Britain
by Amazon

40504515R00162